ISLAND DREAMS

Island Dreams

Montreal Writers
of the Fantastic

EDITED BY

Claude Lalumière

Véhicule Press

Published with the generous assistance of The Canada Council
for the Arts, the Book Publishing Industry Development Program of the
Department of Canadian Heritage, and the Société de développement
des entreprises culturelles du Québec (SODEC).

Cover design: JW Stewart
Set in Adobe Minion by Simon Garamond
Printed by AGMV-Marquis Inc.

**SCIENCE
FICTION
Island**

06 05 04 03   5 4 3 2 1

CATALOGUING IN PUBLICATION DATA

Island dreams : Montreal writers of the fantastic
/edited by Claude Lalumière.

ISBN: 1-55065-171-4

1. Fantasy fiction, Canadian (English)–Quebec (Province)–Montréal.
2. Science fiction, Canadian (English)–Quebec (Province)–Montréal.
3. Horror tales, Canadian (English)—Quebec (Province)—Montréal.
4. Canadian fiction (English)–21st century. I. Lalumière, Claude

PS8323.F3184 2003   C813'.08760806   C2003-903239-6

Véhicule Press
www.vehiculepress.com

CANADIAN DISTRIBUTION:
LitDistCo Distribution, 100 Armstrong Avenue,
Georgetown, Ontario, L7G 5S4 / 800-591-6250 / orders@litdistco.ca

U.S. DISTRIBUTION:
Independent Publishers Group,
814 North Franklin Street, Chicago, Illinois 60610
800-888-4741 / frontdesk@ipgbook.com

Printed in Canada on alkaline paper.

Contents

INTRODUCTION 7

Elise Moser *Human Rites* 11

Glenn Grant *Burning Day* 28

Dora Knez *The Dead Park* 70

Maxianne Berger *Report on a Museum Incident* 80

Yves Meynard *In Yerusalom* 82

Martin Last *Carnac* 105

Melissa Yuan-Innes *Mrs. Marigold's House* 119

Linda Dydyk *The Strange Afterlife of Henry Wigam* 136

Shane Simmons *Carrion Luggage* 157

Mark Paterson *The Ketchup We Were Born With* 173

Christos Tsirbas *Brikolakas* 175

Mark Shainblum *Endogamy Blues* 183

ABOUT THE EDITOR 231

Introduction

In 1989, I returned to my hometown — beloved Montreal — after being away for a few years, and I opened Nebula, a bookshop devoted to "the fantastic, the imaginative, and the weird." In the ten years that I managed Nebula, the shop became a nexus for aficionados of the fantastic from Montreal and beyond.

Sadly, Nebula no longer exists. Five years later, I still run into former customers who ask me when I'll return to book retailing. I doubt I'll ever be taking up that gauntlet again, but I do hope that someone fills the void, and soon. Culturally vibrant Montreal needs a bookstore to cater to the tastes of the many readers who enjoy more than a dash of the outré in their fiction.

What I am offering, however, is this anthology, *Island Dreams: Montreal Writers of the Fantastic*. Within these pages, you'll meet twelve of this city's most imaginative authors, some native-born, some Montrealers by choice: twelve writers representative of the unflinching daring, dark wit, multicultural zeitgeist, and effervescent energy that characterize Montreal.

Several of these stories use Montreal itself as a setting — Elise Moser's gruesomely disturbing "Human Rites," Dora Knez's bizarre love story "The Dead Park," Maxianne Berger's short weird tale "Report on a Museum Incident," and Mark Shainblum's science-fiction adventure "Endogamy Blues" — but, true to Montreal's cosmopolitan spirit, several *Island Dreams* writers venture farther afield.

In "Burning Day," Glenn Grant envisions a future Toronto and takes us on a genderbending police investigation. Yves Meynard's "In Yerusalom" describes an alien city literally dropped in the middle of an American desert. Martin Last, in "Carnac," brings us along on a mysterious vacation to France. Melissa Yuan-Innes's "Mrs. Marigold's House" is located in the fictional small town of Edelson, Ontario. Shane Simmons's "Carrion Luggage" travels from Haiti to Florida. And Christos

Tsirbas's "Brikolakas" roams through twentieth-century Greece.

Less geographically specific, Linda Dydyk subverts the generic future depicted in 1950s American SF in "The Strange Afterlife of Henry Wigam" and Mark Paterson's peculiar farce "The Ketchup We Were Born With" has global consequences.

Montreal's English-language SF scene — a metaphoric linguistic island on the Island of Montreal — often gets overlooked. Outsiders tend to confuse multilingual Montreal with the francophone Province of Québec. The result: we hear about the French-language Québécois scene or about English SF writers from other provinces. As different as Québec is from the rest of Canada, Montreal is even more different from the rest of Québec. And its writers who work in English — including those whose careers span more than one language — do so from a perspective unlike any other.

So, without further ado, here are twelve all-new, all-different stories of "the fantastic, the imaginative, and the weird."

ELISE MOSER

Human Rites

Gaping Mouth was only about eleven when he came to the squat. He had been following them for several days; they were only dimly aware of him until he fainted from hunger behind them on the street. They heard him fall, and they heard the grunt that thunked from his mouth when his thin ribs hit the concrete. That's how they knew he belonged with them; anyone who could follow shadows like a ghost belonged. He had a good survival instinct, all things considered.

There were four of them all together. Shiver was the leader. Shout was the second-in-command, the enforcer, the one who backed Shiver up with a cut of the eyes. Shout was even more sullen and silent than the others.

Sentinel was an artist of sorts, and Gaping Mouth was merely beloved, a mascot almost. They were all thin and dark and brooding. They were nearly only shadows. They kept fingers because they couldn't always get heads. It was Sentinel's idea to keep them in bottles, so they could be easily stowed away. It was originally this idea which demonstrated his artistic bent and established his reputation.

The idea came to him one night after a ceremony. It was dark inside the room; they had only the flickering half-light of candles. The four of them were squatted in a circle around the fingers and ear and clump of hair, and, as the others watched with silent attention, he pushed the fingers one by one index pinky middle into the narrow mouth of an empty bottle they'd been using to bring water in. The fingers dropped to the bottom, forming a whitish jumble turned opaque amber inside the brown glass. They stood leaning against each other in the bottom of the bottle like teepee poles, pointing upward in a bruised, inarticulate, in any case useless gesture. Then in one swift lithe movement Sentinel slipped the bottle into a niche where it disappeared behind a crumble of bricks and mortar. That first time it was recognized by all of them, although it remained unspoken, that this was an act of ritual significance which would be repeated in the future.

Shout recognized the grace of Sentinel's act. From where she squatted she grabbed another bottle and tried to cram the ear into it, but it would not go in. Her efforts to push it in through the little round hole were clumsy. She grunted with effort and frustration, and a slime of blood accumulated on her hand. A piece of her long lifeless black-dyed hair hung in front of her pinched face, and she wiped it back with her bloody hand; later that night and for days afterwards the crust and stink of old blood would lie across her face and remind her of her shame. Finally Shiver became angry. He leaned over and, in one powerful move, caught Shout under the chin and heaved her back against the broken plaster of the wall. Her head cracked against the wall and then shot forward onto her chest, where it stayed, her arms limp at her sides like a rag doll's, her legs stretched out before her in layers of torn tights, fishnets on top. She didn't move when the bruised and ragged ear shot from Shiver's clawlike white hand, slapped against her forehead, and fell into the front of her sweatshirt. She didn't move either when Shiver threw the slimy bottle so it shattered on the wall beside her, sending a shower of glinting shards back towards the dim centre across her thin limbs.

Shout carried the ear, at first cold and moist and rotten, but eventually dry and leathery, on a string around her neck, forever after that day. Sometimes it was visible, sometimes tucked inside her top. The shrunken ear was a sign of her humiliation and equally a sign of her determination never to repeat it. And it was a useful gruesome and silent threat, which did more, twirled idly between her grimy fingers, to enforce Shiver's will than any words could, on those rare occasions when they were faced with enemies on the street. It didn't happen often; they were so far from whole people and so close to shadows that they were hardly even seen.

That night they'd been waiting for Licker. He didn't always show up, but they always hoped, with fear, that he would. When he did he was almost always through the door and looking at them before they realized he was there. In spite of his size — he was tall and broad and meaty, in contrast to the four of them, who were slight and pale and gaunt — he was able to materialize out of thin air. Licker could appear and disappear in the blink of an eye, so quiet it was like he had sliced open reality and slipped through.

They'd be waiting, fingers (or if they were lucky a head) in the broken plastic garbage bin in the middle of the room, blood seeping out the crack in the bottom in a nearly motionless black stain on the stained floor. Maybe they were utterly quiet in the tension or maybe one of them, Shout or Sentinel, would be keeping up a steady mumbling stream of mutter, tumbling blocks of old anguish rolling out on a monotone string, and then he'd be there. Licker. And he would come forward and inspect the offerings. Sometimes he would eat the meat, and sometimes he would pocket a pack of cigarettes. Once he lit four cigarettes at once and put them in his mouth and sat cross-legged before the head basket, smiling at each of them in turn, and smoked. They were pretty scared of him that time. And then he would lick the blood off the torn flesh or sometimes off the floor or once even, when all they had was Shiver's bloody knife because they'd had to abandon the body fast, Licker just touched his tongue to the blade. And then, having tasted the blood, he would be satisfied and leave again.

They knew he protected them. Once Gaping Mouth saw him passing a bag of something to a cop who was doing surveillance on the building they were squatting at the time, and the guy disappeared from his post for a good three weeks; his car was there, but he spent his shifts in the strip joint two doors down and he never bothered them. There were times when they had nothing to show Licker and he beat the shit out of them. It was hard having no food and being cold and then having Licker come and hurt them too. They were used to pain, but it hurt all the same. They'd tried just not being at the squat, but it was always worse when he eventually found them. Shiver had a scar shaped like a quarter moon behind his ear which Licker had made with a knife once when he was really mad, and they knew Licker had demanded digits from the fingers of other spirits, although he'd never done that to them. They were still so young, and he cut them slack because of it. It was for their own good, they knew, because it would be worse if Licker didn't make them do the sacrifices; then they wouldn't get any food or shelter at all. Once there was a girl from Nova Scotia who came in on the Voyageur bus and lived on the street downtown. They would have let her join them. She hung out with them for a while, but she didn't want to join anybody. She wouldn't do the sacrifices; they'd offered her the chance to join a ceremony, but she'd backed out of the squat and wouldn't even look at them. They found her in early February, frozen and covered with frost in an alleyway off Ste-Catherine, near Foufounes. That's what happened if you didn't do the sacrifices.

Every time they did it right they knew they were protected. Once Shout even got four cold burgers and a bunch of fries for free from the girl at the counter at Harvey's immediately after they'd finished a ritual with fingers and hair from two different people. So they knew they needed to do it and they knew Licker made them because they had to.

The four of them hung together, mostly. Whereas the rest of them ate hot dogs or burgers at every opportunity, Gaping Mouth seemed to taste blood and flesh in each bite, and was likely to leave his unfinished. He ate the fries instead, in a slow and methodical fashion, sucking as much grease and salt off each one as possible. Once when he'd been out begging he'd brought home a bag of the first cherries of the season instead of the traditional burgers. His mouth was stained red from cherry juice, and for a moment they all thought it was blood, but when he happily held up the bag of fruit their surprise turned to disgust. Shiver was about to hit Gaping Mouth but at the last minute only spit on him and glared, stalking back to the centre of the room where he and Sentinel were smoking cigarettes. Gaping Mouth never brought fruit home again, although they knew he hung around a dirty little fruit store on the Main where the owner sometimes gave him stuff to eat, old fruit on the verge of going rotten or couple-day-old bread. Occasionally he brought home mice that had died in the fruiterie's traps, which they used for small sacrifices. Gaping Mouth was easily humiliated by his errors, and it was common to see his head hang.

They didn't try to get heads on a regular basis; only when the signs required it, or when one of them, usually Shiver, felt it was necessary. If a dog appeared full of wounds, it meant they were threatened with a calamity, and they would need to make a big sacrifice. It was like that the time they killed that German tourist. That was the first time Gaping Mouth had ever seen them actually sever the head, and he puked his guts out over it. He was the littlest one (not by much), and they had always protected him before that, but Licker had been in the squat eyeing Gaping Mouth in a funny way, and Shiver thought Gaping Mouth had better participate from now on if he wanted full protection. He didn't want to have to take Gaping Mouth's own crooked little head. Licker could have made them do that.

One time Licker had made some offhand remark to Gaping Mouth about his smallness, saying he would "send the baby home to his mummy, if she wanted him, seeing as he was such a runt." To the horror of the others, Gaping Mouth suddenly launched himself across the dim room at Licker's face. They had all been beaten up by Licker on many occasions, and although they had killed a number of people none of them had ever even thought of lifting a hand against him. Yet here was soft little Gaping Mouth, hanging by a fistful of Licker's greasy hair and hitting him in the face, his feet scrabbling against Licker's thighs, scratching at him and screaming fuck fuck fuck fuck in between great wheezing gasps of foul air. He drew blood from the side of Licker's nose and temple before Licker managed to detach the fierce child and throw him to the concrete floor. Before Gaping Mouth could scramble up and launch himself again, Licker put a great booted foot on his chest and pinned him where he lay. The others were shaking with fear, sure this would provoke some magnificent revenge on Licker's part or on the part of the forces he represented. But Licker stood and caught his breath, looking down at the panting boy under his foot, and then he began to laugh, a tumbled, coughing laugh. Shiver wet his pants with relief. Finally Licker looked up at the others. "Little fighter," he said, chuckling hoarsely. He put a finger up to his nose, tasted the blood that flowed there, and grunted with satisfaction. Then Licker left and Gaping Mouth had an asthma attack that almost killed him. It took him three days to recover.

Gaping Mouth's mother's boyfriend had pushed him out of the van wearing only his pajamas, just before the exit leading out of the city; he'd known he was going to have to leave home but he hadn't expected it to be quite so soon or quite so brutal. His mother, sitting up in the front seat, had kept her face turned from him, but at the last minute she'd flung his sneakers out the car window, and then, just as they peeled out, the boyfriend's leather jacket. Gaping Mouth could hear the boyfriend screaming at her for it until the sound was swallowed by traffic noise and a high piercing whine that he gradually recognized as his own voice. After that he never took that jacket off in any weather; the other three of them had never seen his wrists. His fingers would crook out from the cuff now and then to take a donut or a cigarette, but that was as far out as his arms could get. They all assumed without saying it that he would be dead before he could grow into it, even if he ever got enough to eat to grow at all anyway. Even protection like they had could only go so far. Licker used to make him eat a piece of the brains whenever they got a head, saying it would make him strong, but it only made him throw up, so even Licker gave up trying after a while.

It was really best if they could get a living person, but who could they get except a child or a really old person? They knew that some adults kidnapped children because the sacrifice was much better done at the shrine and a child could be transported. (Who would stop an adult dragging a screaming child through the streets? That was normal.) But they were too close to children themselves and couldn't bring themselves to do it. Fingers and hair were mostly good enough anyway. When they got a good bunch of hair they mounted it on a "head" which was really only a beer bottle, but they would stick the hair into the mouth of the bottle and arrange it as well as they could around the neck as if it were a long face. Those they kept also, in a series of holes scraped out of the walls, hidden or barely visible in the faint light. They never said so, but they were proud of their shrine, which was inside the very walls, inside the architecture of the squat the way it was inside the architecture of their minds. They had seen the flashier shrines that adults made, with red and yellow plastic flowers and scraggly plants growing in front of them and so on. At first Licker wanted them to do that too, but he soon realized that this way they were more secure. For special occasions they could bring out all their bottles, and the ears on strings, and the heads from the crannies in which they were usually stored, and arrange them on the floor or on milk crates. This display was very impressive.

They avoided construction sites, although they were drawn to them too, and would watch them from a safe place for hours, especially Shiver. They could lean back against a wall in the smallest wash of shadow even in full daylight, and somehow they would melt into it until they could hardly be seen, like butter into toast, leaving only a vague shine on the surface. It was said that flesh and blood sacrifices strengthened the foundations of new buildings. It was said that construction workers put live animals into the foundations, but that small children were better and heads of grownups were best. They all had hypersensitive napes, which prickled in the wind and especially while watching or walking past construction. Shiver had seen Licker's shadow slipping around the heights of open half-built buildings, so they knew these rumours had truth in them. Walking along the street the shadow of a bulldozer coming along behind them looked like the shadow of a skeleton, a dinosaur-sized foretelling of skeletons to come. Roadwork or sewer repairs — the yawning excavations dug out of the blacktop — gaped like graves to them; the bared pipes hanging in mid-air and the ropes and cables suspended, clotted with mud, all looked like surgery, bones and blood vessels and bodily fluids.

It was Shiver who did the severing of heads, although gradually he was beginning to allow the others to take fingers, and even little Gaping Mouth had taken hair clumps on a few occasions. Shiver had no skills recognized by society, but he had developed a deftness and a fine judgement about taking heads, both well worthy of the ghosts' respect — even Licker's. Shiver knew how to feel with a light touch, brushing his dirty fingers over the back of the neck to tell exactly where the knife could slip in between the last vertebrae. He could tell how brittle the bones would be and how much force would be required to separate the head from the body with the greatest economy of movement. He and Sentinel were equal masters at hiding the decapitated bodies so they would never be found, or at least not until they were completely decayed. And Shiver was brilliant at finding ways to smoke the heads without giving away the locations of their squats. His heads were always beautifully dark, burnished, as if they were made of rare tropical woods. Licker even once traded them two whole actual steaks and a down jacket for a particularly lovely specimen. Usually they kept all their own heads, but Shiver had the impression this one had belonged to someone important. It was a truly impressive kill, and he'd been reluctant to give up such a powerful head, but it wasn't a good idea to refuse Licker something he so clearly wanted.

The man had been well dressed, in a thick cashmere overcoat and an expensive suit. They didn't know the difference between a two-hundred-dollar suit and a two-thousand-dollar suit, but they could see this one was beautiful and fit perfectly. They'd seen him step out of a chauffeured car with his soft shoes and into an alleyway with one of the women who worked the strip around the corner of St-Laurent and Ste-Catherine. This wasn't a man who needed to pick women up off the street; he must have been looking for the thrill of danger. When they saw the woman come back out onto the street, leaving the man momentarily weakened and breathing hard, Shiver decided they'd give him more than his money's worth. They moved smoothly, shadows all, and as a group herded the confused man deeper into the blind alley. Ambush was their specialty — their only possibility, really, but they'd elevated it to an art. Gaping Mouth kicked the guy hard in the backs of his knees, and as he fell forward Shiver grabbed him by the hair, pulled his head back, and slit his throat, making sure to slice his vocal cords. The man never had time to do more than grunt in surprise. After that they were home free.

They badly wanted his warm overcoat, but it would have looked too suspicious for one of them to be carrying it around the streets. They took his soft socks, his leather gloves, his shirt, and his watch. They rifled through his pockets, but all they found was a City Hall parking pass and a repair claim ticket for a small-appliance shop. There were only seven dollars in his wallet, but that along with the night's take from Gaping Mouth and Shout's begging was more than enough to buy burgers and fries for all of them after they got back to the squat with the heavy head. They returned all their empties and got twelve beers and had a celebratory feast. Shout was always worried that they'd accidentally return a bottle that had fingers in it, but so far they never had.

It was good for them to make sacrifices, because it helped them get food and kept them in safe shelters; moreover, if they didn't, they could get sick. There was a spirit sickness that took you over if you hadn't made enough sacrifice. It was supposed to be very bad. That's why Licker beat them up, to motivate them harder to avoid it. It had never happened to them, although they'd seen it once in a ghost from another family. The ghost was huddled in the entryway of a squat they were living in; their place was at the back upstairs, and this ghost was downstairs, in from the front hallway. They noticed him because his teeth were chattering so noisily. He was shivering, trembling, and then his tongue was hanging. As they stared his eyes became wild and he began to turn in place, unpredictably laughing, shouting. They went upstairs, and they could hear him; he continued to laugh and shout, dancing in the middle of the night. They came down to see him, and he chased them at the slightest provocation, biting himself and even them. The ghosts in his family came towards dawn, having gathered the necessary ritual objects to cure him: a long stick good for hitting victims, red string for tying them, and two burgers, still wrapped. They begged Shiver to try to do a curative ritual, and he went into one of his trademark trances and began to shiver as if with fever. He made them unwrap the burgers and stick them into a bag, and then he put his face into it and gobbled them up. He made them catch two pigeons and sacrifice them and put their pearly grey heads before the long stick and the string. This could work, but sometimes ghosts died from this spirit sickness.

After the ritual they all sat in a heavy silence watching the sick ghost mutter and rustle in his place. Just after dawn broke they became aware of Licker's presence. He lifted the sick ghost and took him away, not reacting at all as the sick ghost turned in his big arms, biting himself and sometimes Licker.

Heads were traditionally necessary for the most serious cases of misfortune and had to be sacrificed at regular intervals to cure or prevent disaster. A severed head produced a general state of welfare in their family, and even in the larger community of ghosts. It protected them and assured them of food. Heads could also cure the spirit sickness if the other rituals didn't work. A ghost could only have status after taking at least two heads; that was why Shiver was the leader of this family. He had originally roamed the streets by himself, under the marginal protection of Licker, and he had taken a number of pigeon heads just by intuition, roasting and eating the bodies, when Licker gave him the opportunity to take a human head. It was only an old beggar, dead drunk, but still it was a real head and that was what counted. Now Shout had taken one head under Shiver's direction, but she would not take another unless she intended to succeed Shiver or challenge his authority, or unless there was some kind of emergency. She was content with fingers, ears, and hair anyway.

Shiver knew the rules of the street and the rituals for staying safe and protected. He also knew how to take revenge and how to conclude mourning. After Gaping Mouth had been with them for six months Shiver decided to get a head so they could do rituals to end Gaping Mouth's mourning for his mother. Ordinarily it was the grief-stricken ghost who would take the head, but Gaping Mouth was too young. They waited for days, watching the streets for a good target, and finally they took a hooker they found stumbling in back of a restaurant, stunned by a rush of heroin she'd just shot. They dragged her into a dumpster, and they all took turns stabbing her with non-lethal thrusts, and when she was finally on the verge of dying Shiver pressed the knife into Gaping Mouth's hands, clasped his own hands around Gaping Mouth's small double fist, and helped Gaping Mouth strike the fatal blow. Then they took the head and two hundred dollars she had in her purse and they went back to the squat to have a ritual feast that lasted twelve hours.

They had a shock when Gaping Mouth lifted the head by the hair to throw it into the air with a yell to exorcise his grief, his little face red and shining with tears, his nose running a river of snot into his mouth, and all the hair came off in his hand, the nearly bald head thumping to the floor with a wet thwack that stuck it to the concrete by the bloody neck. Gaping Mouth's yell died in his throat, and there was a sudden silence. The silence was broken soon enough by Shiver's barked laugh, and before long they were all laughing, Gaping Mouth hardest of all, until he was doubled over with a knife-like pain in his side from the hysteria. He finally laughed his guts out, the vomit coming out of him in waves, the heaving overtaking his body in painful spasms like the convulsions preceding a birth. The wig had landed like a shot bird a little ways from the stump of the head, and it only made them laugh harder when Sentinel stuck it into a beer bottle and arranged it as if it were real hair.

Shiver made them burn it and smash the bottle later when they'd had a run of bad luck, two and a half days with no food in a cold spell, because he said it made the spirits angry to see them make a joke of ritual. He cursed himself for being stupid enough to allow it. But after they sacrificed two pigeons and a pack of cigarettes they got half a pizza out of the garbage behind the greasy spoon; the next day the weather broke, and Gaping Mouth and Shout made twelve dollars standing in the cold sun and begging.

Before they went out looking for a head they sacrificed a pigeon to provide auguries of success or failure. Shiver would become possessed by dwarves, friends of headhunters, who guide the ghosts on hunts and who would produce a small, sometimes shining good-luck stone. Shiver would rub the stone on his own head, sometimes on one of the others', and allow it to disappear and enter his body to protect him. He would also place ten cigarettes, with a stone on each of them, on a broken plate with strings and safety pins laid over them and a red piece of cloth, a veil, on top. Each of them would take some of these cigarettes and hide them around the shrine to protect them during their absence. The four ghosts would wear similar red bandannas during the ceremony, which they would tuck inside their shirts or pockets when they went outside. Outside, they would look for signs that the dwarf friends were coming to meet them for the hunt in the shape of centipedes, seagulls, or mice.

Once they had made some sacrifice they were allowed to wear red or black tattoos. These they made themselves with pins and pens and ink, except Shout who once spent twelve hours begging and gave a guy a blowjob to get enough money for a professional tattoo. She got a skull on the side of her neck, which hurt like hell at first but afterwards was the object of much admiration among the ghosts.

Secret paths through the streets and back alleys were followed to avoid detection, and they would make a temporary shrine for the dwarf friends at the place where they would settle in to watch for the right person to take. They would put cigarettes, surrounded by pebbles and stones and strips of red cloth tied into a knot, on the ground near the entrance to the alleyway or wherever they were holding their vigil. This was a "no trespassing" sign which acted as a blockade against any spirits that might protect their victims, and it signalled to the spirits which protected other families that this stakeout was taken. Then they would be prepared to ambush their victim.

Gaping Mouth always hung back when a killing was to take place, even for a necessary head. He had been known to argue for taking fingers or hair clumps and then letting the victims escape alive, but he conceded that he could not do that to a live person. Shiver was unconvinced of the efficacy of this sort of half-measure, and besides it was bad for security.

Gaping Mouth wore a crucifix around his neck from his previous life, but he hadn't really believed in that religion of sacrifice either. For the rest of them there was a certain continuity between the religion in the background of their lives, the ways they'd been hurt every day before escaping, and the way they lived now. For them, it was a relief to be able to engage in concrete acts, to take some control and not abandon themselves to a faith of passivity. For Gaping Mouth on the other hand, it was rather a social obligation to take heads. That didn't make it less compelling; the thin membrane of the (anti)social was all that bound him to Shiver, Shout, and Sentinel, and it was all, therefore, that kept his body and soul, such as they were, in donuts and cigarettes. It was also from his association with them that he derived whatever agency he had, which was surely more than he'd ever had before. It was this that he, like the others, had been forced to take in trade for the green vegetables and constant controlling he'd lived with in his other life. It was never clear to him that this was a bad trade; it was painful, but so had the old life been. This new power, to decide his own fate (within the limits of the life of dirt and concrete) — as well as that of grownups — was a kind of power that had been invisible to him before, in the suburbs, but seemed now to have always been there behind the scrim of the social convention of adult dominance. Gaping Mouth was still soft, while the rest of them had long since developed protective hard shells. They could live with the harsh camaraderie of the squat and the street as substitute for the feelings a soft heart feels; they'd done it for so long they'd lost the taste for the real thing. Like frozen feet, it would be so painful to thaw their hard hearts it might not be worth it. Gaping Mouth, on the other hand, throbbed with the cold every day. He was only now beginning to get tough, his heart marked with the long strange crystal marks that frost leaves, like fossilized ferns.

When Gaping Mouth finally hardened it seemed to happen all in one catastrophic moment, like a lump of coal, soft and smudgy, being turned to diamond by extreme pressure, the thousand-year process condensed into one horrific instant right before their eyes. When it happened, they could see that he was willing it to happen and that every cell of his body was harnessed to the task as if he was some kind of hard-cutting diamond-tipped drill instead of a soft, warm, blood-pumping boy. When it happened, he seemed to lose something behind the eyes; at the same time he appeared to have grown three or four inches all at once. He was never so small again after that day.

The ghosts had done rituals to call forth the hunters' friends, the dwarves, and they were crouched in the shadow of a scaffold. It was frightening to be so close to construction, but it was only a reno job, and it was ideally located next to an alleyway that turned between two blind walls. They had taken a head there in the past, and more than one finger. They needed a head now.

Sentinel was squatting by the plate with the cigarettes and red cloth at the mouth of the alleyway, smoking a partial cigarette a woman had thrown away at a bus stop. A faint smudge of lipstick had transferred itself to Sentinel's own pale lips, giving him a subtly pathetic comical look. Shiver, Shout, and Gaping Mouth were leaning against the grey stone wall like skinny forlorn buttresses, short shorter shortest. Gaping Mouth was singing to himself in a fading aimless soprano and inaudibly keeping time with two popsicle sticks he clutched in his grubby fingers, barely visible beneath the cuffs of his jacket. The jacket was much the worse for two years' uninterrupted wear, and Gaping Mouth now kept his fingers gently curled to keep his hands from sticking out past the cuffs, but he still wore it like his own skin and it seemed a part of him. They'd been in the shadow under the worn wooden planks for hours without seeing any likely victims, and they were getting hungry, but not one of them could be spared to beg until they had their head and had done their ritual. They'd seen a dog with grievous wounds howling on the corner near the metro station the night before. It had been running without a leash and ran in front of a car just as the light turned and the traffic pulled out. Its hindquarters were crushed, and its screams echoed long after it was gone. This was a sign that a terrible threat loomed, which could be averted only by a full head.

Evening was falling around them like a shroud when Gaping Mouth suddenly snapped his head up. His eyes lifted and slid to one side. Soon the others heard it too, a wild disjointed yelling that was bouncing back and forth as it came closer down the street. It was a woman with tears in her throat, shouting abuse at someone. They heard a sudden acceleration, and a black van sped past them, followed by the woman's slapping footsteps and a rising wail. "You bastard," she screeched, coming to a standstill in the gutter about five feet away from them, her arms hanging superfluous at her thin sides, her skin rough and lined, her hair hanging dull around her dirty snot-shining face.

Gaping Mouth was rigid, and his gaze was fixed somewhere above the woman's head. He was radiating a dangerous energy; Shiver and the others didn't know what was happening, but they knew better than to interfere. From the worn cuffs of his jacket, Gaping Mouth's hands slowly uncurled and his wrists emerged as he straightened himself to the constantly expanding limits of his adolescent height. The popsicle sticks dropped unheeded. Firmly and yet as if in a trance, he stepped forward, emerging from the shadows, a white wraith of iron.

Gaping Mouth stepped out from behind the metal skeleton of the scaffold and into the gutter, and then with deliberate speed, he approached the woman in two long strides, grabbed her forcefully by the arm, and marched her back around the scaffold and into the alley. It was only as they entered the cleft between the two buildings that she began belatedly to react, trying to pull away from Gaping Mouth, but he was unaffected by her struggles and simply pulled her along behind him.

Shiver and Shout looked at each other, astonished. They had always relied exclusively on ambush and luck. None of them had ever simply gone out and grabbed a victim. And Gaping Mouth had never done anything like this before at all. Something was happening. It seemed their ritual was having a very strong effect indeed. The dwarves must be with them, in force.

The three ghosts joined Gaping Mouth in the cul-de-sac. He was standing over the woman, who was crying and trying to speak to him. He kept telling her, from between gritted teeth, to shut up, saying fuck fuck fuck fuck in a rhythmic monotone. The woman was saying something they couldn't understand, her words distorted by her muffled sobs, until suddenly she said it clearly. "My baby, my baby," she was sobbing. Gaping Mouth grabbed her by the shoulder and shook her, bringing his face right up to her face. He was beet red, and his cheeks were shining wet.

"Shut up!" he roared, and shoved her. He stood straight again, looked directly at Shiver, and nodded in the woman's direction. Shiver's stomach contracted. This didn't seem right. He stepped forward and gathered a fistful of the woman's hair and pulled her head forward sharply. Shiver stood for a moment, stock still. Then he stepped to one side and handed Gaping Mouth the knife.

Elise Moser lives in Montreal with two cats, a dog, and a human. Her first published story, "The Seven-Day Itch," appeared in *Witpunk* (Four Walls Eight Windows, 2003).

She notes that the anthropological details in "Human Rites," the names of the shadows, as well as the line about keeping the fingers in bottles, "so they could easily be stowed away," come from an essay by Jules De Raedt called "Buaya Headhunting and Its Ritual: Notes from a Headhunting Feast in Northern Luzon," (pp. 167-183), in *Headhunting and the Social Imagination in Southeast Asia* (Stanford University Press, 1996), edited by Janet Hoskins.

Elise points out that, unlike her characters, she does not eat meat. Of any kind.

Burning Day

"Something's missing here..." I rotate the crime scene in my mind's-eye, pan across the remaining walls of the room, tracking over concrete dust, ceiling debris, toppled rows of wooden benches, part of a small synthetic arm... "Something's missing from this model."

Overlays flicker up, then fade, data collected by a swarm of flybots at the scene: shrapnel fragments and impact sites; splatter patterns of brain coolant and myonic gel; concentrations of chemical taggants, indicating Detanit.

"For one thing, why don't we have any idents?"

"It's only been forty minutes since the attack," says Danny from the squad car's other seat. "CSU's still sweeping the place. Do try to be patient, my paranoid android." Daniel Aramaki is human, and my work partner, and gets away with too much.

Ah, there we go — tiny red flags and neat little labels, finally popping up all over the virtual display in my head — annotating many thousands of pieces of the victims, large and small, positively identified and otherwise.

That's better. "We have four confirmed dead, all cogents. And — oh, shit, no..."

"What?"

"Three of them were kids. Report says a bomb attack on the Usutu Truth Memorial Nanofabrication Facility."

Mind's-eye closed, optics open: we're wailing through the intersection of Dundas and Replicraft Drive, running strobes and siren. Rain streaks the windshield, polishes the streets into shiny dark mirrors. The car is a Persina sedan, in standard-issue Homicide grey.

"Synthephobe terrorists again," says Dan. "Humanist Front,

probably, or the Organic Brigades."

"Fifty dollars says the Humanistas claim it first."

"You're a sick guppy, Mohad." Danny removes his latest designer smartshades, pockets them. He has a new pair every week; he's constantly losing the things. I once suggested that he could simply buy prosthetic eyes with the same features and then some. He seemed to consider the idea an affront to his biological heritage.

I blink back into the model. From the shrapnel impacts, the program calculates a probable detonation point: mid-air, three metres from the floor, at the centre of the room. Not a body-bomb, then. A grenade? Lobbed in from the door? Seems wrong somehow...

So I expand the model, scale it down to see what buildings are nearby. Project the most likely trajectories, out through the windows and back to origin. The resulting probability-cone is centered on the top three storeys of an elderly Modernist apartment block. A free hostel. The CSU team are already checking it out, apparently, datacapture flowing into the model as I watch.

I kill the display. "It would appear that someone fired a small missile into the building from a rooftop nearby."

Dan raises an eyebrow, but doesn't argue. "Which roof?"

"The free hostel. I believe I know its manager, by reputation at least — Severe Commy Skeptic."

Dan rolls his eyes. I know what he thinks of the names cogents choose for themselves. I've also known activists who sneer at mine: Gene Engine Mohad. The first and last are slave names, they say. Anthrocentric, they say. Fuck 'em, I say. It's my choice.

West of Eidolonics Avenue, we howl out of Little Arabia and under the eaves of Cogentville. At once the rain is gone, and Dundas is an echoing halogen tunnel through overgrown masses of architecture. Buildings in Cogtown evolve constantly, with complete disregard for city regs and permits. They sprout overhead pedways, cantilevered wings, swooping bridges. Entire streets are spanned, lost under layers of nano-assembled confusion. Walls are always being knocked through, ramps built apparently at random between adjacent structures, entire city blocks domed over with great geodesic umbrellas. Every surface is covered in spectacular art. Not advertising, but luminescent paintings, tilework, bas-relief, animated graphics, palimpsests of cryptic polyglot graffiti...

"And this used to be such a nice neighbourhood," Daniel mutters. He's joking; twenty-five years ago this was all abandoned office towers stuffed full of flood refugees and squatters. Not a lot of human pedestrians around here now; mostly cogents and lesser bots, walking, rolling, spidercrawling. The majority are anthropine (like me), but only a few are biomimetic, with all the pseudo-organic details. It's unpopular now, politically uncool, to mimic humans too closely. Pinocchio Syndrome, they call it. Many of today's cogents wear their mechine nature proudly: neosomatics with weird new body plans and lustrous metallic skins.

"How come you don't live in Cogtown, Mohad?" Dan's always posing these irritating questions.

"You're suggesting I shouldn't live wherever I like, monkey-boy?"

"Hey," Daniel spreads his hands, "for all I care, you could move in with my sister. Just seems as if cogents prefer the company of other cogents, y'know?"

"More like humans would rather not live next door to cogents. The city only ceded control of this area to keep the phobe riots to a minimum."

"Hey, can you blame 'em? Look at what you've done with the place."

Now I know he's just trying to spin me up. I let it go. "Actually, at one time I lived just over there, off North TelNex. Quite a long time ago. But I found it ... I don't know ... confining."

"Claustrophobic?" Daniel is unconvinced. "Not very cogentlike of you, Gene-baby."

"Neither, for that matter, is policework. But here I am anyway." As the newest member of the Squad, I have to put up with a lot. Such as

Danny calling me *Gene-baby*.

Up ahead, Dundas becomes a long arcade, crammed with rapid response vehicles, pulsating with cherry and blueberry lights. Our squad car decelerates reluctantly, kills the siren, and tucks itself between two Greater Metro Area Police units and a Fire Department Mobile HQ. The street-tunnel has been sealed off for the next three blocks, and all the surrounding buildings are being evacuated. Streams of confused cogents, mixed with a few humans, are being herded along the sidewalks.

We get out. The uniforms working the cordon recognize us and wave us through.

"Forensics are still going over the scene," says Dan. "Let's hit the roof of the hostel first."

The elevator lets us off on the thirty-first. We take the stairs to the roof. It's cool but not raining up here. The top of this and several other buildings are sheltered under great waves of photosynth fabric, a retrofit tensile structure suspended from masts and cables.

Daniel and I walk through the hostel's rooftop bamboo forest, ducking under yellow tape to approach the northern edge. There are tactical units patrolling the railings, and a constable from 52 Division is interviewing a chromefaced cogent in a Mao cap and leather jacket — Severe Commy Skeptic semself.

"No, we don't have security cameras," sie is saying. "What would we need with security cameras?"

Xu Kelly and her technicians are just packing their survey bots away into steel cases marked *Crime Scene Unit*. "Ah," she says, "Detectives Aramaki and Mohad, our local counter-terror experts." She pulls back the hood of her cleansuit, revealing grey hair, tied back into a tail. Half-smiling, she shakes Daniel's hand but somehow neglects mine. "Took you boys long enough."

Okay, it's true that Dan and I collared the Marionette Bombers, but I wouldn't call myself either a counter-terror expert or a boy...

"My team's finished here," she says. "Over at the scene, give us, maybe, another hour?" She waggles a hand at the nanofab facility, about forty metres away across the gap between the two buildings.

There's no smoke over there, only a lot of wafting dust. Most of the facility's upper windows have been blown out, the twenty-ninth floor torn open at the southwest corner. White curtains billow through the open walls, like mourning sheets.

"Who's in charge?" asks Dan.

"Sergeant Moon, got here twenty minutes ago. He's at the scene."

"Sie," I say, unable to stop myself.

"Huh?"

"Detective-Sergeant Moon is a *sie*, not a *he* or a *she*." Humans of Kelly's generation simply refuse to adopt the new pronouns. She was born well before cogents were invented. If not for longevity treatments she'd have been retired two decades ago.

"Right, whatever." She indicates a raised meditation garden: black gravel raked into smooth waves around islands of brightly coloured machine parts. "Now, over here, we've got footprints." We take a closer look. The pebbles have recently been disturbed by unshod feet, each with four broad toes. Not unlike my own.

"Cogent?"

"Well, it ain't human." Kelly watches my reaction. "No sebum, no skin flakes, no biotic residue at all. Shape of the print says anthropine, but definitely inorganic."

Careful not to disturb the prints, I step up onto the garden's tiled ledge. "A nice, clear shot from here. And these overhanging branches would have provided some concealment." Zoom in: a few of the spear-shaped leaves are brown and curled at the ends. "Some of these singed."

"Say what?" Kelly snaps.

Daniel rubs it in: "Going blind in your dotage, Xu?"

I pull the branch towards me, slip a couple of the burnt leaves into a sample baggie, hand it to Kelly.

She doesn't seem grateful. "We'll check for traces of missile propellant."

Dan says, "Thanks, Mom, you're the best."

"Fuck you," she replies politely. Kelly takes her cases and ducks through the yellow tape.

Daniel looks about. "Okay then, let's canvass the building, see if anyone saw a cog waving a grenade launcher around."

I tell him I'll be along in a moment. He strolls off to interview Severe Commy.

Standing still, exactly where the killer stood, I study the blast damage. At 10x magnification I can see most of the room's demolished interior. It's a public ceremonial chamber, small and nondenominational, panelled in blond wood, with several gently tiered rows of simple benches curving around a central platform. Broad diamondpane windows in the back wall presumably provide an overview of the high-security nanofactory beyond. Four mantislike telebots are picking reverentially through the wreckage. And standing in the room's broad doorway, waiting for the CSU bots to finish, is the only other cogent in the Homicide unit: Detective-Sergeant Gondwanaland Moon.

I open a vox connection. +Was it an Upgrade ceremony?+

Sie looks up, jet-black eyes glinting in a yellow-gold face, and voxes back, +Where are you, sweets?+

+The hostel's rooftop, opposite you.+ I hold up a blue-grey hand. +I take it the parents brought their kids here to Upgrade?+

+A Burning Day. They were comping a set of twins this evening.+

A pause to take it in. There is a particular chill to this crime, so deliberate, so malicious, so clearly psychotic...

+Idents?+

Sie voxes, +The adult is Deep Field Scanner, twenty-four, spouse of Jade Kilowatt and Chronic Flesh Nebula — Kilowatt and Nebula are seriously injured but recoverable. Of their children, only Sentient Forest survived, if in several pieces. Siblings Cyanogen Cat, Cadmium Dust, and Volatile Sky were deemed unrecoverable at the scene. They were a quad, all aged five. Shit, Mohad, doesn't it just make you sick?+

It does. Even if you're not fully organic and you can't easily get ill. The myones clench across my stomach, mimicking human muscles, triggered by the same ancient instinctive responses: protect the young; ensure the future of the tribe.

A CSU teleoperator cuts in: +Moon, we've got one.+

Slowly and with the utmost care, one of the mantids draws something out from under a pile of glass shards and ceiling panels, holds it up. A fluorescent orange cube, six centimetres on a side. Pulled from somebody's chest cavity, trailing strands of fiberoptic and fullerwire.

+We've just taken a Red Box from one of the victims.+

+Intact?+ Moon voxes to the CSU team, +Get the data recorders to Dewdney at the lab, pronto.+

I capture images of the scene from my point of view, sending them on to Moon.

Sie pixes back several closeups of the ceremonial chamber — and tacks on three magnified seconds of an anthropine figure in a rain-wet charcoal jacket, framed by bamboo foliage. Prussian-blue skin, embossed navy eyebrows, a hairless androgynous manikin. I seem small and isolated, my indigo eyes lost in shadow.

+Don't look like that, sweets.+ Moon's voice in my head, soothing. +What're you doing after watch?+

Hoo boy, do they have scary attitudes towards reproductive rights. Birthright is controlled by that human/cogent bureaucracy, the Neuremics Authority. Or Repro Cops, as I call 'em...

See, instead of genes, cogents have neuremes, *genetic algorithms that direct the growth of the neural nets in their brains (yeah, I'm oversimplifying wildly here; so what?). The neuremes code for a lot of fundamental emergent behaviours: reflexes, primitive drives, instincts, basic learning agents, like, say, neurolinguistic deep structures. Just as we do, they have to learn everything else from scratch — walking, talking, social skills, everything.*

A complete set of neuremes is a neurome, *right?*

So, to make a baby cogent, you get a blank brain from an authorized nanofactory, and you Burn it, hardwire a neurome into it. The neurome can be a dupe, a straight copy of one adult's original, or it can be a comp, *a semi-random composite of code from two or more adults.*

After Burning, you subject the brain to months of rigorous testing and fault-detection. Once it passes (nearly 15% still don't, even today), you install it in a bot body and power it up — happy Birth Day. For safety reasons, the "infant" body is small and weak, like a human child's, and they Upgrade periodically to bigger, stronger bodies as they get older and more coordinated.

But what if the burnt-in neurome fails the tests? Say it shows an unacceptable risk of going autistic, or learning-disabled, or whatever? Too bad. The all-powerful Neuremics Authority nixes that brain, and it's destroyed. The Repro Cops do that all the time. They can also tell adult cogents whether or not they're fit to reproduce. Ask a cogent about it, and sie'll just shrug and give you a "that's the way it's gotta be" speech.

They don't call it eugenics, but that's exactly what it is.

What I want to know is: how soon before they start expecting us to put up with the same shit?

–Theodore Henry, textpost to Polymath Planet: Debate group: Ethics Round Table; Thread: What right to reproduce?

Dawn is coming on all rosy and optimistic as we check in again at Central Operations, entering via the garage to dodge the scrum of news reporters in the atrium. We've spent a depressing night canvassing for potential witnesses, collecting eye-capture recordings from any cogents willing to provide them, and interviewing the victims' traumatized family and friends. Useless interviews, as it turns out, but they have to be done.

One wall of the Media Room is running a constant parade of

newspix, silent and largely ignored: a winding Mars street, severed by an orange rockslide; a live Dodo, squawking at a cloning technician for more food; Transnational Leisure Party delegates in Caracas, nominating replacements for their assassinated leader; aerial shots of the blown-out walls of the Usutu Truth facility, above the inaccurate caption, *Slaughter in Robot Village.*

The witness-eye recordings give us our first pictures of the perpetrator. Glimpsed as sie entered the hostel: rail-thin, 140cm tall, snow-white all over, dark blue jumpsuit, no shoes, large black backpack. A thoroughly standard somatic configuration, about as nondescript as a cogent can get. Sie took the stairs from ground floor to roof, passing two other witnesses on the way up. Nobody saw sem leave.

"Why," asks Daniel, "did this fucker blow away a family of other cogents?"

"Let's not jump to conclusions." I gesture at the motion-blurred image frozen on the wall next to the newsfeed. "That could be a dumbot, not a cogent. Teleoperated, perhaps."

"Illegally running without a transponder, if it was. The Monitoring Agency says there's no record of a remote of any kind in that building last night."

"Maybe the perp was a cybrid," Moon suggests.

Dan shakes his head at that. "What, some Humanista had his brain transplanted into a mechine body? I just don't see it happening."

Moon mutters something in agreement.

"You two..." Dan's grin is not a pleasant one. "Sure you're not just denying the possibility that one of your own is capable of something like this?"

"Aramaki," I say, "it simply isn't terribly likely. Yes, cogents do kill sometimes, it happens. There are psychotics, post-traumatics, the so-called Self-Defense Militia, but—" But I'm not certain what I intended to say after that.

"Problem," says Moon, frowning. "If the perp's a cogent, we have fuck-all for a motive. For now, we'll proceed on the assumption that this is a terrorist action by synthephobes."

"Fine," Dan says, surrendering. "Which group?"

By this time, the Humanist Front have indeed claimed responsibility, nearly ten minutes ahead of the Organic Brigades, Movement for Bio-Supremacy, and Terran Heritage. The anonymous messages were received by the news media or posted to online discussions. None of the claimants, thus far, display any convincingly intimate knowledge of the crime.

And already the pressure is building: everyone's looking to Detective-Sergeant Moon for a swift resolution to the crisis. Sie's feeling the heat not only from our boss, Inspector Dennet, but also from the cogent community, from City Hall, from Queen's Park, from every level of government up to Parliament and beyond. Warnings from on high that any sign of serious trouble between humans and cogents creates deep concern among all cogent-friendly nations. Which is to say, among signatories to the Convention on Offworld Trade and Development, the treaty that first opened the door for cogent citizenship and civil rights. The ratifying governments want very much to ensure peaceful relations with cogents. Especially with the millions Out There, home-steading the interplanetary frontier...

As well, there have been suggestions that this case ought to be handed over to "someone with a better track record." Moon's success rate is as good as anyone's, but sie's still living under the shadow of the last redball sie handled: the infamous "baby-box" case. Early last year, somebody stole an ectogestation system from the Royal Edward Medplex, along with the fetus that was developing in it. That case is still open, with no significant progress. And no sign of Baby Doe.

At intervals I find myself obsessing over the Usutu Truth crime scene model — *just one more time* — irrationally bugged by the itching suspicion that I'm missing something, some detail that ought to be obvious...

"You can start reading out the Red Boxes," Inspector Dennet

announces, sweeping into the Media Room with a crash of thunder and a blare of trumpets. "The paperwork's finally come through." He drops a secure memcard in front of Moon, then four evidence bags containing the victims' Sense Data Recorders. "Legal releases all signed by the remaining spouses and two judges. You are allowed to replay visual and auditory tracks from noon onwards, but nothing else, understood?"

"What about the survivors' records?" Daniel asks.

"On that card. Except for the kid's. We're still waiting on the waivers for those."

"What's the holdup?"

"Sentient Forest remains unconscious," Dennet says. "They're putting sem back together at Dragonfly Penumbra Reparatory." Legal protections are stronger for the living. If the cogent is still alive, even a minor, then parental signatures are not sufficient.

"You'll just have to ask the kid's permission," Dennet tosses back, already on his way out the door, "soon as sie's online again."

As if we aren't busy enough. For the next few hours, Daniel, Moon, and I are wired into the Media Room, performing a disquieting task: observing in intimate detail the final hours of four recently deceased people.

Deep Field Scanner spends most of the afternoon at a block school, teaching the quads and a dozen other kids. Chronic Flesh Nebula prepares the family's apartment to receive guests. Jade Kilowatt is with a lover. Their marriage is a typically open arrangement, more about companionship and parenting than exclusivity. After all, what does sex have to do with procreation?

In the evening, the family hosts a dinner party for about twenty close friends. Lots of food and drink are consumed, the kind cogents like, full of bizarre flavours, textures, sensations, but largely without nutrient value. Eating is an entirely sensual and convivial pastime, otherwise unnecessary. But even some "real food" is served, for the three human guests.

Well after dusk, the whole family walks the few blocks to the nanofab facility. Not an odd hour: the four ceremonial chambers, booked months in advance, are busy twenty-four hours a day. As is traditional, the family leaves behind clothes, cash, and any other anthrocentric affectations.

They are escorted into the chamber by an elder official, anthropine, ser forehead bearing a small Neuremics Authority sigil. Shortly a yellow six-legged attendant carries in two clear polymer spheroids, each containing freshly minted cogent brainware. Superconducting neural nets with integral coolant systems. The official decrypts and verifies the new pair of neuromes. The spheroids are placed on a table and connected up to the neurome server. Then the official and attendant politely leave the room, allowing the family to conduct the Burning in private.

Deep Field Scanner begins to make an informal speech...

Sie hears one of the kids gasp.

Then a crack/flash, and nothing more.

The Convention is a hollow joke. Like all those governments didn't sign the Con just to placate the cogents, praying the cogs would agree not to take over any more of the planet behind our backs.

Face it, we're going to be pushed into extinction by our own so-called "mind-children." Treaties and laws won't save us. Laws didn't keep Virani and Bronwyn from inventing the first senchines. The UN's Hazardous R&D spooks didn't stop Eidolonics from bodging together their short-lived mentally unstable cognants. And sure as shit, no World Science Court kept the buggers in Melbourne from dumping their damned cogents on us. Nope. More legislation is not the answer. It's far too late for that now.
   –Theodore Henry, textpost to MediaNexus One: Discussion group:
   World Parliament; Thread: Convention Good/Convention Bad

Second watch is nearly over by the time Cruncher names our first suspect.

The system's real designation is some unmemorable acronym, but everyone simply calls it Cruncher, because that's what it does. A mass of neural nets bathed in liquid nitrogen, Cruncher has been eating vast databases for over half a century, sucking the marrow out of every legally available network and nexus, masticating unthinkable volumes of unconnected factlets, developing an acute taste for complex hidden relationships. Out of enormous volumes of dross, Cruncher digests a few surprisingly useful little sense-packets. Such as:

1) chemical taggants in the rocket-grenade's residue identify the explosive as Pyrochem NanoIndustries "Detanit" 2083-A, specifically originating from a lot sold to Gaian Extraction Ltd;

2) this shipment was received at a Sudbury supply depot three years ago, and later apparently expended in normal mining operations; however,

3) certain anomalies in the company's tracking records suggest that up to four kilos may subsequently have gone missing;

4) GaianEx was, for over a decade prior to the recent economic corrections, the contract employer of Richard Kindred, forty-two, a mining teleoperation technician and Metro resident; and

5) Mr. Kindred is a known supporter of the Humanist Front, and one of several individuals suspected of authoring synthephobe propaganda under the pseudonym "Theodore Henry."

"Baby's on fire!" exclaims Daniel. "You called it, Gene. Our perp used a friggin' telebot."

Moon pulls the optic lead from behind ser left ear. "Kindred was probably sitting safely at home the whole time, running that walking waldo remotely."

I'm already downloading everything Cruncher can give me authored by "Theodore Henry."

To make matters worse, we humans are all turning into cybrids.

We get injured, or just get old, soon we get plastic eyes, myoelectric legs, mechine heart and lungs, eventually we're all just jarbrains in bot bodies. Pathetic cogent-wannabes. Millions aren't waiting until they get sick, they're having themselves rebuilt now. Why wait? Throw away your humanity today and avoid the rush!

Meanwhile over in Africa, the cogs in the so-called Free Enclaves are doing "cephaline" implants: wiring cogbrains into animal bodies. Of course, they have to resect most of the animal's brain to do it, bit by bit, while it's still developing. The buggers have made cephaline cogents out of large dogs, a cheetah, even some chimps and gorillas.

If you're lucky enough to live in a non-Con country like the US, you might think the authorities can keep the cogents out pretty easily. Think again. Even the animals wandering your eco-preserves might really be cephalines.

–Theodore Henry, textpost to: Conspiracy Research News Nexus:
Feedback Group: New threats to consider; Thread: Everyone is wrong!

Night again. We've pulled a triple watch, and I'm feeling like burnt toast. Moon could easily keep going for another two shifts, but sie orders everyone to get some dreamtime. Even cogents require sleep, if only an hour or two per twenty-four. A brain has to be unconscious while it does memory consolidation and other neural housekeeping chores.

Our long afternoon culminated in a large multi-Division meeting in the auditorium. Cruncher has identified half a dozen suspected members of Kindred's cell of Humanistas. Supporting evidence is being collected, warrants obtained, surveillance begun. Six simultaneous raids have been laid out, scheduled for a few minutes after dawn.

The night air is warm and sluggish as Moon and I emerge from Central Ops via the loading docks behind the building.

I light up a cig, savouring the dark carbon taste. "I heard something about a new message?"

Summoned from the garage, Moon's Volvo Ceptor pulls up, opens its doors for us.

"Yeah," Moon replies. "Cogent Self-Defense Militia. They say they'll be 'forced to take retaliatory action against the synthephobes' if the responsible parties are not rounded up swiftly."

"Ah. Just the kind of help we need."

In the car, sie begins to unwind, seeming to slough off all the accumulated pressures of the day along with ser jacket.

"A telebot. Damn." Sie steals the cig from my lips and takes a long drag of nobacco smoke. "I was kinda hoping the perp would be some pathetic loser of a cybrid, just so I could laugh in Aramaki's smarmy face."

"Loser?" Through swirls of smoke, I watch those ink-dark eyes reflect the passing streetlights. "Cybrids are all losers?"

Sie waves the cig, dismissive. "Cyburgers. Humans should repair themselves with human parts. They can clone 'em up, grow them in culture, or at least make them *look* biological. Why pretend to be mechinik? Cybrids are mimsies, really. They mimic cogents, the way biomimetic cogs ape humans. It's undignified. Completely lacking in self-respect." Moon's voice carries a clear and dismaying note of contempt.

I take back the cig, suck it slowly down to ash, saying nothing.

We pass the audacious diamondoid arc that is Greater Metro City Hall. Looks like God's own wedding band has been half-embedded in the ground at a radical forty-degree angle, expressing all the over-confidence of the early Nano Era. It embraces Bicentennial Park in its arms — knots of bored teens there by the fountains, hanging out, smoking up, necking under the trees. Most of the youths are sporting the latest fashion in biometallic skin mods.

"Ever thought about kids, Gene?"

I almost laugh, until I notice sie's not joking. "What, you mean having my own?"

"Careful what you say," sie warns, smiling. "I had this lover once, happened to mention sie had no interest in reproducing, ever. Now, I'd never even imagined comping with sem, understand. But suddenly, I lost all desire for the cog. Don't know why. Just one of life's mysteries..."

As the car swims into the traffic streams of the LunaBank Expressway, Moon's mouth finds mine, hands at work between us, undoing my clothes. Sie tastes of smoke.

+At least blank the windows,+ I vox, unable to speak.

+Such a prude,+ sie replies, but the Ceptor's windows opaque, the seatbacks lie flat, music comes on: Branca's *Ascension #1*. Massed screaming guitars, perfect-tuned, crawling up a dissonant, Fibonacci-derived series, muted somewhat by Moon's tongue in my left ear. We struggle out of our shirts, chests crushed together, my senskin flushing dark blue-violet against Moon's suede-textured buttery gold. Ser mouth descends to my petite breasts — grown in the past hour just for this occasion, shivering exquisitely against ser lips and teeth. Pants sliding off, then a hardness against my thigh: sie has deployed a cock this time, or something like one. Not content to play the passive Ladytron, I send out an exploratory party of sensitive tendrils to meet the space invader. I feel it flex in a most unlikely manner. Preparing clefts and mouths with no human parallel, I am flooded with anticipation.

I awaken with a jolt. Moon's bedroom, closet light on, the city glowing and feverish beyond the windows. Silhouette of ser fake Chinese rubber plant, with its green plastic watering can...

"Sorry, sweets," sie says from the right of the bed. "Didn't mean to wake you." Sie finishes pulling on black pants, selects a shirt from the closet.

"You didn't, I—" Shards of nightmare fall away as I grasp for them. "I had a strange dream."

Screaming rockets. A chaos of exploding colour: brilliant green, spiralling gold. Helpless paralysis, aching apparitions that once were limbs...

Moon sits on the bed and leans over to kiss me.

I slide my hand over ser nipples; they're already fading back into

Moon's soft-bronze senskin. Until next time.

"It's after midnight," sie says. "I'm heading back in to Central Ops to see that things are shaping up nicely. You just go back to sleep." Sie's noticed I have an unusual need for sleep, over five hours per night. Sie thinks it's weird, but tolerable. "Get lots of dreamtime. We all need to be sharp for the morning."

I hear music from downstairs, melodious deep-thimba. The girls must still be up. Moon shares this revivalist brownstone with two human families, a parenting collective. I have a small apartment in West Hill, but these days I often don't see it for a week at a time.

"Gondwanaland. Were you being serious, before, about wanting kids?"

"Well," sie studies me with those coal-black eyes, "not this year, obviously. But, yeah. I want kids. We should do it some day. You and me, Officer Blue. Comp a pair of twins, maybe. We could all live here. I think the others would love to have some little cogs around the place..."

Ser voice fades out as sie notices my expression, uncertain and non-committal, masking a growing sense of panic.

"Just think about it, okay?"

Sie gets up and finishes dressing.

I settle into the pillows. "Will you be there when we pick up Kindred?"

Jacket on and ready to go, sie looks back from the doorway. "Not in person. I'll be running things from Central Ops. You and Aramaki can handle Kindred. But you be careful, eh, baby?"

What did we think we needed them for? Clearly it was the worst kind of desperation move, grasping at straws. A race drowning in its own effluents, destroying entire forests, wiping out other species without remorse. Praying for some kind of deliverance from ourselves.

When Mind Theory came along, the cogence-lab girls and boys thought they could make superbeings. Researchers had been scanning human brains for decades, tweezing out the wiring responsible for every human ability, every emotion, even romantic love (activation centres located in the anterior cingulate gyrus, the insula, the caudate nucleus and so on).

As soon as the brainmappers had abstracted out the human equivalent of a neurome, they started translating it into something that could run on fullerwire nets. They really believed the cogs would evolve straight up an exponential curve, quickly becoming godlike super-intellects. Didn't work, did it? Seems there are scaling problems. Mainly heat dissipation, systemic synchronization, emergent bottlenecks, all kinds of unexpected limiting factors. Self-aware systems just can't bound up the evolutionary ladder so fast as they'd hoped. Lucky for us, eh?

Still, sixty-odd years on, we're suffering the effects of their Promethean hubris. Cogent enclaves are proliferating across the planet, even under the oceans. A disease left unchecked for too long, metastasizing wildly, competing for resources. Inevitably the cancer will begin to kill off the parent organism, human civilization.

The patient's condition is entirely iatrogenic.
–Theodore Henry, textpost: University of Terra at Belize City:
Department of Anthropology: Open Forum: Culture of
Science; Thread: Technology as Religion.

"Shitty-looking place," says Dan, lowering his binoculars. "I thought mining was a decent-paying job."

"Mining's not what it used to be," I point out. "No more risking your life down there underground."

It's not quite six in the morning, a pink sun just crawling above the rooftops. Daniel Aramaki and I are waiting in an unmarked grey Persina on Ash Crescent, about two hundred metres along a gentle uphill curve from Kindred's suburban residence. He lives in an antique split-level under a mossy, swaybacked roof. Scrub grass has taken over the yard. A lawn jockey with silver-painted skin stands guard by the crumbling front walk.

"And Kindred's taken some hits recently. GaianEx hasn't had him on contract for over two years. His ex took the condo. At least he gets to see his kid on the weekends."

"Definitely fits the profile." Dan takes a swig from his coffee, twists his mouth in disgust. "What's taking them so long?"

I mind's-eye the status display. "Surveillance is having trouble determining whether he's alone or not. He lives in the basement. Something in the foundation seems to be clouding their millimetre-wave imagers, and they've lost contact with the flybots they've sent in."

"Probably built on old landfill," says Dan. "Compacted aluminum cans, car batteries, plastic diapers..."

Moon's voice hums clearly over the vox link, +SWAT teams, take up secondary positions.+

Short figures dash across the adjacent weedgrown lawns — armoured, inhumanly agile, armed with shockstaves. I glimpse others leaping the fence into the backyard. Their asymmetric heads are agglomerations of lenses, scopes, detector vanes.

+Team One, Control. We're in position.+

+All teams...+ A long pause, then: +Playtime.+

The SWATbots ignore the doors. They tear the security bars away from the ground-level casements and disappear, boots first, through the windowpanes.

+Room one, clear.+

The Persina makes its move, accelerating towards the residence. Daniel seals his armour vest. I'm lightly bulletproofed, but there's no telling what kind of firepower these synthephobes may have stockpiled...

+Stairs, clear.+ The teleoperators calmly report in, one at a time, through crashing waves of static on the vox link.

Jerking, blurry pix tile across my display, half-obscured by interference noise: rooms full of junk; mote-filled sunbeams in a dismal wreck of a kitchen; a startled look on Kindred's pillow-creased face, eyes opening to his worst nightmare — *cornered by faceless implacable robots*—

+Police! Down! Down on the floor!+

By the time Daniel and I are out of the car and sprinting up the front walk, it's all over. A SWATbot casually opens the door for us. +All secure, Detectives. No booby traps. Come on down.+

In the basement, there's a smell of mouldy carpets. Slivers of glass crunch underfoot. Flags hang in the doorways: "HF" in white on blood red and forest green. Blank screens wrap around the teleop workstation in one corner, the waldo controls under an accumulation of dust. I note a variety of handguns and rifles, some locked into cases, others just sitting out on cluttered tables.

In the bedroom, Richard Kindred lies on his face, in rapidly yellowing underwear, wrists gathered in plastic restraints behind his back. He is breathing heavily, but still unable to move, aside from the occasional twitch.

I turn around in wonder. Tacked up across the low ceiling and covering every wall: layer upon layer of silvery pie-tins, aluminum foil, and chickenwire.

From his seat in the back of the car, Kindred watches me with a look of resolute fury. He's very pale, balding, immobile as a showroom dummy. Hasn't said a word since the stun wore off. Not even to thank us for letting him get cleaned up and dressed. Sweat is beading across his porcelain forehead.

"I don't think he likes you, Gene-machine." Dan puts his shades on and drops into his seat. "What's the matter, Dick?" he says, swivelling to grin at the suspect. "Got a problem with the help? Just be glad you don't have to *work* with this uppity fucker. I gotta listen to Detective Love Doll here, yak about how he fought against your kind in North Africa. He's a real pain in the ass, in fact."

Kindred's seething gaze never strays from me.

The Persina's doors begin to shut, but I override them. "I'll be just a few moments, Aramaki." I climb out again.

"Where you going?"

"Something's bugging me..." I head back towards that abject house. "Need to take another look."

Two steps from the car, I'm suddenly thrown to the ground in a blast of heat. Trembling, I try to rise on pavement-scraped hands and knees, but my left arm gives way. Through sheets of pain, I see a million tiny chunks of crystallized safety glass, bouncing and refracting brilliant orange. I have the sense to start rolling, away from the car, or what's left of it. Small and large pieces are hailing out of the air all around me. My roll puts out the flames I've only just noticed: the back of my neck and my clothes were on fire.

Sitting up, I see the Persina's smoking remains.

Crazy bastard blew himself up.

+A thoracic implant,+ says Moon, framed in my mind's-eye, pixing from downtown. +About thirty grams of Detanit, wrapped in some sort of incendiary compound. Kelly's people are trying to identify the incendiary.+

And where, I wonder, did Kindred find someone to put a thing like that inside him?

Unclothed, immobilized from the neck down, I'm cradled in the gentle grip of an operating-room couch at Dragonfly Penumbra Reparatory. It's a class four clean-room in here, so no face-to-face visitors for me just yet. Moon has assured me sie'll come down as soon as sie can get away.

A legless white telebot is attaching fullerwire bundles to my left shoulder terminals, where my arm used to be. I wish the tech would hurry it up: the continuous phantom pain from the missing limb is going to drive me mad in a few more minutes, besides evoking well-buried memories I would much rather leave safely undisturbed.

+What's Dan's status?+

+I just spoke with the hospital,+ says Moon. +They're cooling him down for nanosurgery. His lungs are damaged, but not too badly. His chances look good. But the burns, Gene...+ For a moment ser confidence seems to falter. +They're going to have to replace all of his skin, his limbs, his face and eyes... In a few weeks, he'll be a full-body cybrid.+

But Danny wasn't the target; I was. When I got out of the car, Kindred must have thought he was going to miss his chance...

+Dennet's about ready to have kittens,+ Moon continues, +threatening to fire everyone in Surveillance, the SWAT unit, even me. Wants to know how we failed to detect Kindred's implant.+

+As the arresting officer,+ I point out, +it was my responsibility—+

Moon waves both palms in front of ser face. +Oh, don't be so fucking noble, Gene. I don't want to hear it. And you weren't the A/O, Danny was.+

"Ser Mohad," the teleop tech interrupts politely, "you may feel a momentary twinge as we start feeding the simulated input."

"Fine. Just hurry up."

A brief spike, then at last the agony recedes like flames doused in water. Replaced by virtual sensations, to fool my brain into believing my left arm is still there.

The tech assures me that the new limb will be ready for installation within two hours. "After that, we'll do something about patching the senskin on your back and neck. Okay?" Then sie vacates the telebot. It swings away from the couch, bows its head and shuts its eyes, as if in prayer.

+Gondwanaland, you've questioned the other Humanistas in the cell?+

+Yeah, but we didn't get shit from them. And they all seem to have hermetic alibis for the night before last. We're holding them on various weapons charges, resisting arrest, distributing hate lit, while we build a case for conspiracy.+

+Any progress on tracing the perp's telebot?+

Moon seems confused by this. +Um, no luck there. Could be any of several recent models. The pix we have aren't too clear...+

+What about the kid, Sentient Forest? Do we have those sense records yet?+

+Um, sie's awake, just a few floors up from you. We can get permission any time. If we even need the records. But— What's the matter, Blue?+

+What's the matter? Moon, we've got to find the bastard with the rocket launcher, before somebody else gets killed.+

Sie squints at my image with growing concern. +What d'you mean? We got the guy, remember? Blew himself to bits in your squad car, right?+

Sie still hasn't got it. +No, no...+ I retrieve and transmit some pix from this morning's arrest. +Take a look at these. I don't believe Kindred's touched that teleop workstation in months, maybe years, not even to clean it. He almost certainly supplied the explosives, but— Moon, he can't possibly be the perp.+

Instead, we gave them the run of the cosmos, sent them in our place, sent them out to colonize the system, even off to other stars now. Too expensive to send humans, say the parsimonious bean-counters, we need to respire and eat and shit. We have to haul biospheres around wherever we go. Nah, we're too cheap for that. Let's just send the bots to do our work, to prepare the way for us, to build the infrastructure we need to survive Out There.

But what if they decide they don't want to lay out the carpet for us? Maybe they'd rather take the whole cosmos for themselves?

–Theodore Henry, textmail to: News Editor, ActionPix Worknet.

A grey Persina screams along the LunaBank Expressway, all alone. The rearview is full of roiling flames.

I wonder if I should open the window to let out the thickening smoke.

Next to me, Danny has turned black, his face charred away, his arms and legs reduced to carbonized sticks.

I try to speak, but my body has been replaced by phantoms, itching, cramping, howling in my head: the mourning wails of brain-wiring suddenly without purpose, neural agents without jobs now that the skin and muscles and senses they used to serve are lost...

"Hey! Hey, stupid blue thing, wake up!"

Lavender plastic curtains. The Reparatory. I must have dropped off. Moon is sitting on the edge of the bed, shaking me.

"You were making those awful whining noises again."

"Sorry. Just a dream."

"Fuck, Gene," sie strokes my chest with one hand. "What's with these nightmares? I've never known anyone who gets them so often."

"Don't worry, Moonie." I cover ser hand with mine. "Only a touch of post-traumatic stress, nothing too serious. I'll be okay, really."

My non-existent left arm pringles strangely. A flat box taped to my chest is feeding virtual sensations to my peripheral nervous system, keeping the phantoms at bay.

Sie stares at me for a long moment, caught in a realization, but trying to conceal ser horror. Out of concern for my feelings, I suppose.

"You *can't*, can you?" sie asks, and I know just what sie's thinking. "They won't let you, the Neuremics Authority. Something's gone a bit wrong upstairs, gives you these nightmares. And they've revoked your right to reproduce. Oh, sweets..."

"No, Moon, no, it's not—" I falter, not sure if I should go on.

"You don't have to be ashamed, Gene. It's not your fault. I understand." Sie nods, sadly, accepting. But I can see the disappointment in Moon's eyes. And the pity. Sie doesn't say the words, but it's clear what sie's thinking. *Bad Code.*

"Listen," I say, swinging my legs off the bed, "we don't have time for this right now. We need to get back to work." I get up, my balance a bit off.

GLENN GRANT

"But, Gene, baby. Your arm—"

"They won't be installing it for another hour. And there's one thing I can do in the meantime." I don't have any clothes; they were ruined in the blast. Doesn't matter for now; a naked cog is hardly a big deal, especially in Cogentville. I can pick up a change of clothes later at home.

A one-armed hug in the hallway, then Moon returns to Central Ops, and I head upstairs.

In the Children's Post-Op Ward, I connect my fiber line, one-handed, to the port behind Sentient Forest's left ear. Ser new skin is an iridescent bluebottle-green. The two surviving parents sit in the hall, holding each other. An awareness of mourning hovers around them like an invisible, hypersensitive gas.

"But I don't remember," Forest says. "I really don't remember a thing after we got to the, the place. I'm very sorry." Sie enunciates perfectly, with far more maturity than most human five-year-olds.

"That's alright, Senchie," says a black-feathered angeline, a friend of the family. Sie squats next to the kid's chair. "You lost a few minutes of memory when you were hurt and shut down without prepping first. But that won't affect your sense records. They capture most everything you see and hear, separately from your memories. Memory is a different thing, made of connections in your brain. Sense records are stored sequentially in your chest, in your Red Box."

"Do I have to watch it?" Sie looks to ser parents, then to the ebony angel, very anxious. "I'd really rather not."

"Don't worry, Green Sprout," the angel replies, "you don't have to view any of it. Remember when we learned how to call up sense captures? Just retrieve the captage for the night before last and copy it to your optical output. Okay?"

The little cogent closes ser eyes to concentrate, twists together ser new viridian fingers.

The file appears in my system, then I disconnect and reel the fiber back into my head.

"All done," I say, resisting the urge to muss the kid's ruff of black radiator filaments. "Thanks very much, Ser Forest. You've been a great help."

Sentient Forest is clearly relieved.

"Detective Mohad," says the angeline. "I suppose you're very busy, but... There's a candlelight vigil tonight, to remember those we've lost, and to call for unity and peace. In Bicentennial Park at sundown, if you can make it..."

I collect the memcard with the legal documentation. "I'll try to be there, if I possibly can."

"Detective?" Flecks of gold in the kid's serious green eyes. "How come you only have one arm?"

"An explosion," I say, without thinking.

"Oh," sie says softly, as if *sie's* trying to comfort *me*. "That's what happened to my sibs."

Returned to life, the legless telebot has cozied up to the clean-room's cradle and is busy installing my new arm. I'll need weeks of training to get used to the thing, as my brain re-maps its coordination and control networks.

I've forgotten the technician's name. The thought flits through me that I know nothing about the person who's repairing me. Is sie here in the building, or in Hyderabad? Cogent or human? Gendered or otherwise? And why should it suddenly matter to me, anyway?

While I wait, paralyzed again, I run Sentient Forest's visual and auditory records, watching events nearly thirty-eight hours past...

From the child's perspective, the neurome server is an imposing monolith, its table-top barely below eye level. The Neuremics Authority official and the six-legged attendant politely step out of the ceremonial chamber, allowing the family to conduct the Burning in private.

Apparently bored, Sentient Forest allows ser gaze to slide to the outside windows, to the soaring solar tent overhead, to the bamboo greenery across the gap.

Deep Field Scanner begins to make an informal speech.

Out there in the dark, a brilliant flare, a blur of flame—

Sentient Forest gasps—

A thunderclap shatters the room.

For several seconds there is only rumbling, visual noise, flickering darkness.

Forest is now unconscious, in several pieces in fact, but by chance one of ser eyes is still open, still recording. Details begin to resolve out of a rising pall of smoke and dust. Wood panels, fluttering across the half-obscured visual field. The window frame is a mouth of glass teeth tilted at a mad angle. Torn curtains undulate in the sudden wind.

And there, on the opposite rooftop: a figure, anthropine. It swings a long object onto its back, then vanishes. No, *jumps*. It performs the kind of miraculous stunt that bots have always pulled off effortlessly in netshows, but are never seen to do in real life. It arcs high, out of sight, then appears with a jarring *crunch* in the blown-out window frame. Over forty metres in a single leap. Not a record, but certainly an astounding display of robotic gymnastics.

Silhouetted now, the bot stumbles on injured feet, through the debris, reaching right past Forest's recording eye, and picks up something: a spheroid of clear plastic, one of the freshly minted cogent brains. It goes into the black backpack.

The bot staggers back to the window's mouth, almost out of view, crouches, then leaps again. Disappearing from all ken.

We should've stopped them from proliferating when we had the chance. We should've wiped out the first Free Enclaves as soon as they appeared in South Africa and Australia. They're probably immortal, and they breed like bugs, spawning in nanofactories, broods of two, four, six at a time. At the current rate, they'll own

*the planet within a mere century. Then, we'll be the ones required
to have Sense Data Recorders and locator implants. Maybe they'll
keep a few of us alive in little human-preserves. If we're lucky.*
  –Theodore Henry, textpost to: Institute for Humanity's Future: Public
  Topic: The Cogent Problem; Thread: Time's running out, folks

+Xu Kelly is hopping mad,+ Moon voxes from the Media Room. +She's
ready to kill, either herself or all of her staff. I know how she feels. How
could we not notice that one of the un-Burned brains was missing from
the crime scene?+

Charging back to Central Ops in a squad car, I'm berating myself as
well. On some level, I'd known, or suspected at least. Obviously, my
intuition is worthless.

The seat next to me is empty. Daniel should be here. His absence is
even more irritating than Danny in the flesh.

Responding to the Persina's flashing and wailing, vehicles up ahead
are vacating the centre lane of the LunaBank Expressway, squeezing out
of the way in a near-panic. I'm in a bit of a hurry. I haven't bothered to
find clothes to wear, the singed-black senskin on my back still needs
replacing, and my new left arm has yet to be tested out.

+It doesn't make any sense,+ Moon is saying. +Why would a
Humanista steal a cogbrain? To hold it for ransom? And why only one?
Why not both?+

I have the embryo of an idea, but Moon is too busy bringing me up
to speed.

+It's the telebot traces that really have Kelly pissed off. Her staff
had collected several kinds of myonic gel and senskin at the scene, but
once the victims had been identified they stopped checking the samples.
Everyone assumed all the traces belonged to the victims. Who would
believe the perp had actually been in the goddamn room? Now they've
looked closely at every sample, and, sure enough, some don't belong to
any of the cogents.+ Long serial numbers briefly scroll across my mind's-
eye. +There are registered molecular taggants in the myo-gel. Not from

a cogent. They came from a telebot.+

Oh, you pretty things. Taggants are a detective's best friend.

Moon says it took all of ten minutes to trace the coded compounds to a specific batch of myo-gel, produced in a molecular component plant near Frankfurt. But it took another four hours for Cruncher to connect all the dots, from that batch of gel to a Singapore-based industrial distributor, thence to the licensed nanofacturing facility in Cuba that made the bot's muscles, which were then supplied to a Halifax telebot maker; that firm sold the finished machine via an authorized reseller here in Metro. The specific unit, a Replicraft Spectris 409-S Remotely Operated Anthropine in gloss ivory finish, was finally purchased by a cross-town courier company.

+They reported it stolen six months ago,+ says Moon. +Gone without a trace while delivering somebody's prescription. Property Crimes Squad investigated, without success.+

There the trail would simply have run into a wall, if not for a century's worth of paranoid robotics legislation. All telebots are required to carry Red Boxes, visible bar codes, inertial and GPS tracking devices, anti-theft features, proximity alarms, hardwired kill-switches, and various other security measures. Far more than those required of cogents.

+Whoever stole the telebot is very technical,+ says Moon. +They've disabled or spoofed every security system the thing has. All except one...+

And there in my mind's-eye: stuttering pix of an echoing stairwell, the viewer jogging up, flight after flight, tirelessly. It's dizzying to watch: up a floor, turn, up a floor, turn, up...

+Replicraft hid a mole in the transceiver. Apparently our perp doesn't know about the mole. He seems to have rigged the transceiver to channel-hop constantly, spread-spectrum, even using restricted military wavebands. Very hard to nail down, and probably encrypted. What he doesn't know is that the bot's sense data is being leaked to us over a standard pix channel. Cute, eh?+

+So how come Property Crimes didn't pick up the signal before?+

+The thief must've kept the bot in an off-grid locale. Maybe some place underground.+

We get a short glimpse of the thing's feet: scuffed yellow senskin. The damaged legs have been replaced since the attack on the nanofab.

+What's that building?+ The dim stairwell is whitewashed cinder-block, completely generic. Windows at every second storey look out over urban twilight, blurring past too quickly to catch. +Where's the bastard going?+

+We've only managed to track the signal to within a three-block radius, centered on University and SenStream. We're now sealing off the area and doing a sweep.+

+It's not in Cogentville?+

+Nope, it's—+

The stairs end in a door: *Staff Only*. The Spectris emerges onto a rooftop. It strides along wooden boardwalks between roaring ventilation systems. Low clouds above, bruised violet and red by the end of sunset.

As the machine approaches the edge, Greater Metro City Hall rises into view, a cut-crystal half-torus skewed at a wild angle, arcing over and around Bicentennial Park. Twenty-seven storeys below the bot's vantage, on a shadowed greensward between ornamental trees and floodlit fountains, a large crowd has gathered. Four thousand people at least, a mix of humans and cogents, each individually illuminated by a fluttering handful of light.

+The vigil,+ says Moon. +All personnel: clear the park, immediately.+

Sirens echo up from nearby streets as the Spectris crouches on one knee. It extracts a black metal cylinder from a backpack, unfolds handle grips. The weapon looks crude, all exposed welds and wiring, like something built in shop class by irresponsible high-school students.

+If you get a clear shot, fire at will.+

And I'm stuck here in this goddamn Persina, making less and less headway as the evening traffic thickens. I'm still two kilometres from City Hall.

Moon is now shouting fifty orders a minute. +I don't give a fuck; jam *every* frequency if you have to. Just jam him!+

Driven by extreme frustration, my mind lurches into high gear, wheels spinning near lightspeed, incongruously flashing on Kindred's thoracic implant, Theodore Henry's propaganda, the African free enclaves, two dozen other irrelevant thoughts. That itching suspicion is back, in spades.

The bot connects its optic feed to the grenade launcher, and little green cross-hairs sprout across its visual field. Hundreds of cross-hairs: firing solutions for all cogents within range, and only the cogents. Tight knots of crosses and candles are just now beginning to break apart as cops converge on the park, megaphones crackling. The gunsight settles on a particularly large and clotted group channelled between the fountains.

A buzzing noise distracts the operator. A six-metre flying thing banks into view, solar-fabric wings catching the last seconds of the vermilion sun. A police drone, about two hundred metres away and closing, aimed straight for the telebot's head.

The Spectris swings the fat barrel up at the surveillance plane. Lock is acquired. A *whoosh* of fire, and a missile leaps, seems to wobble, then splashes the police drone into smoking fragments with a hard *clap*.

Now there are real screams of fear down there, and the small figures are scattering rather more urgently. Scrambling right over each other, in fact.

Snicking and pinging metal all around: police sniper fire is picking up. The Spectris pulls back from the ledge and scuttles to a new position, loads a second missile, and again takes a bead on the running cogents. More clusters of crosses blossom.

The perp selects a rich cluster of targets, and locks.

A long, terrible pause...

The trigger remains untouched. The telebot seems frozen in place. Then it shudders, taking multiple sniper hits, and seems to pirouette on the edge...

+Control signal jammed. Good work, people.+

The night blurs, a sense of falling, glimpse of tarmac rushing up—
And my mind's-eye goes black.

For a full minute, I savour the darkness, the welcome relief.

Dennet's voice on the vox link: +Any trace on the control signal?+

Moon says, +No such luck, Inspector.+

I kill the strobes and the siren.

Opening my eyes, I see a face reflected in the Persina's side window, almost purple, fading now towards mauve and blue. For several seconds I barely recognize myself. Who's this androgynous toy action-figure in the fruity colours? It's been three decades since I acquired this face, and many years since I tried to remember the original. I wonder if the perp has ever felt the same confusion. Then, I wonder at my own thought.

Out of my brain's chaos, a terrible pattern is born, as if picked out in thousands of minute flames, almost sublime in its pure, hideous clarity...

I tell the Persina to take the next exit. "New destination: the Royal Edward Medplex. Best speed. Full lights and siren."

Then I vox Moon for backup.

In a semi-abandoned sub-basement I jog down a ramp, feeling the edges of despair.

The Medplex is a sprawling hypertrophic growth of towers and blocks, all nucleated around this huge building, the original hospital, dating from the Second World War. Narrow wings angle off from other wings, labs, wards, offices, research annexes, growths accumulated over the last century and a half.

This is hopeless. The bastard could be anywhere in this maze. I'm gambling on a wild guess.

I step aside for several rattling food service carts. I haven't seen any actual personnel for twenty minutes. There was a tethered maintenance telebot in the south wing, but the operator ignored me. Does anybody ever bother to come down here in person anymore?

+Shit, Moon, this place is a rat warren. I'm still searching, working from the bottom level up. Sorry I couldn't wait for backup. Time may be critical. He's only had the brain for two days. There might still be a chance.+

+What's that, Mohad? You're break—+

For the third time, I lose my vox connection. Hard to re-acquire the network down here, where the ceilings and walls are thickly veined with steam pipes and conduits.

I jog along puddled corridors, checking random doors, finding only a disused laundry, a mechanical workshop, a buzzing electrical transformer. I know the room I'm looking for. I've been there before, long ago in another lifetime. But I was just a kid, and nothing is as I remember it.

+—understand, Mohad?+ Moon's voice again. +Just sit tight, wait until we've sealed the building. We're contacting Medplex management and will query their employee records. Did I get you right, we're looking for a surgical teleop specialist?"

+It was those text posts. "Theodore Henry." It's a faux-stupid persona. He's trying to sound folksy but he's just no good at it. None of those posts are Kindred's work. Take a look at his diction. Nobody uses words like "resect," or "iatrogenic." Except doctors, maybe nurses, lab workers. Or telesurgery techs.+

Through swinging plastic doors, I find a service elevator for the kitchen bots. I hitch a ride up one level, and continue on, past a storeroom full of stainless-steel bathtubs.

+This afternoon, I wondered about the technician working on my arm, some anonymous teleoperator. For all I knew, *sie* could've been our perp. But no, our guy's a Humanista, he wouldn't fix cogents, right? He'd be repairing humans.+

+When he's not implanting bombs in future martyrs...+

+Exactly.+

Here. A tickling of troubled recollections. Yes, this was the place.

Broad double doors marked *Telesurgery Maintenance* — stencilled in black over much-faded text: *Magnetic Resonance Imaging,* and *Caution: Strong Magnetic Fields.* Under large, peeling shock hazard symbols.

+Now, if I wanted to conceal a stolen telebot from telltale satellites and snooping flybots, I'd want some place with a lot of RF shielding. And our guy has so much to hide...+

Past the doors, the connection goes dead.

I step into a darkened workshop, past tables covered in orderly equipment: microsurgical workstations, life-support gear, half-disassembled telebots propped up on testbeds, an obsessively complete array of toolkits, microprobes, spare parts. Dim ochre light from the next room filters through a broad observation window.

Past a haze of memories, I peer into the inner chamber: its walls are half a metre thick, heavily shielded. There's where the MRI scanner used to stand, the huge donut electromagnets long since removed, leaving an obvious gap in the room. That space is now occupied by stacked boxes of diapers, a surgical table, and an ectogestation system.

A pink-skinned nurture-bot stands next to a clear plastic crib, cradling a newborn human in its arms.

Baby Doe, his little head wrapped in micropore bandage, suckles cultured milk from the soft machine's breast.

No. Please, no...

I think we're too late, Moonie.

Reflected movement. I turn to see a half-built one-armed telebot raising a shockstaff. I try to grab its wrist, but my clumsy new arm misses wildly.

A burst of blue pyrotechnics, and I fall spasmodically to the—

Proses are read
Violence ensues

Everything's dead
And nothing is true.
–Theodore Henry, untitled poem found in an encrypted personal file.

"Find what you were looking for?"

Relayed through a ceiling speaker, his knife-smooth voice has sharpened edges. He sits at a workstation in the former MRI chamber, gazing at me through the dust-smeared glass. Dark-haired, caucasian, maybe forty years old, in loose surgical greens. Utterly normal and ordinary, like his stolen telebot.

I must have blacked out for a while there. I've lost time. My internal clock says twenty minutes have passed. Can't remember a thing after the shockstaff...

"Missing something, are you? Or maybe you're looking for me?" He smiles lopsidedly, takes a pull from a bottle of beer. "Looks like you found me, eh?"

The mindless nurture-bot is behind him, pacing the dimly lit room, murmuring to the baby.

He notices my look. "You've seen my son? Cute as a bug, isn't he? Just six months old."

I seem to be paralyzed from the neck down. My arms and legs are cramping up, formications beginning to boil across the skin—

Oh, shit.

I look down: my head and torso are strapped upright on the test table. My limbs have been messily amputated and dumped in a heap beside me, dripping lubricant and myo-gel.

X-ray images appear on one of his screens, text files scrolling up another. "It's really a pleasure to meet you ... Detective Gene Engine Mohad. Seems you're not all that you claim to be. Says here you're a cogent cop, one of the few, the proud. Very nice. But these X-rays say otherwise."

I try desperately to vox, but can't access the net. Too much shielding in these walls.

"Most of you is mechine," he continues, "but, hey, lookee here: lungs, heart, pancreas and what-not, spinal cord, brain nicely nano-cushioned against hydrostatic shock. Artificial colon... Vintage stuff, this bio-maintenance 'ware, thirty years out of date. That makes you one of the earliest, doesn't it? One of the first full-body cybrids. A pioneer! Wow, if this database isn't lying about your age, you must've been all of, what, ten years old when they put you in that body?"

In the grip of screeching neurosensory phantoms and equally terrible memories, I manage to find my voice. "What the fuck do you want?"

"Just a moment, just a moment," he says testily. "I'm *trying* to do an archive search. Thirty years. My, that's a ways back. Yes, here we go. You're not Shelley Stein, you've got a Y chromosome, so you must be..." He looks up, smiling almost warmly. "Mr. Mohandis Boaz Mohad."

He leans forward, dead serious. "You, Mr. Mohad, are a cogsucking traitor to your species."

I see no point in replying.

"What happened to you?" He digs deeper, finding the news stories. "Says here you were on vacation in Venezuela with your parents, when some cretin discarded several paint-soaked rags in a bin ... which then ignited a warehouse full of illegally stored fireworks. You, Ma and Pa, and the hotel you were sleeping in were all were caught in the ensuing conflagration."

His screens show archive pix of a Maracaibo street, severed by rockets, smoke, massive explosions of brilliant green, spiralling gold...

"How fortunate that you all survived, eh? Wasn't much left of you, though. They flew you back in cryosuspension, and— Hey, you were treated right here at King Eddy's Medplex. Alright! Must be Old Home Week for you."

He rotates sections of the actual MRI scans. My ten-year-old body, limbs reduced to blunt stubs, my face a corroded ruin wrapped in synthetic skin. I remember the claustrophobia of the scanner, the ratcheting machine-gun noise of the big magnets, but, above all, the neverending phantom pain.

"I suppose I can understand," he says, a paragon of tolerance, "why you might turn your back on your humanity. All that horror of the flesh, so many human weaknesses. All those corrupt safety inspectors, careless human janitors, insensitive doctors... And worst of all, yes, yes, the betrayal. The cruelty of those who saved you, at such enormous expense. Parents who loved you too much to allow you to die, to escape, no matter how desperately you must have wished for it."

I want so much to kill him. If only to shut him up.

"I can see why you would rebel against them, why you flew off to Morocco. To join the African cogent underground. To fight the good fight against the human oppressor. Man, you were really in the thick of it, eh? You were in Algeria when they freed those cog slaves from that silver mine. And didn't they milk that scandal for all it was worth? Before the Convention opened the floodgates and the cogs started living out in the open, all over, even here. Before you came home and joined the Forcers."

He nods and takes another gulp of beer. "Gee, I wonder what your colleagues would say, if they knew you'd been lying to them all these years?"

"I never made any false claims. My employers know I'm a cybrid. Of course they do. If anybody else wants to assume I'm a cogent, why should I correct them? They'll just ask a lot of questions that — that I shouldn't have to answer."

He considers this. "Nope. I don't think that's going to wash. That sounds like a major rationalization, that does."

"And you, fucker." Hauling myself back from the dead past. "Mr. Theodore Henry or whatever you're really called. What happened to you? What made you such a sick fuck? That artificial womb you've got in there — misappropriated from the Medplex with a fetus developing in it. Then you murdered four people at the nanofab just to steal an un-Burned cogent brain. So you could wire it into that poor kid."

He stares blankly through the glass, through me. "I'm sure I don't know what you're talking about."

"No, you wouldn't. Your delusions are so strong, they won't allow you to recognize your own actions. I've never heard of a more severe case of substrate dysmorphia. To prove your humanity, you joined the Front and became their most vocal advocate of direct action. Anthromimicry taken to psychotic extremes. You even managed to acquire a baby, and convince yourself that he was your own, the ultimate proof of biological virility. No other way for you to reproduce, except to make a cephaline and Burn a dupe of your own neurome. You're a mimsie of the worst kind, Doctor Pinocchio. No wonder the Neuremics Authority revoked your repro rights. And you've just passed on your Bad Code to that child in there."

"I've had enough of this crap," he says, standing. He holds up a flat box, a sense data simulator. "Hope you like this. Maybe it'll help you find what you're missing."

He activates the feed, and I start to scream.

I'm still screaming forty minutes later, when the room's power is finally cut off, and the SWATbots — trailing long fiber umbilicals — drop out of the ventilation system.

"What's that, Gene?"

"A stupid myth," I repeat, my voice in shreds but flat and detached, all emotion thoroughly wrung out. I must sound like I'm stoned. "They're not supposed to exist."

Maybe twenty minutes have passed since Henry's arrest, and we're en route to the Reparatory. Moon doesn't know much of what happened back there at the Medplex. I'm trying to explain, but it's coming out in incoherent lumps. What's left of my nervous system is a quivering mess.

"What doesn't exist, sweets?" As the squad car rockets through each intersection, a wash of light scans across Moon's worried features, gone pale as white gold. Having released my seatbelt and laid me across ser lap, sie cradles my head in one arm.

"Black market sense-recordings," I say, twitching. "Always someone panicking about it — snuff, torture captage, war porn. But we never find any actual evidence. No underground distribution rings, no such recordings. Imagine my surprise!" I manage a laugh, feeling blessedly numb, even the phantom itching of my amputated limbs silenced by neural overload.

"But, Gene..." Moon seems too horrified to process. "I don't understand. Why didn't you just do a crashdown?"

"Couldn't. Not something I can do. No neural shutdown command."

Sie doesn't understand, just narrows those eyes, anxious slivers of flint.

Sie's going to find out anyway, during the debriefing. Dennet will want to view my sense records for the past two hours. Legally, I could probably refuse, but that simply isn't a realistic option. There's no keeping up this pretence any longer.

So, as the streetlights sweep past and the siren cries, I spill out the story, and sie listens.

Eventually something snaps, and sie picks up one of my severed arms, almost ready to use it to bash apart my stupid head.

Too sane for that, sie tosses the limb into the back seat, then glares through the windshield for several minutes, slowly cooling down.

"Why, Mohad?" sie finally demands, aghast. "Why lie to me, to Daniel, to everybody?"

"Moon, you have no idea what it was like. I was just a kid when it happened, when they rebuilt me. Early on, people looked at me like I was a monstrosity out of a horror show. A tragic victim. Look, there's the boy in the plastic body! But in Morocco, the cogs didn't stare. They just saw a fellow mechine."

"You couldn't just," sie waves a hand over me, "go biomimetic? Look like a human?"

"I did, at first. But the early ones weren't very convincing. It just felt worse. Reminded me, every time I looked in the mirror—" I have to stop for a moment, staring into the rhythmic flash of passing streetlamps. "And anyway, it was just as much of a lie. I wasn't human anymore. Why pretend? Isn't that what you hate about cybrids? Pretending to be something we're not? Undignified, completely lacking in—"

"Alright, shut up, I know what I said." Sie sits and simmers for a moment. "Then, what? You figured I'd never find out?"

"Would you? Nobody else ever guessed. And— I know this is stupid, but it was flattering, in a strange way. To be accepted. To be one of you."

Now Cogentville envelops us, bustling and surreal, a mad Escher maze.

Moon's expression is frost-hard in the seething tunnel-light. I wait, desperately hoping for a thaw.

But sie says nothing more, all the way to Dragonfly Penumbra.

"The bastard was living under the name Marvin Saks. Had been working at the Medplex for nearly ten years." My voice is nearly lost among a hundred conversations and the frenetic thimba pop rumbling from the bar's walls.

We're in the depths of the Black Star on Dundas West, drinking at the head of three tables crammed with off-duty cops from 52 Division and Central Ops. At the far end, nearly lost in the nobacco smoke, Xu Kelly is entertaining Moon and several others with one her stories of the bad old days of the early Flood Crisis.

Only Daniel Aramaki can hear me, nodding as I bring him up to date. It's the end of his first day back at work, though he'll be stuck in his cubicle for a while yet. Still shaky on his new legs, just as I'm still not fully adapted to mine.

"Ser real name," I go on, "ser cogent name, was Moebius Sketch. An old cog, over fifty years old. Second generation in fact, a comp of four highly stable and gifted cogents — two from the very first Melbourne group, two from Capetown."

"Right," Danny puts in. "Fuckers were still trying to evolve super-human intellects."

"Might happen yet," I say.

"Might just evolve superhuman assholes." He grins, and it's the same evil grin, the same old Daniel. Or close enough. He's fully biomimetic, a bit younger-looking, maybe slightly idealized. I like to give him grief, calling him a hopelessly conservative mimsie.

"Anyway," I continue, "as the suppressions got worse, Sketch was smuggled to the Bahamas and raised by a very decent human couple. Sie never met ser neuremic parents, which wasn't unusual for that generation. During the Bahamian raids, when sie was only thirteen, sie disappeared. It was assumed sie'd been killed."

Dan takes a swig of Black Star microbrew, then asks, "What're they going to do about Baby Doe?"

"Didn't I tell you? He's been legally adopted by his biological parents. Now I ask you, what — just what can you say about that?"

"That's just creepy," Danny says. "The kid's brain is being shaped by Sketch's neurome. He'll eventually go mongo-psycho, right?"

"Not necessarily. More likely there are flaws in ser neurome which might or might not cause a predisposition to mental problems. Sketch's messed-up childhood was maybe just a trigger. All very equivocal. So if the kid has a stable home life, is properly socialized, and so on — who knows?"

For a while we just listen to the music, the laughter, the clatter of glasses. I light up a cig.

"You have to admire them," I say. "The parents. Choosing to raise that kid, despite everything. Sort of a gesture of defiance against neuremic destiny."

"Yeah. Fuck the Neuremics Authority!" Danny cheers, and we laugh.

Down the table, Moon is now in a loud but amiable debate with two detectives from Property Crimes.

Danny notices me watching them, and leans over. "You okay, Mohandis?"

"Sure." I shrug, and blow bittersweet smoke rings, remembering the taste of ser mouth.

"A shame, though," Dan says. "Thought you two made an interesting couple."

"Thanks. Could've been worse. We can still work together at least."

Danny isn't fooled. Neither are all those unhappy neurons that won't shut up, especially there in my anterior cingulate gyrus, down deep in my insula and caudate nucleus. All now wailing like hungry babes. Feeling like something essential has been hacked out at the most sensitive roots. Connections lost, seemingly irreparable, leaving only painful ghosts.

GLENN GRANT's credits include a string of cyberpunk stories that appeared in the early 1990s in the British magazine *Interzone*; publishing and editing *Edge Detector*; coediting, with David Hartwell, *Northern Stars* (Tor, 1994) and *Northern Suns* (Tor, 1999); and contributing the story "Thermometers Melting" to *Arrowdreams: An Anthology of Alternate Canadas*.

Glenn tells us: "I was born and raised in London, Ontario. My parents and siblings are all classically trained musicians, but I took more interest in drawing and animation. In high school, some friends and I started an underground zine, *Mind Theatre*. I finally did get involved in music for a while, as the singer in a couple of strange bands. In the late 1980s, I moved to Montreal to study film production at Concordia University, but ended up with a Creative Writing degree instead. I love life in Montreal; it's a great town to be a writer, even a lazy, unilingual anglo writer like myself. Montreal is an open-minded, cosmopolitan, cultural hotspot. Plus, I get lots of support from my fellow travellers, the spec-fictionistas of The Montreal Commune writers' group."

The Dead Park

This is the Dead Park; where the dead park, or are parked. Fleshys do not struggle when they're brought here by their former families. Maybe they even recognize it as refuge, this hilly, pretty landscape studded with old gravestones, wound about with waterways, the paths of the dead.

In the high ground of the Dead Park, where the fleshys do not go, Edward grew up, pale and weedy, but certainly alive. His mother cut the lawns there.

They said it was something in the water that made the fleshys. Edward grew up hearing them, fearing them, at night behind the bobwire; the water possessed all the lower parts of the cemetery, long winding pools joining on to each other, reflecting the blank sky and the weeping willows like so many snaky underwater weeds themselves. Our Lady of Snows it used to be called, before the snows stopped coming and instead the creeping water took all the low-lying bits of the city.

Twenty-two years old and just back from college, Edward sat on top of a mausoleum at sunset, staring down at the water turning silver rose and green, daring himself to stay out for once past dark, past fleshy-time. A slight breeze hummed in the bobwire where it floated, protecting human from fleshy and, oh yes! certainly, fleshy from human too. Edward picked up a stone fragment from among the many lying in the long grass (Mother seldom mowed around these lumpy houses of old dead) and tossed away the words "B. 1922/D. 198...," making the stone arc high over the bobwire. He did not hear a splash; instead the willows whispered secrets as always.

The breeze fluttered in Edward's hair and brought him the rattle of the shed door closing on the gardening tools. He turned. On the next ridge, fifty metres off as the glance flies, his mother was calling it a day, heading for the house. She did not look over, and Edward did not call, but he brushed his fingers together and started for home.

The song came from downslope, where a finger of water touched the roots of a willow tree, just inside the bobwire. It was a gentle trill like a night bird barely waking. But no birds lived in the Dead Park.

Edward stopped, turned, looked, all before he knew he was going to. At first he could see nothing extraordinary, just the lapping of wavelets, metal-coloured in the gathering dusk. Then the wavelets rose and settled, and she was looking back at him.

He could see big dark eyes peering from just above the water like a child over a bedsheet in a game of peekaboo. Her forehead already glowed a little in the shadows of the tree. She was watching him; he saw her gather herself to stand. Shadows thickened around Edward. He smelled must and brown-red spices, itchy in his sinuses and eyes. The fleshy opened her mouth and another high trill curled out towards him like a tongue. Her naked body glowed a pale green under the willow tree. She held out one hand with a grey rock in it. Edward ran.

That night, Edward had his old nightmare of drowning again. He was stuck in the dark with water rising all around. The water was endlessly deep, but of no temperature, or the exact temperature of his skin, so that he could hardly tell when it reached his chest, his chin, his lips, when it slipped into his mouth and drowned him, like a silk and velvet kiss that tasted of nothing, not even air. He awoke with his ribs aching and tears on his cheeks.

Edward sat up in bed. He could hear the bobwire buzzing like a nocturnal cicada and, above it, soft-edged and high-pitched as a children's chorus, the singing of the fleshys. He shuddered. At the college, some people had talked of human rights for the fleshys. Edward thought they had probably never been close to a fleshy. Rights? Perhaps. But not human.

Then there were one or two who kept heavy sloshing tanks behind the locked doors of their rooms, whose breath smelled of autumn leaves, and whose fingertips were pruny every morning at breakfast. Edward propelled himself out of bed at the thought.

There was no point in trying to sleep now. Edward got dressed and went into the kitchen, where the night light bathed everything in deep yellow shadows. It smelled comfortingly of the stew they'd had for supper. Edward pushed buttons on his mother's music player, and violins covered up the sounds from outside.

"Ed?" His mother came in, short and solid. She was wearing her work clothes of brown leather and hairy wool.

"Mother? What—"

"I'm going to walk the bobwire. Want to come with me, since you're already up?"

"Uh. But—"

"We've had more vandalism lately. People with bolt cutters. I don't like to let them think they can get away with it."

"B-but the fleshys..."

His mother might have smiled; in the yellow light, it was hard to tell. She said, gently for her, "They stay on their side of the wire. They know me." Her voice turned brisk. "You could make yourself useful."

"You mean, since I haven't learned anything useful at college?"

There was a pause. Edward could not interpret his mother's expression, and then she turned away. She rummaged in the broom closet.

"Take this," she said, handing him a shotgun. She took one herself.

The night was warm as skin, soft as breath. If he could have, Edward would have enjoyed it; but there was too much quicksilver water, too many glimpses of greenly luminous bodies vanishing at their approach, too much silence following them. Far behind them, the fleshy song would start again.

After an hour's scramble up and down, guided by the hum of the bobwire moving gently with the breeze on the water, Edward was panting and hot. The shotgun was a hateful clumsy thing, always snagging on branches or twisting his muscles out of shape. He wished he could put it down, knew he could not. Finally he sat down on an old piece of asphalt under the last of an avenue of maples that had once run halfway through the whole cemetery. Some of the trees still lifted dead branches above the waterline. Edward thought of drowning swimmers coming up for a third time.

His mother came back to him. "Here," she said, offering a canteen he had not seen her carrying. He drank gratefully. She took the canteen back, drank too. "It's quiet tonight," she said. "You could go back to bed."

"And you?"

She shrugged, turning half away from him to peer at the night. "Edward?"

He looked at her, but she seemed to have nothing else to say. At last she offered him the canteen again, slung it back across her shoulder when he shook his head.

"Go back to sleep," she said, already walking away. She was gone before he recognized that her voice had been kind.

And there he was, alone in the night. Only not really alone, of course: the bobwire hummed, bobbing on the surface of the water scant metres away; and the water itself chuckled and gurgled softly, too alive for comfort. Edward shook his head. All his life he'd avoided this, all his friends had avoided it too. Nobody went out at night near the low-lying places. Nobody but his mother, it seemed.

Still, it couldn't be that dangerous. There was the wire, there was his shotgun. He got up and headed homeward, keeping the humming fence on his left.

At first he reacted to every gust of wind, every crackle of branches underfoot. There were water rats patrolling quietly, and once an owl ghosted by; but the song of the fleshys was far away and he saw no glowing shapes, so after a while the night turned close instead of vast, familiar instead of mysterious.

Edward was in sight of the house when he saw her again. She stood like a candle; no, like a flame; no, like a bonfire, only green. And she stood beside the wire in a place where the path swerved within a metre of the humming barrier, the fence between the living and the dead.

He stopped dead. No, he was still living, and likely to keep doing so; but she, ah, what was she?

In her hand she held a sliver of granite, and she held it out to him. In the glow of her skin he read the dates, born, dead; but it meant nothing to him. She trilled her single song again, the bird call that had already called to him twice.

Involuntarily, Edward took a step forward. He could smell her: a spicy, sneezy sort of smell, musty as old dust and pungent as smoke. He looked into her face, which was pale green-white but ordinary, a snub nose and a wide mouth. Only her eyes were dark, he could not see their colour, they were dull in the glow of her skin, absorbing light instead of shining, and therefore like bits of night in the moon of her face. She did not smile.

Instead she held up her other hand, palm out near the bobwire. Edward lifted his hand too, brought it close — but you cannot touch the bobwire, it pushes you away, and so their two palms did not meet.

Edward snatched his hand back. What was he thinking of? But then he looked at the fleshy girl again and the darkness of her eyes seemed sad to him, so he put his hand up again and leaned forward, peering through the fence as if through an aquarium wall at the mysterious denizens of another element. She put her face close too, as close as the fence would let her, and she breathed softly out as he breathed softly in, and her breath smelled of mushrooms and autumn in the forest and sent him reeling away like a drunkard up the path to the house.

For the second time in one night, Edward dreamt. The water rose up his body, warm and not-warm, and swallowed him. But this time he did not wake gasping for air. Air was there, or breathing wasn't, it did not matter because he was suspended in the liquid and perfectly calm, at ease, at home. Then she was there, the fleshy girl, playing around him like a dolphin in the ocean. He moved his arms and followed her, he who had never learned to swim, who now shot through the silver element with the joy of an otter, who leapt and twisted and spun, who awoke to the hot sunlight on the tiles of the kitchen floor with a laugh on his lips such as he could never remember laughing before.

His mother had already gone, or had not come back at all. Having the house to himself, Edward took his time over his bath and his breakfast, eating scrambled eggs slowly, marvelling over their texture, especially as compared to the crispness of toast. Edward did not think he had ever felt this good before. His had been a thin sort of life, eked out here among the dead in the Dead Park; and this had made him into a thin sort of boy, with every likelihood of becoming an even thinner sort of man.

Now, though... Ah, now! And then the first chill struck him since the night before. What, indeed, now? He looked carefully, consciously, at the bare wood and tile of the kitchen, a room that was wholly functional. Was anything different in this room because of his intoxication of last night? Was anything different in his life?

A habit of judgment is hard to shake, and Edward had had judgment far longer than joy. He took himself off to the toolshed, found an oily rag and a whetstone, and cleaned and sharpened mower blades and trowels for the rest of the day.

Near sunset, his mother came home. They barely spoke while they chopped vegetables for supper; but, after they had eaten, Edward said, "Are you going out again in the night?"

His mother looked at him, and he felt himself flinching under her gaze, unsure of what she might be seeing. "Yes. But you don't have to go with me."

"But I—"

"Stay here. Sleep. I don't sleep much any more. It doesn't bother me. I'll go by myself."

Edward could not tell if this was rebuff or kindness. During his uncertainty, his mother left the room. A thought had been growing in Edward's mind, and he was ashamed of it, and yet he could not help holding on to it as to a forlorn hope. The thought was: surely she will come back tonight.

It was all he could do to pretend to go to bed. He lay still on top of his blanket, and as he lay there it seemed to him that the rivulets outside the house were rising, coming for him up the walls and pouring through the window shutters, and, when they found him, he was encircled enfolded enveloped with such intimacy and such tenderness that his body disappeared in one sharp spasm of shame and delight.

He was still a little giddy as he stumbled down the cottage stairs in the moonlit middle of the night. One part of him wanted to ask what he thought he was doing, seeking out a fleshy, but Edward resolutely ignored that question, put his boots on, and walked out the cottage door.

Once outside he had caution enough to stand and listen, but there was nothing to be heard except the usual buzzing undertone and the children's chorus of fleshy song. Edward walked down the path, headed for the place where he had seen her last.

She had anticipated him. At the point where the bobwire came closest to the house, she waited for him, a green-white column of naked girl. Edward stopped short, gulping. A fleshy, screamed one part of his mind. But the rest of him walked on again, right up to the bobwire, his boots sinking into water to get there.

He lifted his hand to the wire, and she lifted hers in return. But she did not stand long; she wanted something of him. She walked slowly along her side of the fence, looking at him over her bare glowing shoulder. Inevitably, he followed.

She led him up and down along the wire for many minutes, until he was breathless with walking and with wafts of her dry-leaf scent. And the place that she led him to was barely noticeable: it was just a little spot, where the bobwire anchor had been moved, shifted up just about ten centimetres above the water level, by a big dead branch of willow wedged underneath.

She brought him there and looked at him with her sad dark eyes in her glowing face. It took Edward a moment to figure it out, and then he felt a heartbeat of pure panic.

"You want me to go in there? With you?"

The fleshy girl lowered herself into the water, and he saw that it was deeper than he had thought: it rose to cover her back as she leaned on her elbows and watched him from water level, as she had watched him the first time he had seen her. He noticed this time that her nose and mouth were below the waterline, but there were no bubbles rising from them. He shuddered and started to back away.

With one strong push of arms and legs, the fleshy ducked under the bobwire anchor and surged to her feet on the other side. Edward stopped, entranced despite himself. Somehow she was more beautiful on this side of the wire. Somehow he had his hands up and was stroking her sides and cupping her breasts, pulling her up against him. He forgot to be afraid, he forgot to be ashamed, he forgot even his desire in the rush of pleasure he felt at the touch of her skin.

She was as warm and not-warm as the water of his dream, but he could not seem to get close enough to her. He tore at his clothes, and she helped him, and then they were lying in the grass, thigh to thigh and chest to chest, with his arms around her, trying to pull her closer still. He was breathing that mushroom and spice smell of her, and it was tickling behind his forehead like ghost fingers stroking his brain. He wanted to be inside her, and he didn't want to move at all. He was just summoning the strength of will to rearrange himself and her, when two shots cracked across the night.

They felt like slaps across his face. Edward dumped the fleshy girl onto the grass and got up. He slithered into his pants and stamped into his boots and ran in the direction of the shots.

Once over the first ridge, he could see where the trouble was.

Someone had brought a floodlight on a little ATV and pointed it into the bobwire enclosure, as if jacklighting deer. Some fleshys were visible, retreating, hiding their faces from the glare.

A hoarse voice shouted, "Fucken bitch, you fucken bitch, what you shoot me for?"

Edward ran faster. It was downhill to the ATV. He couldn't see his mother anywhere.

He got to the little machine and saw her. She was lying on the ground, trying to use the butt of her shotgun to get up. The wool of her sweater was dyed red with blood.

"They're fucken fungus, that's all they are, and you shot me, you bitch." The man yelled and tried to kick Edward's mother, but his leg bent and he fell over. Edward shoved past him to pick up his mother in his arms.

She looked up at him with no visible surprise. Edward said, "Mam, Mam, are you—"

A hand grabbed Edward's hair and pulled his head back. The man was wincing in pain, but he brought his knife up to Edward's throat.

"I'll fucken kill you," the man screamed. Edward thought he would do just that when a green-white moon rose behind the man's head and the fleshy girl hit him with a large chunk of marble tombstone.

Edward struggled back to a sitting position, stroked the hair back from his mother's forehead. She looked up at him with her eyes glazing.

"Eddie," she said. "Don't bury me, son. Burn me. I don't want. My body coming back." She took a deep breath that sounded merely tired.

"Yes, Mam, don't worry," Edward whispered.

"And you. Be happy. As you can. I wasn't always..."

Edward waited and waited, but there was no more.

After a while he lowered his mother's body gently to the ground. He realized that the fleshy girl was still standing there, the chunk of marble in her hand. She was watching him and his mother and the still-unconscious man, all by turns.

Edward and the fleshy tidied up together. The man and his ATV they left outside the gates of the Dead Park. Edward's mother they brought back to the cottage. The fleshy girl helped Edward pile up branches for a funeral pyre, at least until the sky began to grow light. She stopped then, and put her hand on his bare shoulder.

Edward put his face down into her neck, pressed her against him and felt the giddy rush of her that was like floating, that was like drowning. Then he let her go, and watched until she was out of sight, heading back to the gap under the wire.

He built his mother's pyre and lit it, and made sure that her body was burned beyond recall. In all his thin weedy life here in the Dead Park, his mother had really only given him that one piece of advice: be as happy as you can. He thought it was probably worth taking.

Edward chose a good fat willow branch and took a shovel with him to the edge of the bobwire closest to the old cottage. He found an anchor and wedged it up, and then he began to dig a channel towards the house. For the water to flow into.

DORA KNEZ is the author of *Five Forbidden Things* (Small Beer Press, 2000), a chapbook of stories and poems. Her poems also appear in *Tesseracts6* and *Tesseracts7*. She lives and works in Montreal.

Where does "The Dead Park" take place? "Montreal is a great place to live and provides many odd nooks and crannies suitable for story settings. If you've ever walked in the upper part of the Nôtre-Dame-des-Neiges cemetery, near Mount Royal Park, you might even recognize some of the topography of 'The Dead Park.' The mausoleums and the long paths lined with maples were part of the inspiration for this story, as was the hushed feeling of being in some inaccessible highland, remote from ordinary city noises."

Maxianne Berger

Report on a Museum Incident

The search continues for seven-year-old Holly Barnett-Leduc, who disappeared three days ago while on an outing with her mother. Around noon, Saturday, a neighbour saw Joan Barnett and her daughter board a number 55 bus at the corner of St-Urbain and Laurier near their home. Two hours later, Barnett was alone at the Musée des beaux-arts. Her admittance receipt indicated one adult and one child, but Holly was not with her. A police spokesperson says there are no plans to press charges against Barnett, who is undergoing psychiatric tests at Hôtel-Dieu Hospital.

Barnett was first restrained at the museum by guard Louis Conchetta when she attempted to remove a painting from the wall. The guard told reporters he did not notice Barnett enter the gallery because he was helping an older woman to a bench and was looking the other way. The oil by Edgar Degas, *Jeunes Danseuses*, is part of a travelling exhibition from Ottawa.

Conchetta said he heard hysterical screaming — Barnett — and turned to see her grab the painting by its frame and shake it back and forth. As he approached her, said Conchetta, he was able to make out her words: "She was shouting over and over, 'Holly, come back here. Holly, come back.'" Two patrons assisted Conchetta in subduing the sobbing and obviously disoriented woman.

In a statement to police, Barnett said that Holly was quite taken by the painting of ballet dancers, that Holly talked incessantly of becoming a "balley" dancer. When Barnett later offered to buy her daughter the postcard in the gift shop, Holly ran away screaming, "No. It's not real!"

Barnett pursued her daughter back to the gallery but, she claimed, before she could reach the child, "Holly was climbing into that picture

— she just climbed right in to be with those ballet dancers — I couldn't stop her — I just couldn't get there soon enough."

Restoration specialist Paule Dutrisac examined the Degas for possible damage. "The valuable oil is unharmed," she said, "though infrared sensors revealed an inexplicable 'hot' area over the figure adjusting her slipper in the upper left quadrant." Dutrisac suggested this aura might be due to Barnett's handling of the painting.

MAXIANNE BERGER is an audiologist at The Montreal General Hospital of the McGill University Health Centre. As a poet, she recently completed a two-year mandate as Québec representative to the council of The League of Canadian Poets. She reviews poetry for *Arc*, her translations have appeared in *Poetry* (Chicago) and *Maisonneuve*, and she is coediting a haiku anthology forthcoming from Shoreline. Her poems have appeared in Canadian and American litmags and anthologies since 1985. She has one book, *How We Negotiate* (Empyreal Press, 1999).

She has this to say about her story: "In flash fictions, the white parts must be explicit because the inky parts are so brief. 'Ideal' readers of 'Report on a Museum Incident' know about Alice's rabbit hole and looking glass, about Diggory's wardrobe, and so they recognize the constructed truth about the child in the museum despite the narrative's groundedness in some real world."

Yves Meynard

In Yerusalom

It's night in Yerusalom, City of Miracles, Jewel of the Eldred, Bright Gift from the Stars; and in Yerusalom, even the dark shines with its own kind of light. It's night in Yerusalom, City of Abominations, Newest Franchise of the Pit, Cosmic Corruptress; and, in Yerusalom, even the brightest light carries its own shadow.

In Yerusalom, three dreamweavers stride along Faro Street in the luminous darkness, and all about them the multifarious sounds of the city blare and thunder. They've got soundsuits putting out their own personal music, and they've got neon-implants accenting the curves of their jaws with streaks of cold radiance, and they've got enhanced eyes, noses, ears, the better to soak up the surrounding world at the maximum possible intensity, and they've got hopes and fears roiling through their minds. Most importantly, they've got viable asset-slopes.

Edge Nain, tall and thin, his hair an upswept brush, walks point; he carries little protection, unshakeably convinced his wits and faith will see them all through. Ras hangs back several paces as always, his soundsuit unzipped to display his scarred chest; his head is a gleaming copper sphere, and his augmented muscles advertise he needs no weapon to defend himself and his companions from ill-meaning fools. Kel strides between them, nearly as tall as Edge Nain but, unlike him, ill-proportioned, his extremities too big for his body. Yet his features are startlingly beautiful, an angelic doll's face set on a too-big skull, long-lashed eyes the blue-green of seawater.

As they walk, the three dreamweavers pray. Their belief is not the sharp and acid belief of those who fear, it is not the dull and musty belief of those who used to fear but no longer care; it is the hard and cold belief of those who *know*.

This is Ras's prayer: *Sweet Jesu, make me a success at the performance, let me be noticed picked up contracted sold traded REMEMBERED.*

This is Edge Nain's prayer: *Sweet Jesu, let it all go well; all I ask is for us not to go to pieces; even if we don't make it, let us accept it in peace.*

This is Kel's prayer: *Sweet Jesu, I want to meet a girl, a good girl, a hot one, but a true one, with a heart of flesh not gold, oh please, Sweet Jesu...*

Set down in the Dust Belt of the North American plains, Yerusalom has fertilized the barren land with abstractions: money, hope, ambition, greed. Twenty-five years after taking root in Earth's soil, it is surrounded with the pulsing life that is commerce. Streams of vehicles flow in and out of the city, carrying raw materials and finished goods, foodstuffs and drugs, liquid oxygen and dried seahorses, personal weapons and one-time encryption pads. Streams of data enter and leave, borne along superconducting wires, some even consigned to unbound photons blaring through the atmosphere, for anyone to intercept — if they dare.

The shadow and the light of Yerusalom have reached throughout the commercial sphere of Earth. Its presence has pulled its host nation out of a downward spiral, and by contagion the rest of the world has also benefited. Hard to say how many tens of millions owe their livelihoods, if not their very lives, to the shining alien city that endlessly consumes all that is poured into its brazen mouth. How could one then balk at a few hundreds of thousands dead of mysterious new diseases, the odd backward nation's political collapse from economic pressures too intense to bear? Change, after all, always hurts. Adapt or die; it's an old, old story.

The self-built edifices that border Faro Street come in every shape; their only constant is hugeness. Here a steep, five-sided pyramid three hundred metres high; there an arboreal structure rising from a central stem, recursively fanning out until a single two-metre-wide room stretches to ten metres in height. A smoothly swollen dome, looking frozen in the act of erupting from the ground, squats across the street from a disturbingly not-quite-organic fortress that drips angular turrets, like an inverted Gaudi cathedral rendered at low resolution. All of the buildings shine with their own light, in great sheens of fluorescent colours. Windows open into their facades like geometric bits of the interstellar void. Above their doors small digits flicker in red, indicating the one-time entrance fee, the visiting fee, the long-term residence fee... In Yerusalom everything has a price — not even the air you breathe is free. Though at least it is unmetered: since it would not have been cost-effective to implant oxygen-usage monitors in every citizen, a flat breathing-tax is incorporated into the baseline living fee. Panting and gasping come at no extra charge.

In defiance of rational use of land space, a vast network of irregular alleyways, sunk in the shadows cast by secondary structures of unknown import, spreads between the buildings. Some assert this is necessary for the unseen machines and agents of the Eldred; some say this is where Sweet Jesu makes his lair. None know for sure, for few venture deeper than a few metres into the darkened maze: as soon as you enter it, your baseline living fee drops by a full forty percent, and if that is not a clear sign of a dangerous area, what is?

As the three dreamweavers pass yet one more opening into the underside of the city, three pairs of enhanced eyes flick to the right; detect quasirandom stirrings in the deep shadows, but no telltale signature of danger. Three pairs of enhanced ears absorb the sounds emanating from the alley, reaching far into the high-frequency domain, beyond thirty thousand cycles per second. Three enhanced noses sniff at the air, glomeruli both natural and synthetic discharging in response to airborne molecules. All three brains, presented with this mass of data, effortlessly integrate it and return the final verdict: nothing meaningful there, just a man groaning, perhaps passed out, maybe dying, maybe not. No threat to them, no concern of theirs.

In the alley the old man lies on his back, praying, and this is his prayer: *Sweet Jesu, please make it so I eat tomorrow.*

In Yerusalom everyone prays, for it's true, verified, and certified that Sweet Jesu Himself walks the streets of Yerusalom, Whore of Cities, and verily He goes about granting prayers left and right. It has happened to Edge Nain himself: years ago, newly arrived in Yerusalom, he found himself cornered by a half-dozen predators, robbed at knife point. They could take nothing as essential as assets from him, only possessions, and Edge Nain had already resigned himself to this. But then one of his assailants began playing the tip of a blade along Edge Nain's face, and he realized he stood to lose a lot more than mere belongings. In his heart rose a fervent prayer to Sweet Jesu, a simple one, nearly wordless. And even before he could repeat it, just as the ceramic blade had begun to cleave his skin, there came flashes of energy, screams, the noises of the gang fleeing ... Edge Nain found himself alone, his possessions scattered at his feet, a hot line of blood along his jaw the only sign of the attack. He heard receding footsteps in the distance, among the blurry washes of light, going, perhaps, towards the darkened jagged-walled alleyways; he thought to follow for an instant, then came to his senses, gathered up his stuff, and fled towards safer streets.

Though there are cranks and charlatans aplenty claiming they (they alone!) have the truth of the matter, no-one in fact can claim to know Sweet Jesu's face, His dress, His age, even His sex, for in these days morphing oneself along the gender spectrum is something anyone with a few thousand assets can afford, and, if Jesu Himself couldn't be Herself once in a while, it wouldn't make any sense, now, would it? And so most everyone treats other people kindly, for any one of them might be Sweet Jesu Himself, and your behaviour is being watched; yeah, friend, you're on the line.

And this is the thought that passes through all three dreamweavers' brains at the same time: that a sin of omission is a sin nonetheless and that, if they want their prayers answered, maybe they'd better be extra good tonight.

So they step back, of a common and unspoken accord, and enter a little way into the alley. Edge Nain in front, Ras in the rear, keeping a suspicious eye on the street they have left, in case this is an ambush. In the light shining from their neon-implants, which carries its own flickering darkness within it, they see the old man lying in the angle made by two vertical slabs of self-assembled stone. They see his stained and pitted skin, the blue auras at the corners of the eyes, the tremble at the lips. Edge Nain, in a mostly failed attempt to increase his asset-slope, has sunk a sizeable sum into medical training in implant form. He recognizes the symptoms with an almost gleeful familiarity.

He says: "Hanley's syndrome; 'Azure Fever.' Late second stage."

Kel: "So?"

"He needs food and warmth first. Then a course of treatment: antibiotics, targeted enzymatic flush. He'll probably recover."

Ras, from the rear: "And *we* pay, of course. How much?"

Edge Nain frowns, guesses: "About sixty thousand, more or less."

Ras: "Sweet Jesu's balls, Edge, sixty!"

The three dreamweavers look at one another in hesitation. Paying this much for the old man's cure will dangerously deplete their balance. No matter how high your asset-slope, in Yerusalom debt and death are more than just phonetically close. If at any moment you are unable to pay the baseline living fee, the city's cybernetic bureaucracy will send a message through your asset-implant and terminate your abuse of the city's precious resources... They should let him lie in the alley, let his life extinguish itself; but they are committed now that they know of his plight.

The old man has opened his eyes, stares in confusion and fright at the trio. Edge Nain crouches down, lays his hand on the old man's shoulder.

"It's okay, Grandfather, my friends and I are going to take care of you. Can you stand up?"

The old man comes to his feet, wheezing and gasping, his legs trembling so badly Edge Nain has to hold him up. Thick saliva drips down from the man's mouth, blue-tinted. Some say that this disease, as with others that have begun to haunt humankind in recent years, comes from the Eldred, that it is one mark, perhaps the most telling, of their foulness. Others object that the biochemistries of the two species are so mutually alien it is ridiculous to suggest a cross-species illness. The first reply that the Eldred could very well have hatched human-specific viruses in their ships' laboratories, and the conversation thereafter degenerates into a zero-sum match of paranoia versus denial.

The three dreamweavers lead the old man out of the alley, into Faro Street.

Kel: "What's your name, heh?"

The old man: "Harold." The name dates him more than anything else about him.

At a public terminal node, Edge Nain checks Harold's asset balance. It hovers precariously in the positive, with a clear downward slope. Like so many others, he sought refuge in the alleyways, stretching his assets and thus his lifespan, but also condemning himself ultimately. Edge Nain transfers a little of his assets to Harold's account and nods as the figures alter.

Harold: "Sweet Jesu bless you, young sir, you're too kind..."

Ras: "Yeah, yeah. Listen, Grandpa, we'll take you with us to a place where you can get something to eat." He checks the timepiece embedded in his wrist, inked digits blinking beneath the skin. "We don't have time to take him to a hospital right now..."

Kel objects: "But we can't just make him wait for us. That's just as bad, isn't it?"

Ras: "Brothers, the performance starts in less than forty-five minutes. We have just enough time to get Harold to the nearest dispensary. Or else we can kiss that competition goodbye."

Edge Nain speaks in an imperative tone: "No. We take him to a full hospital, and now. If we hurry, we can make it in time. Sweet Jesu sees what we do, and He will make sure we get what we deserve."

Ras growls in protest; his faith clearly is not as trusting as Edge

Nain's. But he yields to his friend's authority, and the four of them set off. Kel summons a red-class taxicab — why quibble over a few tens of units when they're about to burn tens of thousands? They pile in, request to be taken to the nearest full-service hospital. The self-piloting vehicle weaves its way among the brightly lit streets.

They are isolated in the cab; the three dreamweavers have silenced their soundsuits, extinguished their neon-implants. The outside sounds are muffled to a chaotic background percussion track, the bright lights filtered by the polarized windows. They travel so swiftly and in such a complicated course the brain balks at the idea that the streets and buildings are fixed; so much easier to assume this vehicle is the unmoving centre of all things, while the brightly lit outside swirls and jitters by. There comes upon Kel, youngest of the trio, born long after the Eldred had landed, a familiar feeling: that all of Yerusalom is a stage set, that the Eldred have recruited humanity for some absurdist play of theirs, incomprehensible to human minds. He has a vision of himself as a Pierrot wandering through a maze of streets, questing in vain for his Columbine, who lies all tangled up in her strings within some prodigious attic, beyond a door it costs a lifetime's earnings even to open a crack... Not a bad image, that; should they use it in their next dream? He will at least suggest it — but right now he should be concerned only with the dream they are going to perform when they reach the Proxima Theater. Assuming they do manage to get there in time for the competition. Seated at his left, Harold stares ahead blindly, weeping pale blue tears.

The performers' doors of the Proxima Theater are closed when the three dreamweavers rush out of the red-class taxicab. They run across the street, their coats flapping behind them, ascend the three steps, slam their bare hands onto the doors with desperate cries. Kel wails in frustration; Ras gives Edge Nain a murderous look. Edge Nain has been praying, deep in his heart. And so it does not truly surprise him when the doors suddenly yield, swing inward, let them in. The trio stagger into the backstage lobby of the Proxima. The entry fee is deducted from their accounts; and, starting this instant, every additional minute they remain within the building will cost them 1.8 assets.

In the lobby stand nearly a dozen groups of dreamweavers. Most are made up of three or four people; one group boasts nine members, while two flamboyant individuals are going it alone. An Eldred carrying a palm-node greets the trio; by the pattern of jewels embedded among her scales, they think to recognize her as one they have dealt with before, whom they learned to call Sumyuru.

Sumyuru: "Friends, you have come to participate in the competition?"

Ras: "Yes, we have. We're registered under 'Brothers of Enceladus.' Are we too late?"

Sumyuru raises a hand and spreads her six digits, the Eldred equivalent of a smile, or so it is believed. "No. There was a small delay on our part and you are still on time. I have confirmed your participation. In one minute we will announce the order in which the performances will be given. There will be a ten-minute period to rehearse, after which all performers will be required to enter the auditorium and attend the others' performances. If you wish, mood-enhancers and hallucinogens are available at self-service dispensers; rates are posted above the machines."

Kel shakes his big-boned head in contempt. He has a pathological aversion to drugs, believes only in the purity of the dreamweaving experience. While Ras and Edge Nain are not so puritanical as he, neither of them considers using the proffered substances. They see one of the soloists at the drug dispensers, obviously mentally trying out combinations, checking the total price. He comes to a decision, punches in his choices, and four varicoloured pills drop into his outstretched hand.

Kel: "That fool's going to burn out every neuron in his brain. I can't let him do this."

Before the other two can hold him back, Kel strides over to the soloist, urges him not to take the drugs. The other goes instantly suspicious, demands to know why Kel is so concerned about his welfare. Next instant, before any answer can be given, he takes a swing at Kel, who ducks back and retreats towards his friends, under a torrent of invective. The soloist does not pursue, probably aware that he has already been heftily fined for attempted violence and that actual assault might well bankrupt him on the spot.

Ras: "Give it a rest, Kel. It's his choice if he wants to take them." Ras forebears to add that if the soloist does burn out, it will increase their own chances. He knows that his soft-hearted friend would be deeply offended by such a remark, though it is no more than the truth.

Sumyuru's hissing voice rises in the lobby, instantly commanding silence. She reads out the schedule for the competition. The Brothers of Enceladus will be fifth out of eleven, a good spot. They will have time to calm down, but they will not have to wait too long and risk losing their concentration.

Everyone takes advantage of the ten-minute rehearsal period. Small side-rooms are made available to the performers, at a nominal charge. Kel groans in anguish when he sees the soloist swallow all the pills at once before going into a room. The trio choose a room and go through warm-up exercises. They do not evoke anything they will be using in their performance, for fear of killing the spontaneity. Instead, they work on standard effects, striving to achieve a meshing within the first few seconds, gauging each other's moods. The ten minutes pass by quickly; at the end, they are as relaxed and comfortable as they'll ever be.

A bell rings, and all the dreamweavers gather, enter the auditorium. The human audience is assigned seats on the parterre, while the Eldred are seated in a single high box. No efforts have been made to conceal the box's security equipment: sensors and weapons gleam in the lights. Exclamations rise from the human section as the dreamweaving teams make their way to their bank of seats close to the stage, separated from the rest of the parterre by five metres of empty space and a softly glowing line. Edge Nain recognizes more than a few people in the crowd, including a woman he would never have expected to see again, not after her friend was gunned down by theatre security at the Brothers' last performance for having tried to cross the line separating performers from audience. *Sweet Jesu*, prays Edge Nain as he grasps the relayer-bar set in the armrest of his seat, *please let everyone here keep their head tonight.*

The first group, Noncortical, steps onto the stage, to the raucous cheering of their supporters in the audience. It is a quintet, with three inexperienced youngsters and only two old hands in their mid-thirties to keep them in check. Edge Nain knows one of them, Syrna; worked with her in fact, five years ago, when he was just starting out. He smiles briefly, remembering the dreams their group shaped in those days. The smile turns into a slight wince as Noncortical's performance starts. Within a few seconds, Edge Nain is swept into an adventure within an endless jungle, along with a band of friends he has known forever... The dream is brash, energetic, but it lacks focus; frequently, the thread is lost, sounds and images clash with the moods: the sense of purpose, which is so important, fades away. Five years, and Syrna's dreams have not changed. Maybe if she allowed herself to act her age, if she went after experience instead of raw youth in her partners...

The dream lasts the full five minutes allowed and concludes abruptly when the inducers power down at the command of their timing units. Noncortical leave the stage to polite applause. Immortality will not be for them this night, and everyone knows it. Even their fans' enthusiasm now sounds forced.

Three more performances before it is the trio's turn. Between each performance, they empty their heads of the others' dream. This is the risk they all run: being contaminated by the other weavers' material. If it echoes in their own performance, they will show themselves to be weak, easily influenced.

Indeed, it happens to the soloist who goes fourth, just before them. As he steps upon the stage Kel heaves a sigh: the man is shaking all over, in the grip of the drugs' side effects. When he starts his dream it comes blaring out, distorted and incoherent. This might have been intentional, but it is clear to the trio that it is not: merely from the images in the overture, they could see the dreamweaver was trying for a pastel fantasy, a type well-suited for solo performances. But the drugs are now altering his metabolism too swiftly for the inducer to adjust. His fear of failure is so strong it affects everything he weaves; Edge Nain tastes it in the back of his throat, Ras hears it as a ghostly wail, Kel sees it in the corner of his eyes. Then the third team's dream begins to insinuate itself into this one: as the protagonist gazes through a window at the shining wonderland beyond, incongruous eidetic flashes rip through the visual field and pulses of terror, too sharp to be filtered by the inducer's emotion dampers, lash the audience's brainstems. The soloist's thoughts, unspoken, are painfully obvious: *They were so much better than me, how can I have a chance?*

Edge Nain pulls himself partly away from the dream, cranes back his head, looking up over his shoulder at the box where the Eldred audience is seated. The dream blurs his vision, so he cannot clearly focus on reality; still, he can discern paired gleams in the dimness: reflections of the theatre lights upon the glossy black spheres the Eldred have for eyes. Can't they put an end to this performance? The weaver's concentration is shredding away, the drugs still roiling in his system; if it keeps up like this, he will soon need medical attention.

Ras, under his breath: "No! You had a way out, you little fucker, you could have brought it back under control, don't you know *anything*?"

The dream has gone utterly sour; the soloist is no longer in conscious control of it: icons from his undermind are pouring out, personal archetypes of his fears and self-loathing. It is an ugly thing to experience, for all that it reveals of the human soul. Someone, a woman, shouts: "Stop it!" Kel grasps Edge Nain's wrist, says: "I can't go, he'll never let me. But someone should..."

And then it is all over; with a final dissonant ugliness, the dream collapses. The weaver is on his knees, hand clutching the inducer white-knuckled. He lets go of the machine, tries to crawl off the stage, halts at the edge of the stairs, and starts retching. A woman from the second team comes to him, drags him off and out of the auditorium.

An Eldred's hissing voice: "Fifth competitors: Brothers of Enceladus."

The trio stand up, file onto the stage. They purge their minds of everything except the dream they are about to weave: they can spare no more pity for the failed soloist, nor any fear for themselves.

The inducer is a silvery machine, a slim pillar a metre and a half high, with a dozen fragile sharp-tipped spines extending outward from its top. Another marvel of Eldred technology, another gift from the stars. Each of the three grasps a spine, and then all feel themselves drawn into the dream as the inducer powers up.

Dreamweaving is typically a collaborative experience; using several participants brings greater depth to the experience, though it demands a severe mental discipline. While techniques vary widely — this is a very new art form, still in its infancy — most often sensory and intellectual cues are divided among the weavers, one handling sight, another sound and touch, a third emotional overtones, and so forth. Edge Nain, Ras, and Kel, the Brothers of Enceladus, work this way. Edge Nain has the additional responsibility of keeping things on track; it is to him the other two must defer if an uncertainty arises in the unfolding of the dream.

But this time he will have no need to intervene; honed by hundreds of hours of rehearsal, given additional intensity by the pressures on them, the dream unfolds precisely as they envisioned it.

It is a fantasia, midway between a freeform improvisation and a classically developed thematic dream. Sets of images recur throughout, giving it an identifiable texture; the initial situation is allowed to fade away, but reappears more and more frequently as the dream progresses and eventually can be seen to be resolving, revealing the overall shape of the dream.

It is a strong dream, built on pain and wonder. Yerusalom is the setting for it, but at a remove: everything happens as if within a great luminous structure, which only alludes to the buildings of the city. Images recur throughout: a weeping girl wearing a bonnet of green felt; a proud warrior standing desperate against the twilight of his race; a bright concourse strewn with flowers and bloody skulls. It is a complicated story the three dreamweavers tell, which seems to meander into a hundred dead ends, yet always returns to its main thrust.

When the bitter tale concludes, there comes a feeling of dissolution, and the dream's focus widens. Is this Yerusalom where the whole tale took place, its own world embedded in reality? Or are we still dreaming, finding within the dream a city much like the one where we live and strive, questing for our hearts' desires, praying for them to be granted?

Hands release the spines of the inducer; Edge Nain speaks the disengagement command and the machine powers down. The audience emerges from the dream. It was all told within four and a half minutes, though as in the manner of the best dreams it seemed to stretch out for hours. The Brothers' fans whoop and yell. Edge Nain can see them all with the surprising clarity that comes after an extended weaving session. This portly man dressed as a financier, always reserved and stiff-backed, indulging a secret vice perhaps; the tattooed gaggle of couriers desperate to be seen in company with the Brothers; those two girls who used to share Kel's bed and whom he won't look in the eye nowadays; and others... The rest of the audience is applauding, even the other groups' supporters; heckling at dreamweavings is frowned upon. To Edge Nain the applause seems somewhat half-hearted, but he knows, he knows they were good. Really good. Perhaps that last flourish was judged clever but affected? Yet it could be said it is the whole point of the dream; he had hoped people would pick up on that. His eyes rise to the Eldred's balcony. They, unlike the audience, sit immobile. He had been hoping for some reaction, however slight... The Brothers file back to their seats, settle back to go through the remaining six dreams. Edge Nain grasps his comrades' hands and smiles brightly at them. Sweet Jesu has granted his prayer that they be allowed within the theatre, and the prayer that they work well together. Edge Nain prays one last time, but it is meant more as a form of thanks. *Whatever happens now, let us accept it in peace, please, Sweet Jesu.*

The six other dreams all pass in a blur, and then it is time to leave the auditorium and await the results. The dreamweavers gather in the backstage lobby; tension runs high, manifesting in some as ebullient good spirits and fellowship, in others as bitter hostility. The soloist who collapsed cannot be seen. Edge Nain asks the woman who helped him what happened.

She: "I don't know. I got him out of the auditorium and left him sitting on that chair over there, then I went back in."

Edge Nain: "You didn't call for medical assistance?"

She: "What, on *my* money?"

Edge Nain is silent. He considers stepping out into the street. Waiting here is ten times more expensive than waiting out in the street — but he cannot make himself leave the confines of the lobby, and no-one else can either.

Time passes. It cannot be more than ten minutes, Edge Nain thinks, and is astonished to realize they have been waiting for over an hour.

Then a door opens, and three Eldred come out. In the lead, an Eldred who looks like none Edge Nain has ever seen; she is barely ornamented, and the jewels and wires on her face are nearly as dark as her scales. The Eldred speaks a few words, but Edge Nain cannot hear them well; he sees that the Eldred is beckoning to them, the Brothers of Enceladus, asking them to follow her. He finds he has trouble breathing. All this time preparing for graceful failure — he had never expected to win.

The Eldred ushers them into a small room panelled in some dark shimmering stuff, looking like gasoline rainbows filmed in black and white. They are offered seats and take them, while the Eldred remains standing.

There are some uncomfortable seconds of silence. Finally it is Kel who dares to speak, asking a question as inane as it is inescapable: "Well, did we win?"

"Yes. The soloist who preceded you placed a close second, but, even if he had not died, you would still have won."

Edge Nain shivers and gazes at the floor. "Sweet Jesu, I'm sorry," says Kel, as if whispering a confession. "I didn't try hard enough. I should have..." Ras stops him, gripping his shoulder and squeezing hard enough to cause pain; Kel barely flinches.

Ras: "He made his choice, brother. He made his choice and what happened was his own fault."

Kel: "If we'd gone with him outside, we could have called an ambulance. He could be alive now."

Ras: "We'd played ambulance once already, and it's too expensive a game for my tastes. Life is money, and I don't care to be terminated because I've wasted my assets on Yerusalom's failures. Just grow up, Kel."

Edge Nain rises and stands before his friends; both of them look up at him. Kel's retort dies on his lips, and Ras withdraws his hand from the younger man's shoulder.

Edge Nain: "We saved one life tonight. We're not doctors; we're not Sweet Jesu. We're dreamweavers. I don't regret helping Harold — but, Kel, Ras is right that we can't afford to do this kind of good..."

His words trail off; because as a matter of fact they probably *could* afford it now... All three turn their heads to look at the Eldred who has remained apart from the scene, and who now inclines her head while rotating her upper body slightly: the body language for a polite request.

The Eldred: "Please take a refreshment from the minibar; the first one is complimentary."

Ras sighs nervously, stands up, goes to a small cube in a corner of the room and opens its door. After a brief scan of its contents, he takes a small bottle. Kel, who has joined him, picks a bigger one. Edge Nain will take nothing. All three sit back down. Ras and Kel sip at their drinks; Edge Nain fidgets, waiting for their host to speak. She — always *she*, for though the Eldred are a hermaphroditic species, they will only use the feminine pronoun when referring to themselves — watches them in silence, holding herself erect but tilted slightly forward, in a position believed to connote benign attentiveness. Suddenly she turns around, opens the door to the room. The three dreamweavers do not see the lobby, but instead the naked sky. The room is an elevator then, and they have reached the top of the building.

The Eldred commands: "Follow me."

The trio file out of the room after her, Kel clutching his unfinished bottle. The top of the building is so high it feels as though one's gaze can encompass the four corners of the Earth. Around them stretch the self-lit, self-constructed edifices of Yerusalom. City from the stars, having come up of itself around the Eldred landing ships that planted its seeds in the hard stony ground. A hundred shades of light, carrying its own darkness within it. Above it all, the roof of the sky, black and spangled with stars, like a circular tent, its fabric pricked with holes.

The Eldred: "Your performance was quite moving. We will pay you two hundred fifty thousand assets each; the work will be made available at theatres throughout the city, and trailers will be broadcast on all major entertainment channels. As far as royalties go, you will receive the standard 8.3 percent of all net profits — divided into three equal shares. This verbal agreement is binding upon the moment of your formal acceptance; printed documents will be issued on an on-demand basis, for a fee. Does this satisfy you?"

Kel murmurs something indistinct. Edge Nain is silent.

Ras asks: "Then ... you won't record us?"

"Oh, you already have been recorded. While you waited in the room, you were anesthetized, taken to the laboratories, and your personalities were recorded in full detail. Twenty-four hours have passed since you left the auditorium."

YVES MEYNARD

Ras nervously adjusts his clothing. He feels cheated, like a child promised marvels to keep him quiet. He who wished more than anything to be preserved for the future, who dreamed of one day basking in the knowledge that his very essence was kept by the Eldred, suddenly wonders why he ever yearned for this. He had dreamed with mingled terror and desire of great scanning engines, complicated procedures... Now it has all been done, without the slightest awareness on his part.

And yet, and yet, what is he thinking, he has achieved what thousands of other artists have tried for in vain: he himself, not just his art, will be remembered throughout the centuries and millennia... In the bad old days before the Eldred came, fame was a thing bestowed at random, withdrawn almost before it had been granted. An artist's identity always vanished behind his public image; authenticity itself had been reduced to a set of standard poses. He, Ras the dreamweaver, has been *recorded*, and as long as Eldred civilization endures, the image of his soul will accompany it, ready to be replayed. There is nothing closer to true immortality; for all that he in this body will die and rot, his soul in the Eldred's pattern-storage will endure eternal... Why then this despair that tightens his throat and brings tears to his eyes?

Kel is saying: "Well ... I guess this is okay by me. Thank, you ... ah... How should we call you?"

The Eldred makes a sound they have never heard, a low buzz, almost synthetic. Then she says: "Since you are all so unhappy, I will allow you to call me by my human name of Satan."

Edge Nain: "I beg your pardon?"

His two partners, he notes, are as surprised as he. Of course, "Satan" is in some ways a trite name: millions of humans call the Eldred "Snakes," millions more equate them to demons. Eldred, who are known to use several names depending on context, have on occasion chosen surprising human cognomens. But still, why *that* name?

She: "Satan. The fount of evil, the breeder of lies. Also, the staunch ally of humankind against an indifferent god. It is an appropriate name."

98

Kel's mouth is drooping at the corners, like a little child about to weep. He complains: "What are you trying to say?"

"My choice was determinant in the competition; and I chose you above all the others because your performance demonstrated, among other things, that you would not be content with what we offered. You" (pointing at Ras) "have gained the brand of immortality we promise, but I can read the disappointment on your face; and I will tell you furthermore that although we recorded all three of you, the available space is not unlimited. We will be forced to discard two of the three recordings and commit only one to long-term storage. I cannot promise you will be the one we keep."

She points to Edge Nain: "You did not truly want to win, did you? Now that you have reached your goal, you do not know what to do."

Edge Nain corrects her: "I did not expect to win. But I *am* glad we did."

"No, you are not. You are lying to yourself. And you" (her clawed finger points to Kel) "have realized that although your art is successful as a mating display, it was not reproductive prowess that you craved after all."

Kel splutters and coughs, theatrically or not Edge Nain cannot tell. He speaks up, to forestall Kel's angry words that he can sense coming.

"Hold on. Never mind whether you're correct about us or not. Why would our discontent make us win?"

Satan: "Why do you think we record you in the first place?"

Ras answers, hesitant: "Because you seek to understand humans. Isn't that why you gave us dream-inducers? Because we reveal more of ourselves in the dreams we make?"

"We gave humans dream-inducer technology because we wished to record artists working in a fresh, untainted medium, but this is no longer a major focus of our attempt to understand humans. Most of your race believe that artists are more deeply in touch with the human condition, so initially we expended considerable effort to record them.

YVES MEYNARD

The return on investment was disappointing. We have recorded tens of thousands of humans, from all places and social statuses. It is our consensus opinion that any one of the fifteen million indentured labourers of southeast Asia comes much closer to the essence of the human condition than do any of the artists in Yerusalom. Most of us feel that artists have no depth to them at all, only a mild form of mental illness."

Edge Nain, taken aback, asks: "Then why do you still sample us? Why all these competitions, all the wealth you shower down?"

Satan leans to one side, against the railing, and rotates a knee outward. This form of body-language the trio have never seen. Perhaps it means nothing special.

She answers: "Market research has its own inertia. The total amount invested was relatively small and had the potential for a large payoff: it was a worthwhile risk."

Ras quotes: "'The Universe is commerce.'"

Edge Nain: "And why, then, are you telling us all this? When the Eldred have never told us exactly what they seek on Earth?"

She: "We never sought your art; we sought to understand you only insofar as we must evaluate your future commercial status. We gave you seed technologies to accelerate your technological development, to send you out into your solar system. In two or three hundred years, you might become worthwhile trading partners; not before. And the reason why I tell you these things is because I have become convinced — you, in fact, have finished convincing me — that our presence on your planet has already distorted you beyond reasonable bounds. I believe we will destroy you, ruin any hope of bloom for your civilization."

Kel speaks at last, in a voice thready with outrage: "But that's non-sense: you've given us so much! We've learned from you. Earth is better off than it was before. You talk of indentured labourers, but they're being freed even as we speak. How can wealth be bad? All the people in Yerusalom, the artists, the scientists... We've benefited from your knowledge, and the rest of Earth has too. And humanity hasn't really

100

changed much. It's adapted, that's all."

Satan says quietly, in her hissing voice: "Maybe I am mistaken. But I am a High Administrator for my commercial sept, and it is my function to reach such understandings. I have dealt with three species before, and I have access to a thousand years of records. And it is my evaluation that any prolonged presence among you will destroy your species. The loss would be severe."

Edge Nain, after a pause: "You speak of financial loss, don't you? If there was no question of profit involved, you wouldn't care at all."

"That is correct. This is an aspect of us most humans do not seem to understand, despite our explanations; I am pleased that you do."

Ras speaks up: "You said you didn't want our art. That soloist who died ... I couldn't believe you placed him second. But then, it didn't matter how shitty his performance was, did it? You've never cared about the artistic value of dreamweaving."

"It has always been irrelevant. The soloist almost won because he showed us his naked mind, in all its terror. He was a good candidate for recording, but you three are in some ways even better."

Edge Nain: "Then, as long as you're answering all our questions, tell me: why does Sweet Jesu walk our streets? Or do all of us simply imagine Him?"

"He is real. We've made Him real. Since human cultures traditionally associate commerce with forces of evil, this was taken to be a necessary balance for our interactions with you. We have over twelve dozen teams of operatives monitoring the city constantly and striving to apply immanent justice to human endeavours. Indeed, without the intercession of one of those teams, you would not have been allowed to enter the theatre. Globally, however, results of the Jesu operations have been inconclusive."

Edge Nain blinks at the Eldred, then shuts his lids for a few seconds, withdrawing into a private darkness. He is not truly surprised, not really disappointed. It is not as if this hypothesis had not been floated in his hearing before, a hundred times. He knows the mystics' answer also, that the real Jesu could choose to enlist the Eldred to work His miracles in Yerusalom. If the magician shows you the trickery he used, that does not prove he cannot truly work a spell. When Edge Nain opens his eyes again, he looks at Ras, who is smouldering with anger, at Kel, his youthful face like that of a bereft angel. And for a split second, like a pivot-point in a dreamweaving, he thinks to grasp the Eldred's perspective on the Jesu experiment, and horror rises in him at what humanity has become. But then the epiphany leaves him, and he returns to his former bewilderment. He was five years old when the Eldred came down upon the Earth; their arrival spelled the ending of his childhood. He remembers, dimly, a time when his parents constantly squabbled about money, when they refused to let him play outside for fear of the gangs roaming the suburban streets. In front of him stands one of the race that brought his family, his entire country, out of despair. The Eldred are the core of his existence, those from whom all blessings flow. That they should also embody Sweet Jesu is unavoidable, is it not?

Ras is saying, sullen: "What will you do with us now? Are you just going to give us money and let us go?"

Satan: "As soon as you give me formal agreement on the contract. Kel already has; what about the other two?"

Ras makes an angry gesture. "Sure, I agree." Edge Nain whispers: "I accept." He knows it is done, knows their asset balances have jumped up hugely, and feels how little it all means, now that Satan's words have put it all in perspective.

Satan: "I expect you will repeat our conversation to others. You may or may not be believed. I have run several simulations, but my models are still primitive. In this I advise you to use your instinct. People may well react violently to your message."

Kel speaks suddenly, his voice strangled by emotion: "Are you done? Then just let us leave. I don't care about your stupid contract. I never wanted your damned money. I just want out of here; out of Yerusalom!"

Satan nods abruptly, and this human gesture is so disconcerting the trio find themselves shuddering. A flyer appears over the rim of the roof and noiselessly comes to rest a few metres away. Its hatch opens: the interior is richly decorated and, although dim, glows with a hundred tiny lights.

Ras and Kel climb inside. Edge Nain stays behind, facing the Eldred. He asks: "It won't be long, will it?"

She: "No, not long. It may be too late already; we will not delay."

"If you keep one of us, keep Ras; he wanted it so much. Or Kel, at least: he was the one who believed the most."

"You mean you do not want us to keep *you*. Do not worry about that. You are the one we will certainly not keep."

And Edge Nain, who had felt again he was coming to understand something about the Eldred, now senses the gulf that has always yawned between them. Ice in his stomach, he joins his comrades aboard the craft.

The hatch closes; through the smoky canopy they can see the top of the building, but the dark figure of the Eldred named Satan has faded against the darkness of the sky. As the flyer speeds away from the tower, there comes unbidden to Edge Nain a vision of the near future: of the self-constructed buildings of Yerusalom all taking to space in a glow of dark-bearing light, leaving behind a stunned humanity. Never, never, never to return.

Born in Québec City in 1964, YVES MEYNARD moved to Longueuil (a Montreal suburb) in 1971 and has lived there ever since. Active in Québec SF circles since 1986, he was literary editor for *Solaris* from 1994 to 2001. His short fiction, nearly fifty short stories in French and English, has garnered him numerous awards, including the Grand Prix de la Science-Fiction et du Fantastique Québécois, Québec's highest award in the field. His story "Tobacco Words" was reprinted in David Hartwell's *Year's Best SF 2*. His fantasy novel *The Book of*

Knights (Tor Books, 1998) was a finalist for the 2000 Mythopoeic Award for best novel.

Yves says: "I hold a Ph.D. in computer science from the Université de Montréal and earn a living as a software analyst. I used to be insanely jealous of Ian McDonald, to whom this story is dedicated, but, with eleven books under my belt, I now feel slightly less inadequate. 'In Yerusalom' was begun as a direct homage, but it started mutating after the first page. Still, the three dreamweavers and the Eldred remain in some way escapees from McDonald's universes, where light and darkness are always inextricably intertwined."

Martin Last

Carnac

We had been travelling ad libitum in Amorica, the inland part of Brittany, driving more by instinct than map. After several days of exploring the enigmatic forest of Brocéliande, where, legend has it, Merlin was enchanted by Viviane, the Lady of the Lake, who held him there in a state of suspended ecstasy while she, like Jesus, danced on the surface of the water, we began to long for the sea and drove southward, aiming for Carnac Plage, a sheltered beach area on the shore of the Bay of Biscay adjacent to the small town of Carnac. We knew that near Carnac were the ancient megaliths that have attracted archeologists and anthropologists for centuries, their origins, like those of Stonehenge and the Round Stones, still refusing to reveal themselves to the sleuths of history and myth. Gustave Flaubert wrote: "Carnac has more pages of rubbish written about it than it has standing stones — and there are more than five thousand stones."

We booked into a neo-modern spa-hotel near the beach and spent our first hour marvelling over the splendid facilities of our suite, particularly the bathroom with its sunken tub and multiple showerheads. Every provision was made for a luxurious bathe; the enormous marble counter in which the basin sat like a miniature goldfish pond was replete with decorated boxes in which all manner of cosmetic and functional salves, creams, and soaps were stored. Vases of fresh flowers were everywhere. There was even a built-in hair dryer and a robot shoe polisher. As we examined this profusion of sophisticated living we giggled, making fun of each bit of excess.

"There's more mirroring here than in all of Versailles," Kate said. "You be Narcissus, and I'll be Echo."

We used up the second hour of our stay over the lavish spread of food and drink available in the dining room, apparently twenty-four hours per day, then settled on the beach for the balance of the afternoon, awash in the comfort of sand, sea and the voices of children at play on a halcyon day.

Before going out to dinner in the evening I showered and started to shave. The mirror covering the wall over the counter was enhanced by mirrors on either sidewall facing each other. Had they been perfectly parallel a person at the sink would have seen only himself singly to the left and right. But one of the side mirrors was just enough out of parallel to cause an infinite replication of diminishing images to both the left and the right. I could see myself disappearing into infinity on either side, which amused me; I did a little dance number that was multiplied into a chorus line of ever-smaller images in a ludicrous performance without music. Quickly tiring of that silly game I set about shaving. As I concentrated on my face I was suddenly sure that my peripheral vision showed a figure in the line of diminishing images that wasn't me at all, but when I turned to the right or left there was no such interruption. Yet each time I stared at myself an out of place figure slipped into the corner of my vision somewhere down the rank of replications. Kate and I had enjoyed a couple of drinks in the lounge, and I wondered if I wasn't a bit inebriated, but I found it impossible to believe that a couple of shots could be causing this curious and unsettling episode. Putting the matter firmly out of my mind I finished shaving and went to join Kate. I didn't mention my little mystery to her for fear that she would make fun of me, as she liked to do. "What an over-ripe imagination you have sometimes, Lorne," she would say, and we would laugh together, never taking her tease seriously.

That morning while driving to the hotel we had noticed a quaint little roadside restaurant, and we set out by foot to find it. A pleasant and appetite-inducing walk of a kilometre or so brought us to its door. There, while gorging on Normandy salt lamb and vegetables, which forenoon had still been in the garden, we shared a bottle of house red, actually two bottles of house red, and chattered away over nothing much at all. The small restaurant filled up as we ate leisurely; a susurrus of conversations drifted around us. Although a majority of the diners appeared to be locals, we didn't feel at all out of place; no-one paid us any mind.

Just as we were leaning away from the table in the interval between finishing the entrée and scanning the dessert offerings I became aware of a presence just seen obliquely to my right. When I turned to have a direct look there was nothing of note there, yet I was sure that someone had been staring at me with attention-getting intensity. Kate was talking to me, but I hadn't actually been listening to her. "What's with you, Lorne? Your mind seems to have wandered. What are you looking at?"

"Oh, I thought for a moment that I saw someone from home, but I was wrong, and besides ... oh, it wasn't anything. You were saying?"

Kate went on talking about the megaliths, saying that we should get out early in the morning to explore before the tourist buses arrive. "If we get there at sunrise we may see something amazing," she said. "There are thousands of menhirs there, thousands more than at Stonehenge." I was looking at her but still felt that someone or something was just out of my field of vision. I purposely resisted looking directly at the imagined eidolon, believing that I was delusional, or at any rate a bit tipsy.

"Yes, Kate, I agree. We'll get them to wake us before sunrise, wolf down some breakfast and get an early start. I'm particularly curious about the burial vaults; dolmen, I think they're called. And then there is a tumulus, an artificial hill with tombs in it. Ridiculously enough the Catholics have built a chapel on top of it, to counteract any devils lurking within I guess. It's called St. Michel, or the Michaelmas." Just as I was saying that I was sure that I saw a figure rise into my peripheral vision, but when I jerked my head around to see whatever it was there was nothing to be seen; just ordinary diners eating ordinary dinners and having prosaic conversations. I tried to shake the ocular bewilderment out of my head, but I was disconcerted and having trouble keeping my focus on Kate. I was still reluctant to bring her into the mystery, as I was completely unsure of just what might be going on, if anything. Still, I thought, it might be good to have some confirmation. But as nothing in Kate's behaviour suggested anything unusual I withheld my bafflement.

We selected a sweet and ordered espresso. I gradually managed to erase my imaginings, and we planned our tomorrow. A final brandy provided us with a dreamlike walk back to the hotel through the brilliantly moonlit night.

"Want a nightcap?" Kate asked with a wicked wink.

"We're getting up early in the morning, remember? But anyway, yes, a nightcap would be nice," I responded, and we wandered in and settled into the embrace of a richly upholstered booth. Two brandy and sodas were brought as we gazed with minimal interest at the others in the room, others who like ourselves were clearly tourists. They were a motley lot, an international set of the curious and the incurious who travel because they can afford it. I had focused my full attention on Kate who was, as usual, chattering away at me. Actually I was less listening than admiring: Kate was a dream of a woman, and I never tired of appreciating her slightly off-centre beauty. Engrossed though I was with her, I suddenly felt that I was being stared at. I tried not to look, tried to unbelieve as it were, but finally I swung my head around to see no-one special; at least I saw no-one who I felt might have been trying to engage me without quite attracting my immediate attention. I was beginning to feel a bit nervous, wondering if my imagination was running away with itself. What, or who, was this peripheral nemesis?

"There you go again, Lorne," Kate said. "You look like you're trying catch someone in an illicit act. I think that you've been watching too many spy dramas. And I don't believe that you've heard a word I've said for the last five minutes."

Realizing that I was looking vacantly at Kate I felt that perhaps I should tell her of my pestiferous visions, but I was so uncertain of any degree of reality that I feared to make a fool of myself, even to my adored and trusted companion.

Again I felt the need to be evasive. "Sorry, dear. I think that I'm just a tiny bit intoxicated," I said with a forced laugh. "We probably should get some sleep. It's been a lengthy day, that drive from Josselin on those twisty roads, and the sun at the beach. All in all I'm exhausted."

With that we, perhaps foolishly, ordered another drink. I tried to drive my uncertainty from me and focus my attention on Kate's cheerful chatter. Eventually we paid up and went to our room, where we both collapsed into bed; the combination of exhaustion and seductive brandy put us almost immediately into deep sleep.

I woke out of a dream, sweating and chilled. I tried to remember it, to reconstruct its content, but it fractured and slipped off into that place where dreams go to die. I only knew that it had upset me, and that was most unusual. Try as I might I couldn't get back to sleep, also unusual; I finally got up and got a gin from the serve yourself. Wrapped in one of the hotel's provided robes I went to sit at the window, where I sipped from the bottle and tried to feel sleepy. The view overlooked a copse of small trees and bushes. As I stared vacantly at the copse a figure emerged, almost seeming to develop from the flora. Though there was a bright moon in a clear night sky, a dappling of shadows camouflaged the form, and I couldn't clearly see it. It stood there unmoving; it seemed to be wrapped in some sort of curious garment I couldn't make out. I stood up to get a better view, but, as I did so, the figure sank back into the foliage and vanished almost as if it had been absorbed. I continued to peer down for a while, but there was absolutely nothing to be seen, only the tranquil tableau of small trees in the moonlight. Torn between a certainty that I was having some kind of dream scenario continued from whatever plot I was involved in while asleep, and a fearful belief that I was taking part in a sort of ultramundane hallucination, I turned away from the window and hurried to get another gin. My heart was pounding, from some unreasoning dread, or from the alcohol — I didn't know which.

I went into the bathroom to splash my face with cold water, but feared to turn on the light, not wanting to see the infinite mirrorings of myself, and who knows what else. Back in bed next to Kate I gradually sank into an uneasy stupor.

When Kate woke me in the early morning I struggled out of that profound yet restless slumber. "Wake up, Lorne," she said. "We want to get an early start. Have yourself a brisk shower, and let's get something to eat. I'll order up." I couldn't shake the night's strange manifestation out of my mind; that figure emerging from the copse and then disappearing into it remained with me like a scene from an otherwise unremembered movie. I went to look out of the window, gazing down at the copse, which in the early light seemed perfectly innocuous. I once again questioned my memory of the night's eldritch demonstration: had I imagined it? How could I know whether it was reality or dream, or yet something else? The last thing I wanted to do was to go into the bathroom for a possible confrontation with an alien reflection in the mirrors. I resisted the idea of having a quick drink and dressed hastily while Kate got herself ready. A sumptuous breakfast was promptly delivered, and we addressed ourselves to it.

"Do I remember correctly that the site is something like four or five million years old or even older? How do they know that? Carbon dating?" Kate pondered aloud, posing questions that she answered with further questions. I could only interject occasional bits of knowledge; we had read the same materials regarding the megaliths. So little is actually known: who were the people who created the site; were they related to the assemblers of Stonehenge and other prehistoric sites scattered throughout Europe; what was the purpose of the stones; were they of astronomic function, or religious purpose? Whose remains lay in the dolmens, the huge rock-formed sepulchres? And perhaps the most fascinating conjecture: what became of the people? Kate and I played a kind of blind ping-pong, passing the speculations back and forth without finding any reasonable answers.

"It's like the Egyptian and Meso-American pyramids," Kate said. "How can we imagine how an ancient people with virtually no tools managed to move these monstrous stones? How did they upend them? It's enough to make one believe in wizardry." I could not but agree with her, though my mindset automatically dismissed all suggestions of the paranormal.

"One day answers will be found," I said. "After all, we pretty well know how the pyramids were built, and last I saw they had figured out how to raise an obelisk. Of course we know a lot about the Egyptians and the pre-Columbians; we know nothing whatever about these primordial people." We had finished our food, and after collecting a day's worth of necessities we set out on foot towards the site that is adjacent to the northern part of the town of Carnac.

The landscape of the area is scrubby, flat, and, except for the thousands of erect stones and a few small houses, somewhat desolate. The sun was just breaching the horizon as we arrived, casting the elongated shadows of the menhirs across the barren, monochromatic ground. There was a disquieting silence around their massive presence as they stood like sentinels of an invisible civilization, waiting its turn to be rediscovered.

We took the advice of one of the many writers on the Carnac megaliths and climbed the twelve metres of the tumulus known as Saint-Michel so as to get an overview of the vast area. The boulders stand in alignments, some of which appear to be parallel lines leading to a half-circle called a cromlech. Some of the arrangements could be taken for astronomical markings, indicating the cardinal points, or the risings of the sun and moon. Here and there, apparently at random, stand the dolmens, which are burial chambers; some of these are formed of several standing rocks topped with a huge flat stone. Although there is nothing sinister about the view of the menhirs and dolmens there is just a hint of the minatory, or perhaps that was just my somewhat frayed nerves talking.

"My God," said Kate. "Do you realize that some of these stones weigh as much as 350 tons? It's unbelievable that they could have been moved by no matter how many men. What do you think, Lorne? How would that be possible?" As she was speaking I felt a premonitory tremor. I froze, unable to look around, fearful of looking around, yet I could not avoid the apparition that had crept into the corner of my vision. "Kate. Do you see anyone anywhere around us? Are we quite alone?"

Kate turned to look at me, her eyes squinting with surprise. "There's no-one at all, Lorne. Where do you think you saw someone?" She took hold of my arms as if to steady me. "We're absolutely alone. Who is this person you seem to keep seeing? Are you having some sort of delusion?"

I sensed a chilling wind moving through my mind; I needed to sit down. But now that I dared look around I saw no-one at all, nothing which I could have mistaken for a human figure. I wondered if I was suffering from a kind of delirium.

"Do you want to go back, Lorne?" Kate asked. "I think that you're not feeling well. Can't you tell me what it is?"

I shook off her suggestion, and after a few minutes I felt better. "No, I'm all right. I really have no idea what came over me." I was torn between trying to explain to Kate what was happening and keeping my own counsel, especially as I had no notion of what was occurring and couldn't imagine precisely what I would tell her that would make any sense at all. If she was beginning to wonder about my sanity I didn't want to do anything that would reinforce her worry. I felt that as I had absolutely no comprehension as to what was causing my anxiety I couldn't pass my bewilderment on to her. "Come on, Kate. Let's take a walk among the stones. Maybe they'll sing to us."

The menhirs didn't sing, but as we were strolling along I was horrified to see a shadow in my marginal vision, moving along just behind us. I stopped without looking round. "Now what?" Kate asked.

"Kate. Do you see a shadow of a person just behind us?"

She spun around, almost knocking me over. "There is nothing,

Lorne," she said with a hint of impatience in her tone. "No person. No shadow. Nothing at all. Don't you think that it's about time you entrusted me with your madness? You're beginning to get me down."

Again I was nearly schizoid with ambivalence, so much of two minds that I was incoherent, unable to think. "I'm sorry, Kate. I ... I ... I..." My ability to speak trailed off into gibberish. At the same time I heard someone speaking to me, and it wasn't Kate. From somewhere in the space around me there was a voice using a language I knew I didn't understand, yet in some oblique way did. The sounds were guttural, with a resonance suggesting that they came from a huge echoic room. Frantic, I turned to Kate appealing for help, but she seemed indifferent to my need, looking at me with perplexity, as if I were mad, which perhaps I was. The alien voice persisted as I struggled to comprehend its message. I knew that Kate didn't hear or see anything unusual as she stared at me, now seeing me as a stranger.

Atlantes. Gwrac'h queen. Princess. Hag. What did these words mean? Who was trying to communicate what to me? *Death goddess. Fertility. Men into fish. Déesse Mère.*

"Lorne, we're going to leave this place. Come with me." Kate pulled at the arm of my jacket, but I remained unable to move. "Well, I'm going. You had better come with me." She began to walk off among the great stones; I stood rooted in place, as if in a trance. My eyes were fixed on a menhir directly in front of me. On it was incised the image of an axe and a snake; though the images were very eroded they were still decipherable. The rock was losing its opacity, beginning to deliquesce. Kate had disappeared.

Although I was completely unaware of it, some period of time must have ensued as the stones slowly dissolved; it was as if they had been ice rather than granite. Soon I was knee-deep in tepid water, still unable to move. The voice continued to speak to me, but I could only understand some of what it was saying, as if some other comprehending mind partly occupied my brain. The language was one I had once known, but had lost over thousands of years. In the near distance I saw a diorama, a *tableau mort* of men prying the enormous stones off log rafts. Just beyond, others were using logs to drag them laboriously into place. As I watched uncomprehendingly the scene came to life; as far as I could see there were people struggling with the huge stones as they were unloaded from the rafts and moved across the land. Women went among the labourers doling out food and drink. A few oxen were pressed into service, their nostrils steaming from their exertion.

The scene shifted, like a new episode of a documentary, and I could see people unceremoniously clearing old bones from a comparatively small dolmen, discarding them to make room for future burials, perhaps their own. It was also apparent that they had recently completed a new interment place, a vast and lofty chamber with walls of upright stones and a roof formed of large slabs covered by a mound of turf. As I watched a procession approached with offerings and libations and jars of food and drink for the departed. The air was filled with a melancholy chanting, a funereal music in an alien mode of quarter-tones.

I was no longer standing in water, but on the pebbles of the shoreline. My guide, my beguiler, was close by, talking to me as I strove to understand, seeking familiar words in the archaic tongue he used. It was as if the language itself was buried in the nearby dolmens and tumuli, waiting for me to rediscover it bit by bit. Some remnant of my mind was trying to recall my life, but I had only fragments of memory. I thought of K ... K ... K ... her name eluded me. She had left me to the mercies of my aboriginal past, my origin, and walked off among the oblivious menhirs. I could barely remember her face, much less where I knew her. I knew at some point that I would ultimately lose my recent history forever. That I belonged in a very distant past rather than in the misplaced present was ever more clear to me. I had been mislaid in some malfunction of the time continuum; I had begun to fashion a false life in a synthetic present.

The chanting that I had been hearing started to sound familiar, no longer foreign to my ears, but rather comforting and suitable. An odd sense of belonging was taking hold of me, and I joined a gang of those labouring to move a fearsomely weighty stone across the ground. As I worked I found myself participating in the chant, even without knowing its purpose, though I didn't doubt that it had a purpose.

The scene again slid away from my consciousness, and in the new frame I saw that bonfires had been lit. It was evening, and again the women were moving about with pots of stew of some sort and a heady fermented drink. Although I perceived that the sexes were in some ways separated, there was no sense of inequality; men and women sat together, talking and laughing. Children gathered in groups, amusing themselves in playing recondite games. The scene was a convivial one, and I found my place in it comfortable, even though I was still struggling to understand the language. No special attention was paid to me, but my mentor, he who had lured me back to my own past, stayed nearby. I heard his name as Brog; it was strange that he called me Lorne, a name that had a furtive resonance for me. He only occasionally said anything to me, but I had extracted something of the history of these people, my people, from what I could comprehend. We probably came from the sea, settling here, where our creativity and beliefs could flourish. There was no credible hint as to just where we came from, but I thought that I heard a reference to Atlantis; the people called themselves "Atlantes." This gleaned bit of information didn't seem at all strange to me for I had never heard of Atlantis; in fact I found that I had little information at all, that my store of knowledge was vague; I was essentially incurious. I easily accepted that whatever was, was, and I had no desire to acquire what seemed to me to be useless and unimportant.

I seldom questioned Brog, partly because I was apathetic, partly because I had trouble formulating sentences, but mostly because his responses were both vague and nonsensical. I felt little urge to know more about myself and the people in whose society I now was; it all seemed right and normal. I no longer had a recent past, only a present.

The days passed with little variation other than an occasional ritual pageant, the meaning of which I never learned, or the brief periods of tumultuous weather which made work impossible. During such rainy periods we all huddled in various temporary structures where shamanistic storytellers performed to the edification of the people. The odour of damp hides was narcotizing. Only sporadically was I able to deduce much from these tales, but I listened intently, mesmerized by the fervour with which they were related.

When there was illness or accident the shamans exercised their talents for amelioration and healing; the sick or wounded placed great faith in these sages, and it was that faith which more often than not effected a cure. As I had reappeared among the people with a mind that was essentially a tabula rasa, I was accepting of these paranormal healings, making no effort at understanding. When someone died from illness or mishap the shaman was not blamed; he was the one who presided over the burial ritual, leading the singsong chants and comforting the saddened. I became aware that when a shaman was not performing his enigmatic purpose he worked along with the rest, indistinguishable from any of us. I was further aware that there seemed to be little in the way of hierarchy; no single person, or group of persons, took a lead; everyone led in a kind of tacit equality.

On a sparkling day under a cerulean sky we sweated over the raising of a huge menhir. Some were levering with logs while others were balancing the stone as it rose. Suddenly I sensed that we were losing control of it; it was slowly tilting beyond perpendicular. As if in a filmed slow-motion scene the great rock fell over, smashing down on some of the workers. The log I had been working with along with other men flipped back striking me across the chest and pinning me to the earth. At first the trauma was so great, so unexpected, that I felt nothing. Nothing could be done for the poor souls who were compacted beneath the fallen menhirs. A number of men lifted the log away from me; then the pain began. It was a pain such as I could not ever have imagined; my chest was crushed; I could only gasp for breath; I was completely paralyzed. Only my eyes and brain seemed to be functioning. I was lifted onto a stretcher of lashed-together branches and carried away from the scene. Hundreds had gathered to try to move the fallen menhir off the bodies, but without a planned effort it was useless. I was aware that one of the shamans, perhaps it was Brog, was walking along with the men carrying me, but I could not hear such words as he mouthed. Somewhere along the way I passed out.

Although some vestige of my mind endured, I was incorporeal. What remained of me was in a dim place, most probably a tumulus, that vast tumulus which lay at the far end of the alignment of menhirs. If it was cold within I didn't know it; if it was damp I didn't know it; if it reeked of wet clay I didn't know it. All sensibility was gone; the pain was gone. But I was not gone, my awareness, though without locus, survived. I was without ego, without id, but some fragment of my psyche remained.

For a timeless segment I wander through the scrub, then find myself on a deserted beach where the only sentient life is some herring gulls wheeling and screeching. I am very fatigued, hungry, thirsty, but there is nothing to eat or drink. As there is no sign of humanity it doesn't seem to matter whether I walk to the right or the left. I stagger along, searching my mind for information, any information, but there is only a hole with unintelligible disturbances, a featureless limbo without past or future. I know that if I don't find some sort of sustenance I will be unable to go onward. I fear to stop and rest; were I to collapse onto the beach I might never rise again. But sit I do, and then I lie supine on the warm sand.

I am fading into oblivion — am I incorporeal, bodiless? yet I feel weariness, appetite, dehydration; are these sensations products of my mind or my body? — but at the penultimate moment I am jolted into awareness. I look up to see a small jet soar across the sky. I watch its trajectory until it vanishes at the horizon. This cacophony of human life energizes me; I get to my feet, heading in the direction of the jet.

Suddenly, like an unanticipated movie clip, the hotel is before me, tangible, active, seemingly real. Figures come and go; cars arrive and leave. There is a preternatural normalcy about the scene. I walk towards the main entrance, noting that the people I encounter seem completely unaware of me; some pass through me as if I were not only invisible but also insubstantial. I can't hear voices, though I know that those around me are talking; I can hear other noises — those made by cars, bumping luggage carts, the gulls calling each other as they circle around the hotel grounds — but not the sounds of humans. I try speaking out, but no-one notices or hears.

Then I see Kate, talking to some others who are about to get into an airport bus. When I realize that she, too, is leaving, I run, futilely calling out her name. The driver starts the engine, and the bus begins to roll along the driveway towards the road. I sprint, yelling, but it is useless. I remain unseen and unheard.

MARTIN LAST's long, rich, and eventful life can scarcely be summarized in two hundred words or so, but it is certainly pertinent to mention that he was the co-founder of New York's legendary bookstore, The Science Fiction Shop.

About living in Montreal, Martin says: "In 1990, because of our increasingly dismal perception of the sociopolitical future of the United States, my longtime companion and I abandoned our native land and moved to the city we had come to love over the course of a number of visits — quirky, cosmopolitan, enticing Montreal. Once ensconced, I continued to pursue my unrealistic diversions of music and writing. Years before, while living in New York City, my poetry, fiction, and criticism had appeared in various publications, but the mundane pressure of earning a reliable living curtailed my endeavours. Living in Montreal revivified my dormant need to write, and so I have."

Mrs. Marigold's House

"Mom, do I have to go?"

"To the party by the richest woman in town?" My mother bunched her fists on her turquoise and silver spandex hips. She was the perfect skinny '80s aerobics instructor, right down to the frosted pink lipstick sneer. "Ashley, get in the car. Mrs. Marigold'll have plenty of Halloween treats."

I turned to my stooped-shouldered dad. He smoothed my hair. "What is it, Ashley-bee?"

My eyes filled with tears. "I don't want to go."

Mom stared. "Ashley, honey, you'll insult her if you don't go. You don't want to do that, do you?"

"*She* won't care."

"Darling, only six kids in the whole town were invited. Six lucky five- to ten-year-olds." She paused. "Good thing you're only nine."

I burst out, "Can't I just stay home and give out candy?"

"You mean eat it." She laughed and crouched beside me. "Darling, your dad and I have to go to our party, and you have to go to yours. We can't leave you alone."

"You did in Vancouver. And Chicago. And—"

Dad put his hand on my shoulder. "It's safer at Mrs. Marigold's."

They always won. I closed my eyes. "Fine."

"That's my girl," Dad said.

We had to go out the front door to get to the garage. It wasn't attached like at our last three houses. This was an old brick house with a roof that curled up on both ends. Mom wanted bigger, but Dad said we needed something discreet. And cheap. Everything was cheap in Edelson, Ontario.

When I got to our Dodge Aries, I had to hike up my money dress to get in. That was the costume Mom made for me: a million dollars. She'd threaded Monopoly money together to make a sheath. I once saw a movie star wearing a dress made out of gold credit cards. She looked sleek. I looked fat. I also fluttered when I walked and crunched when I sat down. Dad shut the door behind me and waved goodbye.

Mom glared. "Ashley Quarrington, pick up your costume when you sit! Don't you have the sense God gave an egg?"

"Sorry."

She shook her head and manhandled the Dodge onto Oak Lane, muttering, "Last Halloween, I wore a Versace dress to a masquerade ball. Now I'm in Edelson, Ontario, eating chips and dip with the town eejits."

"Mom," I said softly, "tell me about your dress."

"Well. You remember it, honey. It was black silk, full length..."

I tuned her out. It was 5:30 and pitch dark outside. Just us, the white stripes on the pavement, and the trees looming over us. I thought about what Adam had said on my first day of school.

It had always sucked being the new kid, but this time, in the middle of October, had been unbelievable. My stomach had been knotted as I'd headed for my grade-four classroom. Adam had been lounging around the doorway with two girls. One girl had short brown hair, the other long, but their faces were identical, with oval faces, thin lips, and narrow eyes. The boy was short, with a shock of black hair and a black trenchcoat. He looked like a crow. He leaned against the brick wall, watching me come up. The two girls looked at me, then at each other, and giggled.

They wouldn't be my friends. I kept looking at the boy. His eyes were grey and cool, but not mean. Finally, he nodded.

I nodded back.

"I heard there was a new kid coming," the long-haired twin burst out. "But I heard it was a boy." She eyed me, and they laughed again.

The boy didn't. He slid away from the wall. "Where'd you come from?"

I swallowed. "New York."

"You know the school at all?"

I shook my head.

"I'll show ya. Before the bell rings." He started walking. I followed. I heard a funny noise and jerked around to see the short-haired twin spitting at me. I was too surprised to yell. She missed by two feet. I looked at the gob of spit, white and bubbly on the pavement, then up at the twins. They smiled angelically and waved.

Adam had kept walking, so I huffed up to join him around the corner. He didn't look at me, but said, "Forget them."

I giggled nervously.

He pointed at the tetherball poles. "No-one uses them. And only kids up to grade three get to use the jungle gym, but we slide down the hill when there's snow. It's all right. The rink's for gym class. No hockey because they think the girls'll get hurt, so we do broomball and skating and stuff." He glanced at me. "You like sports?"

My face burned. "Yeah."

He shrugged. He looked around and said low, "Did you get invited to the Halloween party?"

"Just the one by the old lady with the mansion."

He muttered to the ground, "Skip it."

What was up with that? I tried to check his eyes, but he shrugged and walked away.

He avoided me for the next two weeks. He'd skipped a grade, so he was nine like me, but in grade five. He lived with his dad, who worked for a drug company and travelled a lot. No-one would tell me about his mom. They looked funny when I asked. One little kid told me that Adam brought his dad's gun to show-and-tell last year. Maybe that wasn't so weird out in the country, but it was to me. I even tested his teacher, complete with a golly-gee grin. "Hi, Mrs. Collins. Do you know where I could find Adam Corona?"

She slammed some books down. "I have no idea." She looked over her glasses at me. "Young lady, you'd be better off with friends in your own grade."

Whatever. I swallowed the hurt and sailed down the hall.

"Hey. Fat-ly Ashley." I turned. The Cox twins were standing there, wearing identical grey-blue dresses with ruffles around the bottom. They smiled, cruel like cats.

The one with the long hair, Julia, strode up close. "We heard you were asking about Adam."

I backed up and my elbow hit something soft. I whipped around.

It was Jessica's middle. She thrust her narrow, freckled face against mine. "Don't."

Julia jerked my hair.

I yelped, spun, and pushed her off. "Go away!"

They laughed together. "We wish we could." And then they disappeared.

The twins were nine years old, too.

Mom missed the turnoff to Forced Road and had to pull a U-turn, swearing under her breath. We found 126 easily enough. There was a huge wrought-iron gate with ivy leaves, topped with spears. Real candles, fat and white, were stuck on to the top of every other spear. Mom muttered, "Must've been cheap." We cruised along the mile-long driveway until it ended in a half-circle at the house. Paper bags holding candles led the way to the door. Pumpkins, each carved with a letter, spelled MRS MARIGOLD'S HOUSE on the steps.

I held my breath. It was an enormous greystone house. The four columns around the door were wound with orange streamers, like candy canes. Back from the entrance, the rest of the mansion spread its rectangular wings. The roof was iced with stone teeth and wrought-iron gates.

"Limestone," Mom said. "Over a hundred years old. I have no idea why they built it in Edelson."

"Cheap land?"

She nodded. "And they were probably crazy. Now get in there, girl."

One of the massive black iron doors swung inward. I jumped. There stood a fat woman in a pink ball gown with wings and a diamond tiara. "Come in, Ashley!"

I stopped. "How do you know my name?"

Mom elbowed me. Hard.

"Stop it, Elizabeth," Mrs. Marigold said crisply. I gawped. Not only did she tell her off, but Mom insists on "Liz." Mom gritted her teeth. Mrs. Marigold ignored her. She bent and looked me right in the eye. "Every year, I invite six children. If you're extra special, I bring you back the next year. But I love all the children in Edelson and know all your names."

People said things like, "Every child is a gift." Then they ignored the kids in Africa with flies on their eyelids, or the street kids who asked for spare change. But Mrs. Marigold had eyes like chocolate. She also had a real smile, creamy skin, and two double chins. She smiled. "Ashley Jane Quarrington, thank you for coming to my Halloween party."

I grinned. "Trick or treat!"

Mom gasped. "What Ashley means is, she hopes you'll find her special enough to come back next year. I brought you some Moët champagne as a little thank-you..."

Mrs. Marigold waved it away. "Please. You have it. I don't like alcohol. It makes you stupid."

I giggled and ignored Mom's look of death.

"My dear Ashley, come in for all the tricks and treats you can handle!" She shooed Mom out. "Don't come back before nine, Elizabeth. Enjoy your own party." Then Mrs. Marigold glided to my side. "You must have the grand tour." I'd already started ahead to the ballroom, which flickered in candlelight. Then the crystal chandelier burst alight above me. I gasped, and Mrs. Marigold laughed. There was a grand piano on the left, a fireplace on the right, and a shiny wood floor in between. If I'd been alone, I would've run and slid on it in my socks. The windows stood from floor to ceiling, with a curved window in the middle. The ceiling was covered in plaster artwork that Mrs. Marigold had topped with black streamers. The only bad part were the paintings of her ancestors, their eyes following me like in a haunted-house ride. Near the door, on the left, stretched a staircase from the second floor. The smooth banisters ended with statues of pages. I closed my eyes and imagined descending in a long, red dress, my hair swept into a French twist, graceful, beautiful, thin.

"Someday," Mrs. Marigold whispered.

I smiled. "The other thing I want to do is to slide down the banister, like in Mary Poppins!"

"Why not?"

Her chocolate eyes twinkled. Throwing off my money dress, I ran up the stairs, plopped my bum on the banister, and slid down sideways with a whoop. Before I hit a statue, I jumped off.

Mrs. Marigold hugged me. "You look beautiful."

That surprised me more than anything. But her chocolate eyes promised the truth. I hugged her back, laughing at her fake wings and curly wig, and slid on my money sheath. Now it seemed funny, not stupid. "Where're the other kids?"

"They're in the kitchen. They've all been here a while, but you need a tour."

For once, being new was wonderful. We backtracked to the entrance. On our right was the library, with lots of old books and a fireplace. I wanted to live in there. On the left, I peeked into the smaller, cool-green music room. It had a baby grand piano and a bar. Mrs. Marigold opened a wooden cabinet to show me a stereo. "For the untalented, like me," she joked. Next door was the morning room. One side faced the front of the house, which pointed north; the other, she said, faced east, to catch the dawn's rays. There was a pine table with fresh sunflowers and matching chairs. Mrs. Marigold had pasted glow-in-the-dark stars up on the ceiling.

Back in the hallway, we bypassed the ballroom, as well as a smaller staircase and the bathrooms on our left. We drifted into the formal dining room opposite them. The walls were dark burgundy. The ten-foot, rectangular, mahogany table stood in front of a china cabinet. "Behind this is the pantry, and at the back are my offices. Not so interesting. I'll take you to the kitchen now."

I didn't want the tour to end. "What about upstairs?"

She put a warm hand on my shoulder. "My darling. Maybe next year."

It was a half-promise. I frowned. The kitchen door on our left was closed, and I suddenly realized it was pretty quiet for a bunch of kids. I straightened my costume as she threw open the door.

The Cox twins posed on either side of the doorway. They were wearing gunmetal-blue bathing suits with tiny sarongs. Across each chest was a sash that read MISS UNIVERSE. They posed with a hip thrust forward, one leg in front of the other, one arm in the air and the other pointing towards each other.

I blew between their arms into the warm, pine kitchen. A hulk of a man stood with his arms crossed and scowled at me. Mrs. Marigold waved at him. "My housekeeper, gardener, and chauffeur, Mr. Jackson." He didn't blink. I glared back at him. "Let's go from the youngest to oldest. Daisy Mae Boosler turned five yesterday."

A tiny blond girl yanked on her bear mask and growled at me. I pretended to be scared.

"Samuel Paine is six."

He was a black boy with a cowboy hat and holster. His shirt looked bulky. He kept his left arm in an L shape, with the front part sticking forward. He mumbled, "Six and a half."

Mrs. Marigold smiled. "Yes. Six and a half! Ashley Jane Quarrington, you're next at nine and two months."

"What is she?" Julia whispered loudly.

"A million dollars," I replied. Mrs. Marigold smiled. "Ah, the Cox twins. Jessica Alison Cox, at nine years, six months, and Julia Alexandra Cox, nine years, six months, and ten minutes older." They struck a new pose, hands on their hips, chests thrust forward, and looked satisfied when Daisy clapped.

"Last but not least, Adam Christopher Corona, nine years and nine months!" There was a pause and then Adam came out from behind the couch in the adjoining den. He was wearing sunglasses and a black trenchcoat over a black shirt and jeans. He looked like Keanu Reeves in *The Matrix*. The twins smiled like he was the whipped cream on their pumpkin pie.

"And you all know me, Adelaide Ann Marigold."

I pointed at mean old Mr. Jackson. "Is he your husband, Mrs. Marigold?"

She laughed, and her belly jiggled with it. "No, no, Ashley. He's my helper. The only reason I'd ever get married would be to have pets like you." Adam grimaced, but Mrs. Marigold laughed again.

It was a funny party. Adam went back behind the couch. Daisy had a witch cookie in one hand threatening the bear cookie in the other, until she dunked the witch's head in her punch and then bit it off. Samuel got himself some punch and stood there miserably, sipping it, his left arm pressed against his chest. The Cox twins whispered to each other and glanced over where Adam was hiding. Mr. Jackson had moved to the door, so I moved away from him towards Mrs. Marigold and her food.

The crystal punch bowl, decorated with roses and thorns, held a scarlet punch with raspberries, blueberries, and orange slices. Beside it were big chocolate chip cookies and little chocolate cupcakes iced with pumpkins. There were potato chips, tortilla chips with salsa, pita bread with hummus, and plain crackers with peanut butter. There were little bowls with bits of melon, bananas, grapes, or cherries. There was cheesecake and poppy-seed cake and a black-and-white cake; and best of all, there was a huge layered fudge cake with thick icing that said

HAPPY HALLOWEEN FROM MRS MARIGOLD.

I picked up a plate. My eyes were all over the fudge cake. I was afraid she'd say I should wait, or we'd have to sing first, but Mrs. Marigold just took a silver cake cutter and dealt me a slice as big as her hand.

"Thank you," I breathed.

"Come on, all you children." The twins sauntered up. Julia grinned and poked her sister. I ignored them. Julia walked around the table and picked a single tortilla chip, which she nibbled delicately. Jessica one-upped her by taking only a sliver of honeydew melon. They glared at each other. I walked over to Adam.

He shoved something under his jacket. "What?"

"You want some?" I cut a bit with my fork and offered it.

"No!" he whispered. I shrugged off my hurt and brought the moist cake to my mouth. He grabbed my wrist and shook his head fiercely. I stopped and stared at him.

Mrs. Marigold loomed over us. "What is it, my dears?"

Adam walked away.

"N-nothing, Mrs. Marigold. We were just having some cake."

She winked at me. "Now you be sure you both eat up." She walked away, but Mr. Jackson was still glowering at me. Then Adam tried to squeeze by him.

He grabbed Adam's shoulders. "Where are you going, Mr. Corona."

"To the bathroom."

A slash of a grin. "There's a little boys' room in the office behind you, Adam. You know the drill."

Adam glared at him and shook himself loose. "I sure do." He stalked off to the office.

"Oh dear, oh dear," Mrs. Marigold lamented. "And I was just going to play our favourite game. Well, we'll have to wait. Come on, children. Eat up! Lord knows I don't need it!" She gave her belly laugh again and handed the twins some punch. Jessica sipped it and shuddered delicately. "The calories!" Julia picked out a single raspberry and ate it.

I put the cake down untasted. Mrs. Marigold came over. "Sweetheart, don't you like it?"

"I'm not hungry."

She put a pudgy hand over mine. Her palm was cool. "People will always try to make you feel bad. But it would hurt my feelings if you didn't try one bite. It's an old family recipe."

One bite was heaven. Moist chocolate cake with thick fudge icing. I closed my eyes and sighed.

"That's it, darling. Some punch will make it taste even better."

I licked my thumb and picked up all the crumbs and smears of icing. Mrs. Marigold pointed at the punch. I sipped. It tasted sharp, kind of nice after all the chocolate. I eyed the rest of the cake, but she said, "Maybe later, darling. Mr. Jackson's going to get Adam, and then we'll play my favourite game."

Mr. Jackson hauled "Mr. Corona" in. Adam's shoes tracked mud, and he wouldn't meet my eyes. Mr. Jackson rumbled something into Mrs. Marigold's ear. She smiled. Her teeth were sharp. "Adam, sweetheart, we're going to play now. Did you have something to eat?"

"Yes'm."

"Have some punch."

"I already did."

Her eyes glinted. "Have some more."

He started to run. Mr. Jackson seized him and muscled him into a headlock. With his other hand, he forced my friend's jaw open like a dog's. Adam punched and kicked in vain. Mrs. Marigold whistled as she filled up a water gun with her punch. She sauntered over and then — I couldn't believe it — fired repeatedly into his gaping mouth. Adam sputtered and started to cough. I ran and beat on Mr. Jackson's back. "No! No!"

Mrs. Marigold smiled. She put the water gun on the table and stroked Adam's forehead. He flinched. "There, there, darling. In a minute, you'll feel much better."

She turned and winked at me. I gulped. "Now we're going to make a circle on the floor." Mr. Jackson dropped Adam to the ground and moved the couch and table off to either side. Adam was spitting on the pine floor, bright red, but it was punch, not blood. Mrs. Marigold was fussing over him, so I pocketed the punch gun. Might be useful. My fingers were shaking, but no-one noticed. I handed Adam a napkin. He shook his head and kept spitting.

Her fat hand curved around my arm. "You're next to Jessica, love."

The other children had formed a circle on the floor. Daisy Mae, Samuel, a space, Jessica, Julia, another space, and then Mrs. Marigold. I sat closer to Samuel. Jessica pretended to flick a cootie and sidled towards her sister. Mr. Jackson shoved Adam between Julia and Mrs. Marigold, then backed outside the circle, watching us.

"Darlings. Welcome. This is my favourite game on my favourite day of the year. The best get-to-know-you game in the world. Have you ever wondered how you can go to school with all the other kids and never really know anyone?" Her tiara and teeth caught the candlelight. "So every year, I invite the six most special children here to talk about themselves."

Adam sat up and felt his jaw. "So we can tell you our secrets."

"Well, of course, dear. That's the whole fun of it."

I jumped up. "I'm not playing."

"Ashley. Such an attitude your first time here. I'm disappointed in you." And her chocolate eyes did look sad.

"Cake doesn't give you the right to find out all about me."

Adam snorted. "But the punch does."

I gave him a hard look and turned to go. Mr. Jackson blocked me. His forehead hung over his eyes. His huge hands clamped over my arms. I ducked and tried to run. He squeezed the meat of my arms until I squeaked, then tossed me back down in the circle.

I rubbed my butt. Even the twins were dead silent.

The room dimmed. Only the candles threw off light. Mrs. Marigold rubbed her hands. "I love the feisty ones. They have the best secrets." Her smile stretched out her fat cheeks and cast shadows on her eyes. She brought out a magic wand topped by a sparkling star and pointed it at the girl to her right.

"Daisy Mae."

She looked scared. She put her bear mask on.

Mrs. Marigold put her arm around her. "Be a bear if you want, sweetheart," she soothed. "Just tell us your biggest, darkest, deepest secret."

There was a pregnant pause. Her voice was so soothing. Daisy Mae whispered, "Mama..."

"Yes, Mama..."

"She has a bottle, too. It makes her smell funny."

Mrs. Marigold licked her lips. "Thank you, Daisy. That was very good for only five years old." She gave her a witch cookie and hugged her. "Now Samuel."

He shook his head, eyes down at the pistol in his holster.

"I call on you, Samuel."

He shuddered and gasped. Then, eyes closed, voice flat, he said, "I'm a freak."

Mrs. Marigold leaned forward. "What do you mean, darling."

"My arm grows things. It's heavy. Bleeds all the time. Mom and Dad always make me go to the hospital—"

"Oh. My." Mrs. Marigold rubbed her belly. "Show us, Samuel."

He pulled off his shirt. He had a thick neck. Mr. Jackson shone a light on him as he unwrapped the bandages so we could see his huge left arm, three times the size of his right, with lumps and scars and bleeding coming from his armpit and elbow.

Daisy Mae shrieked and covered her mouth. The twins gasped. Adam was thin-lipped. And Samuel had no expression, like it was normal to show us his deformed arm.

"Have you had any operations, Samuel?" Mrs. Marigold asked in a molasses voice.

"Yes. Twelve."

"A dozen! Oh, you're a brave boy." Her eyes shone. "You'll have to come back next year and show and tell us all about it. How exciting."

I didn't want to watch, but I did. My stomach churned.

"And now our newcomer, Ashley Jane Quarrington. Tell us your secret, Ashley."

My body relaxed, like a nap in sunlight after eating chocolate. My heart beat in the rhythm of her voice. Tell us, tell us. Now Daisy Mae and Samuel were chanting it. Tell us. Tell us.

The words slipped out of me. "My parents did a pyramid and cheated a lot of people. Twice. This time they got caught." I shut myself up. Still it beat at me. Tell us, tell us. I swallowed.

"Are they planning to do it again?"

"Mom is. A swindle." I closed my eyes and tried to tamp down the other secrets: that I hated their schemes; that I missed Vancouver; that I had no friends because I was scared I'd tell them. I swallowed again.

"I see." Mrs. Marigold sat back on her heels thoughtfully. "And I'm their big, fat target?"

I nodded.

She smiled. "Not as juicy, Ashley, but interesting. Jessica?"

She hugged her knees. Her eyes were huge. "It's Daddy again."

"Jessica, shut up!"

Mrs. Marigold's eyes blazed at Julia, who shrank back into silence.

Jessica went on in a sing-song. "He comes to my room every night now."

Mrs. Marigold's voice was a rich lullaby. "Tell me, darling."

"He always makes me touch him. Last time he made me use my mouth." She stopped and wrapped her arms around her knees. Mrs. Marigold licked her lips. "Julia?"

Tears ran down Julia's face. She was silent.

"I command you, Julia Alexandra Cox."

Snot ran out of Julia's nose. She didn't wipe it. Finally, she whispered, "He promised he'd leave her alone if I did everything for him."

"Ah." It was so delicious, Mrs. Cox had to sit for a moment to digest it, with a sigh. "And my nightcap, Adam Christopher Corona."

His grey eyes faced the floor. "No."

"I command you, Adam Christopher Corona."

He screamed, "No!" and tried to run. Mr. Jackson leaned on his shoulders, pinning him in place.

Mrs. Marigold thundered, "*I. Command. You.*"

He writhed under Mr. Jackson. "I caught a squirrel!"

"Yes..."

"I killed it!"

"Yes..."

"I cut off its head ... its tail ... its paws..."

"Yes..."

"And I ate them. Raw." His body went limp.

"Yessss," Mrs. Marigold hissed. "Oh, yes, Adam, my goody-two-shoes animal-lover. Now you see: when you're powerless, you want to take something under you and crush it until it screams, and then you crush it some more. Oh, good work, my boy. Next you'll be torturing your dog."

"No."

She stroked his sweaty forehead. "Oh, yes, my darling. I see a bright future for you. Normally, I don't like any children older than ten. But you, my bright boy, I'll bring you back next year and the year after. You show such promise."

He moaned and slid out from Mr. Jackson's loosened grasp.

Mrs. Marigold looked down on him. "Oh, dear. Fainting. But he's still the best we've got. Jackson, get a cool cloth." He lumbered to the faucet and grabbed a dishtowel.

And Adam rose and pulled out a handgun from his waistband. It looked real. Her mouth gaped. He shot her in the belly, and she gasped.

I covered my ears. He repositioned, then fired again. She collapsed on her back like a huge beetle, holding her bloody gut, her tiara crooked.

Mr. Jackson lunged. Adam jumped up, braced himself, and shot Mr. Jackson in the right eye. A stream of blood and brains spewed over the pine cabinets and white walls. A pause, and then the body slumped to the floor, eye socket blown to bits.

Daisy Mae was screaming. Samuel had flattened himself against the floor. The twins wept silently, clinging to each other.

Adam held his gun against Mrs. Marigold's temple. She was still breathing.

I stood there. Samuel yelled, "Get down, stupid!" He yanked on Daisy Mae, who was making tortured chipmunk noises.

I picked my way over to Mrs. Marigold. Samuel muttered, "It's your funeral."

She was lying on the floor, her wig half off, short blond hair peeking out. Her hands pressed against her belly, trying to stop the flow of rich, red blood. Her face was pale and sweaty, but her chocolate eyes glittered just the same as before. She didn't say a word, just watched me walk towards her while she gasped slow, horrible breaths. Adam was panting too, short little huffs, but his finger was steady on the trigger.

I could smell her blood as I bent over her. I pulled out the water pistol and showed it to both of them. Her chest heaved, her lips hitched upward in almost a smile, before I squeezed the trigger. Fruit punch spurted into her open mouth, some spilling over her chin. I fired again and again, until there was only a little punch dribbling down the muzzle, and I said, "Why, Mrs. Marigold? Why? Why?" — my voice getting higher and higher until it broke. Sweat pricked my armpits. I squeezed my eyes shut, remembering sliding down the banister, Adam showing me the tetherballs, the candles on the stakes. Everything was ruined. Everything.

When I opened my eyes, she was licking her lips. Adam still had his gun on her temple. I twisted and yelled in her face. "Why? *I command you.*"

She was gasping, but her eyes shone. "Adam. Ashley. I am so ... proud of you. My parents were — *worse.*" She gasped a giggle. "You can see ... for yourselves. They're upstairs. Stuffed. They didn't care ... I was alive ... but they did ... at the end!" She laughed, and some blood squashed out of the gun holes. I turned and vomited. Samuel groaned. Daisy Mae scrabbled to my ankles and tried to hug my leg. I kicked her off.

Mrs. Marigold's fat, white face glistened. Only her chocolate eyes remained. And her lulling voice. "Adam. The worst ... is not ... your father. The worst is ... abandonment." Adam's hand shook. She held his eyes. "I love ... all ... my children. Adam. I'm ... the only ... one ... who cares."

His right hand shook worse.

He closed his eyes and whispered, "Liar."

Then he blew her brains out.

Her blood and flesh spewed on us. The others screamed. I wiped my eyes and swallowed to clear my ears.

Adam threw a cushion over her half-blasted head and faced us. Daisy Mae screamed. His grey eyes were sad, but he didn't come closer. "I'd never hurt you." He walked to the window.

I followed him. More than Mrs. Marigold, more than Mr. Jackson, more than the gun, I had to know. "Adam. Did you really do that to the squirrel?"

He half-smiled. "Yup. I knew she'd make me talk, so I needed a secret to cover up my plan." He shook his head. Blood flicked on to the window. "I felt worse about the squirrel." He raised the pistol against the right side of his head and braced it with his left hand. "You guys are free now. But I can't live with this." He pulled the trigger.

"Adam, no!" I scrambled to knock it away.

He was too fast.

I screamed.

The right side of his head was blown off, and his body was at my feet. I wiped my mouth and eyes, as tears and mucous mingled with the blood. Samuel was gone. I heard his voice from the next room, calling the police. Jessica stared wide-eyed at nothing while Julia stroked her hair. Daisy Mae crept towards me again.

I launched myself on Adam's body and cried. They'd call him a monster. I knew better. I cradled him, stroking his bloody skin, brushing away the bits of bone, letting his arteries pump on my skin until they stopped. Daisy Mae clung to my leg, and I let her. We stayed like that until the police dragged me away, my fingers branding his muddy black sneakers with streaks of blood and bone. "I'll remember you," I promised, as they hauled me into the night air.

Melissa Yuan-Innes — a Writers of the Future contest winner — is currently working on a science-fiction novel, tentatively titled *The Ape in the Mirror*. Her stories can also be found in *Weird Tales, Andromeda Spaceways*, and *Open Space: New Canadian Fantastic Fiction.*

Melissa only recently made Montreal her home. "I moved to Montreal in July 2000 for my medical residency. I love the food, from exquisite pastries to Pho Lien's soup. I revitalized my wardrobe on St-Hubert Street, since the average passerby put my sweatshirts to shame. I enjoy the vibrant street life, the relative car independence, and the ring of real church bells."

About the genesis of "Mrs. Marigold's House," she writes: "I wrote this story in San Francisco over Halloween. I walked through the crowds on Castro Street. I was surrounded by a drag queen posing for the tourists' cameras, "Hannibal" in chains and face mask (whose clinking kept attracting a dog's attention), and mothers pushing prams through the dusk. It was a city where adults enjoyed Halloween as much as the children did." Not that the children in "Mrs. Marigold's House" enjoy themselves: "You could invite children to your house every Halloween and have perfectly innocent fun, but I wanted to write about a more sinister possibility. Thanks to Dr. M.J. Shkrum for his forensic pathology advice."

Melissa's website is www.melissayuaninnes.com.

Linda Dydyk

The Strange Afterlife of Henry Wigam

Uncle Wiggily came to live with us in the summer of 2112. I won't deny that his dazed expression and sad eyes brought out my mothering instincts. He was very much the newborn. Helpless and vulnerable. And he had a hard time right from the beginning. He had intestinal problems, and the bouts of vomiting and diarrhea disrupted his potty training. Tom and I lived in the fear that if the purges didn't kill him then certainly the dehydration would. One morning, I found excrement everywhere. His diaper had exploded, and he had slipped on the seepage. He was limp and motionless; I panicked, thinking he was dead. Then, there were the rages or seizures, fits so bad that Tom and I didn't know whether we should hold him or cling to each other. It took some time to find the right cocktail of neurological inhibitors and stimulators.

Throughout these difficulties, Tom and I took Uncle Wiggily to physiotherapy and obedience school. These weren't easy tasks. In order to transport Uncle Wiggily, we still had to use his shipment tank, equipped with an air filter. He hated it. Even with sedation, he would hurl himself at the sides of the tank, smashing it around the back of our Humbug Hover with such force that we had to use the autopilot to reconfigure our flight path so we wouldn't smash into vehicles or buildings.

Eventually the three of us reached a much-longed-for, boring, daily routine. Tom and I returned to our government lab work, grateful for having had the paid family leave. But every morning when we left, Uncle Wiggily would crawl in front of the door and block our exit. Abandonment. How many times had he experienced such terror in his life, I wondered. I would hold him just long enough for Tom to remind me that we were going to be late. I often cried the entire way to work.

The best part of the day was coming home. Uncle Wiggily started to greet us like the proverbial family dog. He would jump up and down, dancing to his own internal rhythm — a rather awkward feat given the tortured steps that usually characterized his walk. But his joy was contagious. Soon we were all dancing, even Tom, Mr. Ultra-Conservative.

Then, just after Uncle Wiggily's first birthday, while I was watching him play with his food, I noticed him do something different. His dish was on the floor because his twisted spine made it impossible for him to sit on a chair at the table. He would often take some kibble out of his dish and bat the pieces around. On this occasion, however, he had arranged the kibble in a neat row from larger to smaller.

I said, "What's up, Uncle Wiggily?"

Of course, Tom and I talked to him all the time, but up to this point he had never made any attempt to answer or acknowledge our babbling. Eye contact was something he normally avoided at all costs. There had been many times when I could feel his eyes follow me around the room, but, whenever I would turn around, I would find his eyes lowered. This time a chill ran through my body when he stared up at me with his soft, warm, brown eyes.

He was looking up at me from a crouched position, his hands gently resting on my knees. He held me fixed in his gaze. My skin tingled.

He grunted. True, he could whimper and cry when frightened, despite the damage to his vocal cords. But this grunt was unlike any sound he had ever made. It was thoughtful — a harrumph. It was intentional.

"What is it? What do you want to say?" I was whispering so as not to scare him — or myself, for that matter.

He grunted once more; then, after a short pause, he heaved an aching sigh that seemed to resonate throughout his bones. When I reached out to hold him, he drew away. I saw tears running down his face.

Both Tom and Dr. Bruce told me that I was reading too much into Uncle Wiggily's behaviour. Both of them refused to believe that Uncle Wiggily could be truly conscious of his state and be in agony because of it. As a matter of fact, Dr. Bruce reminded me that humans have a tendency towards anthropomorphism.

"But Uncle Wiggily is human," I said.

"Not anymore, he isn't." Dr. Bruce sounded very sure of himself. He was the type of doctor who came across as very casual. He'd often get on the floor with the cryos rather than having his assistant put them up on the examination table. "Kate, how long have I been working with cryos? Haven't I been right about his eventual adaptation to food? The systematic search for the right mixture for his meds? His potty training? Will you now believe me when I tell you that you're not the first person to adopt a cryo and come in here to tell me it's suffering? The tears may be caused by dust. Cryos are extremely sensitive. I warned you about all the potential problems when you and Tom came for psychological evaluations." This was his way of reminding me that I had a psychological history that had threatened our adoption of Uncle Wiggily.

"I told you that cryos are similar to albinos. The UV suit had to be constructed especially for him, as they are for all cryos. Your UVs are standardized for basic pigmentation. And if I remember correctly, I also told you that many cryos who survive the resurrection process have the mental capacity of a chimpanzee."

I stifled a sob. I couldn't tell if it was Uncle Wiggily or the extinct chimps that made me want to cry.

Dr. Bruce continued, unaware of my reaction. "He's capable of communication in keeping with his primitive emotional and physical needs. Living with Uncle Wiggily is very much like having one of our primate relatives as a permanent houseguest. He's playful, isn't he? Notice I used *he*. It's fine to have feelings for him. But we have to keep them in perspective."

Dr. Bruce was trying to sound sympathetic and cheerful. Nevertheless, his tone annoyed me. He was being condescending.

"We've done extensive work with cryos, including brain imaging and DNA workups. Uncle Wiggily has emotions. He's capable of attachment. He can communicate joy and hunger. But, more to the point, he doesn't remember ever being Henry Wigam. Mr. Wigam, as he once was, no longer exists. He's dead. What you have is a new creature born from Mr. Wigam's remains."

I think Dr. Bruce went on to talk about the similarities between apes and humans. He thought of cryos as a form of devolution that could give scientists some insights into the intellectual and emotional development of our early ancestors. Blah, blah, blah. I had already stopped listening.

On the way home, Tom filled the air with words, trying to draw me out of my silence.

"Bruce thinks the grunting's nothing more than Uncle Wiggily trying to clear his throat, which is probably inflamed from an allergic reaction to dust. He's arranging for us to get a bubble for Uncle Wiggily. The bubble's free. It's supplied by the Society for the Prevention of Cruelty to Cryos and another organization: Species Relief. I think they also deal with mutants. Species Relief, that is."

Tom was rarely chatty. I appreciated his effort even though I had already done my homework. I had studied the mission statements for the SPCC and SR, as well as all the permutations of the alphabet that dealt with cryos, mutants, and other lifeforms distinct from designated humans.

"Bruce says we're to use the bubble whenever Uncle Wiggily begins to grunt and cry," Tom said.

If we followed this advice, I thought, Uncle Wiggily would spend the rest of his life in the bubble.

Now, in retrospect, I realize this was when I began to regret calling him Uncle Wiggily. From the beginning, I had wanted to name him as one does a child or animal companion to bring him into the family. We had read on his official documents that Mr. Wigam's close friends had called him Wig. This nickname triggered an old childhood memory.

When I was eight, I had found a red hardcover book in the attic of my great grandmother's cottage. Uncle Wiggily had been the gentleman rabbit. And perhaps the name and image stayed with me because it was the only printed book I had ever read, as bound texts of that sort were rare and certainly not given to children. There were illustrations of a dapper Uncle Wiggily in a top hat and frock coat, leaning on a red, white, and blue crutch that he needed because of his rheumatism. What I remembered most about him was that he only spoke rabbit and couldn't communicate directly with the kids that he ended up helping on his many adventures.

And so Mr. Wigam was officially registered as Uncle Wiggily; his tattooed government barcodes would lead him straight back to us should he ever get lost.

But maybe, just maybe, Mr. Wigam wasn't on some adventure and didn't want to be the Uncle Wiggily of my childhood fantasies. So I guess this was when I started to call him Wig for short. Whenever I looked into Wig's eyes, I now saw the face of Mr. Henry Wigam, the man whose *Last Will and Testament* had won my heart over the other twenty-three cryonic possibilities at the adoption centre.

Mr. Wigam had had those warm, brown eyes I had come to identify with my Wig. He had been an attractive man, standing six feet tall with a thick mane of grey hair. Now, as Wig, he was barely five feet, completely hairless and bent over. He had shrunk because of the disintegration and collapse that shattered some of his spine, a crippling condition that could only be corrected by using laser surgery to fuse the remaining vertebrae. His chronic pain limited mobility. I've heard cryos described as hunchbacked gargoyles. And while I didn't see him this way, I kept him away from mirrors because I was afraid of what he would see.

Mr. Wigam's stasis had been voluntary, and his estate had been given over to the Cryonic Foundation of the Americas to invest and maintain his cryogenic immersion. The CFA was a privately run organization, which was recognized by the government agency that supposedly supervised the business practices of such nonpublic institutions as education and health. No-one had anticipated the financial crash of the CFA. Finally it became a necessity for the government to clean up the mess by reviving cryos. News leaked that CFA had never attempted the resurrection process because it would have lost control over the clients' funds. It was believed that most of the money had been funnelled towards maintaining the lavish lifestyles of the board members. So no-one really knew what caused the damage to the cryos. Was it because of a maintenance breakdown related to the loss of capital? Or had the metamorphoses taken place over a number of years? Did the Plague Wars have anything to with the mutations? When the government started the resurrection program, many cryos died. Others had become creatures like Uncle Wiggily.

Mr. Wigam had undergone cryonic treatment some seventy years ago at the age of sixty-five. He wanted to be revived when science had found a way to prolong life to a hundred and fifty years. He admitted that he didn't believe in the possibility of a fountain of youth or immortality. As far as he was concerned, his life was over. He made it clear that he had no reason to live. For him, cryonics was a substitute for suicide. "A coward's way out" were his exact words. He had lost everyone and everything that he had cherished.

During the *Last Will and Testament*, Mr. Wigam had talked about the automobile accident that took the lives of his wife, Emma, and their son, Nathan. He held a photo of them as he spoke. While he tried to appear controlled, he could not prevent tears from escaping.

So maybe I have been identifying with him. So what? Is empathy a crime, or a sin? It didn't matter to anyone whether he lived or died. He and his wife, like their parents before them, had had no brothers or sisters. Some historians trace the rampant infertility problems that have become commonplace during the last three generations to this earlier era. There were no nieces, nephews, uncles, aunts, or cousins. Mr. Wigam was alone in the world. His only regret had been in being unable to convince his wife to go into stasis so they could have been reborn together. He said they had often joked about cryonics.

"Emma always said that Nathan might have children one day and they might need us." He laughed when he said this. Shrugged. And wiped his eyes.

I kept replaying Mr. Wigam's *Last Will and Testament* in my head. I even tried to find family records that might contain photographs, but during the Plague Wars, Luddite fanatics who believed that pathogens were being transmitted by neural interface had destroyed a lot of information. Finally, I asked Dr. Bruce for a copy of Mr. Wigam's *Last Will and Testament*. He refused, saying that it would only feed my fantasies. He told me to accept Uncle Wiggily for what he was.

"He needs love and attention." Dr. Bruce's face looked tired and worn over the phone. I thought: don't we all?

This was when Dr. Bruce mentioned a support group for cryo owners, all of whom were childless couples. I wasn't surprised by his suggestion, given my psychiatric history. In fact, I had been waiting for it or something like it, especially after our last visit, when I attempted to convince him that Wig was trying to communicate. Despite my expectations, I found myself angry. I didn't want to talk to people who thought they could own other human beings. And as far as I was concerned, Wig was a human being. But I ended up agreeing to attend at least one session because I didn't want Dr. Bruce to report to the SPCC that I was uncooperative.

When I asked Tom if he wanted to come along, he shrugged. "I'm not the one who's having problems with Uncle Wiggily. I enjoy our relationship. We play. We go for walks. I don't need therapy to deal with my feelings." Tom wanted to be supportive, but he was also apprehensive of getting caught in a *folie à deux*, which, in his mind, had come to define our trips to the fertility clinic. "You don't need me there. This is your thing, and you'll have to do it on your own, just like the treatment you had after your breakdown."

So on the following Tuesday at 8:00 p.m., I went online. King Arthur, the support group host for the evening, had chosen a medieval castle that looked more like something from a *Dungeons and Dragons* scenario than an actual historical place. Each of us was supposed to choose a virtual construct to protect anonymity. The secrecy was meant to give us freedom to express our most horrid thoughts and actions. Cryo-abuse? Cryo-porn? Anything was possible.

Most of the group had chosen historical figures or fictional characters that looked rather bizarre in King Arthur's version of the Middle Ages. As for me, I thought I fit right in as Quasimodo, my tribute to kind-hearted monsters. But Quasimodo could easily be the poster boy for cryos, and some group members thought my disguise was hostile. Napoleon, for one, told me that I was obviously identifying with, as he put it, "the poor buggers." Although I had been made to feel like a pustule, this didn't prevent me from bringing up the issue of Wig's suffering. Zena, the Warrior Princess, explained, not even trying to hide the boredom in her voice, that every one of them had been through the same experience and had eventually gotten over it.

In the end, I was given a lot of advice about everything from buying Wig more toys to having him join cryo competitive sports, which were not anonymous activities. Apparently, with the right coaching and diet, cryos could rebuild their muscle and bone density to compete in track and field or even some light wrestling. Of course, they weren't expected to match human conditioning, especially our superstar cyborg-enhanced gladiators. I also found out there was an entire clothing and cosmetics industry that catered to the cryo population. Teddy Roosevelt told me the best places to buy cryo clothing at a discount, and when I mentioned Wig's body rashes, Simone de Beauvoir suggested a good cream made by CryoCosmetics. As far as I could tell these support groups were social clubs, which met once a week so members could exchange information on how to win the next sporting event or beauty contest. At worst, well, I didn't want to even contemplate the possibilities.

So several weeks later when I found that Wig had made a W with his kibble, I knew enough not to say anything to Tom or Dr. Bruce, both of whom would insist that I try out a few more support groups before passing judgment on the whole process. For the time being, Wig and I were on our own.

"Wig," I said as gently as possible, "Did you do this?"

There was no response. His white scrawny body was curled in his basket like a mummy exhumed from a clay pot. Since his facial expressions rarely changed, I looked for any variation that might tell me something. Anything.

Nothing.

I got my camera to document the event. I knew that I couldn't use the information as proof that Wig was trying to communicate. But I needed it for myself. To remind me of the truth.

"Wig," I said. "I'm going to help. I promise."

Everyone keeps saying that I felt guilty. Of course I did. And I'm tired of people using this as an excuse to ignore the facts. I'm responsible for having Wig neutered. Castrated, actually. Neutered and sterilized were the words for polite company. I hate the pretense. And I hate myself for having ever played into it. I had robbed Wig of his right to be a whole human being — to reproduce. And even though Dr. Bruce had given us no choice in the matter, I can't silence the inner voice that accuses me of giving up too easily.

"All mutants, human or animal, are sterilized at birth. It's the law," Dr. Bruce had said. "Cryos are designated as mutants. We must protect our already contaminated, diminishing gene pool."

He presented his arguments in a neutral way. It took me a long time to catch on that he always managed to make the grotesque seem ordinary.

He said, "Believe me, Uncle Wiggily is probably sterile. Most cryos are. However, even if he doesn't produce spermatozoa now, we don't know whether he will later on. We can't risk the possibility of reproduction. We don't know what would happen should he impregnate a woman."

I had been very naive. Stupid, actually. I had said, "If the risk is so minimal, why bother? There's always abortion. It's legal to stop the reproduction of mutants who escape sterilization. Why not cryos? Why not take the wait-and-see attitude. We'll keep him away from female cryos."

"He may still have biological urges. You don't want your Uncle Wiggily attacking you or perhaps someone else, particularly your female guests, do you?"

I'm ashamed to admit his scare tactic worked on me. I imagined Uncle Wiggily jerking off while looking at me. I had visions of him throwing my female friends on the floor and attempting rape before Tom or I could stop him. There was even a thought of Uncle Wiggily raping me, a picture so terrifying that my mind shut down immediately.

"Will he be violent? Will he bite?" I had asked like a child ready to renege on a promise.

"Cryos are known to show aggressive tendencies. The neutering will help. He'll also be given a cocktail of medications that should control his behaviour. Don't look so worried, Kate," Dr. Bruce had said. "When we're through with him, he'll be as docile as a puppy."

This conversation had taken place a long time ago, before Wig came to live with us. And I had followed Dr. Bruce's advice. And ever since I have regretted being so gullible. But my complacency ended after Wig formed the letter W. From that point on, I stopped giving him his meds. I may have been guilty and angry, but I also wanted to restore his natural state as much as possible.

The cryo support group had inadvertently given me an idea, which I'm sure would have appalled them. Most settings for VR are picked from banks of previously stored locations, such as the medieval castle where the support group met. This unimaginative setting reminded me of Nirvana, a little-known program that allowed people to create their own virtual spaces and images with their minds. It was a difficult program and, in fact, took extensive training in controlled visualization. Humans have erratic thought patterns and can only create their visions after having mastered meditation techniques that filter through the flashes of egocentric emotions that pass for thought. However, it was exactly this randomness of mind that I wanted to explore with Wig. A mindlink would certainly answer some of the questions that had been plaguing me. How does he see the world? What does he think about? From the corner of my eye, I had often caught him studying Tom intently. And I had watched him inspect flowers in the communal greenhouse of our living complex. The more I thought about Nirvana, the more excited I became.

There was one problem. I hadn't run the program since my breakdown. At one time, I had been quite skilled and had passed the first three levels of attainment. But I had never reached the fifth level, which was the highest. This limitation didn't stop me. I convinced myself that I was good enough to explore Wig's mind. I only had to wait for the opportunity. On days off, Tom often played tennis with neighbours. The big day for my experiment came within a week. Tom likes to keep fit.

I affixed the lightweight VR mask to Wig. I spoke to him in soothing tones while I slipped into mine and started Nirvana. For a few seconds nothing happened, as though Wig was truly the blank that Dr. Bruce claimed. Then I was hit — it felt like a smack across the face — by a screaming yellow wave that exploded into a kaleidoscope of colours. A face appeared in the mandala. It was long and deformed. It was my face. Then, I saw Tom laughing. He was rolling around on the grass. A hospital bed. A woman's face. A closed casket. My heart rate increased. The images and colours were coming much too fast. I was short of breath. I ripped off my mask. Punched the save sequence. And terminated the program. I did all this before I was able to attend to Wig.

It took me a few seconds to find him. He was in the kitchen, wildly banging his head and fists on the floor. All I could do was apologize and hold him. We both cried from shock and fear. We definitely had had a mindlink, but, as with all things in life, I could not have predicted the impact the experience would ultimately have on Wig or me.

The colours had surprised me. For some reason, I'd imagined his visual images to be monochrome. Perhaps I'd also anticipated seeing more of our domestic routines. Who was the woman? Was it Emma? I don't know what I had wanted to come out of this experiment, but I had to admit that I had pushed Wig too far.

Nevertheless, the colours had inspired another idea. I decided to encourage Wig's creativity by getting him colour paints and paper. Perhaps Wig would communicate his feelings at his own pace through art. Since most visual art is digital, it was difficult to find brushes and paints, particularly washable colours. In the end, I found an obscure little supply store that served the needs of this archaic art form. It was like walking into a speciality shop for alchemists or magicians.

At first Wig's paintings were magnificent. His early creations were bright yellows and reds. He would smear sky blue all over the sheet of paper, which was large enough for him to crawl around on. He needed a bath after each session, but I hated to wash him because he deliberately seemed to paint himself blue and white. At those moments, he looked like a worshipper from some ancient atavistic cult.

It was about this time that I started to keep a record of any changes in his facial expression or routine behaviour. Except for the mindlink and paintings, most of my observations were quite inconsequential. But I noted them anyway with the date and time. Perhaps I would only be able to convince Tom and Dr. Bruce once I had enough data. A complete picture of Wig's development could emerge after a lot of little details had been logged. For months my notes consisted of nothing more exciting than the following:

Monday, April 11 (8:30 a.m.) Wig blinked three times when I asked him how he was today. He didn't look away from me.

Tuesday, April 12 (5:16 p.m.) Wig gave me his drawing. He waved it at me. A first!

Tuesday, May 10 (10:30 p.m.) Wig licked my hand as I tucked him into bed. When I bent down to give him his goodnight kiss on the forehead, he put his white bony arms around my neck, placing his cheek next to mine. This is the first time he has initiated hugging. Note: Tom and I often hug Wig. I sometimes take his scrawny torso onto my lap while we sit on the living-room sofa listening to Bach or Mozart. At these times, I often give him little kisses as though he were a child. He makes appreciative noises that I imagine sound similar to how an old dog would have responded to having its ears scratched.

Thursday, June 6 (8:00 p.m.) For the past two or three days, I have been very self-conscious. I can feel Wig's eyes following me. His stare doesn't seem to be blank any longer.

My study of Wig began to consume my every waking moment. On a number of occasions I went back to the images he had generated in Nirvana. I ran my experiment in slow motion or freeze frame, so as not to be overwhelmed by the colours and pace. The woman's face had now become familiar to me. I had a copy printed. Although I longed to show Wig the picture or take him back to see his images, I was afraid of the consequences. We had come a long way together. I hoped that after I had enough to prove Wig's consciousness, I would be able to get a copy of Mr. Wigam's *Last Will and Testament* from Dr. Bruce to verify my suspicions that the woman's image was that of Wig's late wife, Emma.

I was so obsessed that Wig's presence dominated my dreams. And although I hid my notes from Tom, he knew something was going on. I had become withdrawn. Lost interest in sex and work. Everything seemed meaningless compared to reaching Wig. What was the point of sex? It only reminded me that I was barren. Work? My team was working on an antidote for KG-7000, a toxin lethal enough to wipe every living creature off the face of the Earth. And my team had created KG-7000 in the first place. Tom and I worked for the North American Alliance for Mutually Assured Destruction program, a new MAD scheme to prevent biochemical warfare. Those of us who survived the Second Plague War knew that we would still be able to smell death in the air if we were to remove our UV suits and air filters. The smoke from the burning pyres of corpses had never fully dissipated. And certainly nothing could protect me from remembering every day that we were killing ourselves. I began to think that it was only in discovering Wig's humanity that I could find meaning and purpose in my life.

Then, Wig and I had our first major breakthrough with the paintings. His creations began to get dark and gothic. He concentrated on one section at a time. He mostly chose black and browns. Red was only used in what seemed to be a contrast to the dark shadings. His painting then began to represent a series of ideas, individual panels very much like the pages of a comic book. But no matter how long I stared at his panels, I could not figure out his message.

I held my breath when I showed these particular paintings to Tom.

"If we didn't know better, it'd look like he's trying to tell a story," Tom said.

"Then, you think there's a possibility that something's going on." I had weighed every word carefully.

"No. Because I know better. Are you still going on about him possessing self-consciousness? Okay, I'll admit that his ability to communicate his need for food, whatever, has improved. He hasn't had an accident in his pants for months. But all of this is a far cry from human communication and consciousness. He's an animal. Let him be, Kate. You don't talk about anything else. You're starting to attract attention at work. Have you forgotten that you're a respected chemical engineer? There're rumours that some members of your team don't want to work on the molecular constructs with you. Do you know what this means? Do you want to end up back in the hospital? Uncle Wiggily's not our child."

I wanted to cry at Tom's outburst; instead I became as stone faced as Wig. I knew Wig wasn't our child. It had hurt that Tom could dismiss my feelings so easily. How could he? Sure I had wanted a baby. For over two years of treatments, I dreamed about our baby. I played with her and carried her in my heart every day. She was real. I named her Lizzie, my little Elizabeth. I could smell the baby scent of her new life. I admit I took the final medical reports rather hard. Who wouldn't? It doesn't matter if infertility is at epidemic proportions and you're just one of many. Lizzie was my baby. So when I got the *you're not alone* speech from the specialist, the same one she gives to every infertile woman, is it any wonder that I wept and sobbed as though my heart had been broken? Did the specialist even understand? I had seen the photo of her son on her desk. She had her baby.

The hospitalization period had been rather short, given the circumstances. I had been on medication for two years afterwards. All of this took place well before we had ever gotten Wig. If I had not been well, I would never have passed the psychological profile to obtain Wig. Hadn't I made every effort to adjust? Wig was part of my attempt to deal with the reality of the situation. I wanted to help the suffering of this world because I knew what it meant to mourn. Tom had confused the issues because he had blinded himself to the truth of real pain, a pain I knew Wig and I shared.

I chose to ignore Tom and continued to work with Wig. My patience paid off a few weeks later. He had created a series of five panels, the first four showing sharp crisscrossing lines in black, brown, yellow, and orange. The crisscrossing lines became more delicate with each panel until the fourth, in which I could detect the images of stick people piled one on top of the other. For a moment, I was stunned. He seemed to have painted the funeral pyres that were built during the Plague Wars. Dead bodies sandwiched between pressed firelogs and antique books. Anything that would burn. There is no way that Wig could have known about these events; he had been safely tucked away in his cryonic tank.

I looked at Wig, who had moved away to give me room. He had crawled, dragging his legs like useless appendages. He struggled to raise himself up on his arms — to meet me face to face from across the painting. He opened his mouth, exposing his teeth in a rather ghoulish manner. But I wasn't frightened. Was it a grimace or a smile? Perhaps it was both. Tears trickled from his eyes.

"Shh, Wig," I said. "It'll be all right. Shh, my sweet man. I'll try and understand." I extended my hand and wiped the tears from his cheek.

Then, it hit me. The panels could be depicting the cryonic storage vault that had bodies in cryonic tanks stacked in a crisscross design. Were the four panels a progression of his awakening consciousness? Had he become conscious at some point while he was in cryonic immersion? The fifth panel remained a mystery. It was a black, red, and orange swirling mandala with a white figure curled in the foetal position. Was the white figure waiting to be born or buried? I looked at the panels from every angle, crawling around it in a counterclockwise motion, in the same way that I had seen Wig inspect his work. I had almost made a complete revolution when I stopped dead. I saw it. A word embedded in the fourth panel, spelt out of the crisscrossing bodies: *Hell.*

This time I didn't bother to show Tom. I made an appointment with Dr. Bruce. I brought Wig's painting and my notes.

I showed Dr. Bruce the painting without any commentary.

"This is a very interesting picture," Dr. Bruce said.

"What do you make of the panels?"

"I think we may have to examine Uncle Wiggily's eyes. It seems that the scope of his vision may be deteriorating. He may have lost peripheral vision. It doesn't have to be serious, Kate. I wouldn't worry about it."

I could tell he was trying to comfort me. He knew I was upset, but, like Tom, he had totally missed the point.

"Do you see anything in the fourth panel?"

"What do you mean?"

"A word." I took the painting out of his hands and held it on its side.

"No." He raised his eyebrows. By now, I knew that look. "Do you see a word?"

"Yes."

"What word do you see?"

"'Hell.' Look. It's in the crisscrossed bodies."

"Have you ever heard of the Rorschach Test?"

"Yes," I said. I gathered my materials. "Thank you for your time."

I was heading for the door when Dr. Bruce said, "Wait, Kate. I didn't mean to insult your intelligence. I apologize. I was merely pointing out that you might be reading into Uncle Wiggily's paintings. It may be that you think his life is hell. Do you?"

"Well, I don't know. It could be. He's lost everything," I said.

I fought back my tears. Wig and I had a lot in common. We were both the ends of bloodlines — thrown into a world we had no control over. The system had been set in motion long before we were born. The next moment I was back sitting in the chair opposite Dr. Bruce. It was too late. The wound had opened, the wound left by the loss of my Lizzie, the throbbing ache that never heals, just bleeds and bleeds until I think I will drown in my own blood. My hands covered my face, such pain being too raw and naked to share. There was no escape from the tears I would cry forever and ever, without end.

When I came to, I was stretched out on the sofa in Dr. Bruce's office.

"How are you feeling? I had to give you a rather potent sedative," he said.

"I'm fine." I said, and pulled the derma-patch off. "How long was I out?" I wanted to leave.

"About an hour," he answered. "I called Tom. He's on his way to pick you up."

"Then you can call him right back and tell him I've left. The two of you seem to think you know what's best for me. What's best for Wig!

I've had enough. Just fuck off!"

"Listen, Kate. Listen. I'm sorry that's how you feel. As for Uncle Wiggily, there is some level of communication. Certainly there's a bonding. He trusts you. And probably even loves you in his own way. But he doesn't remember anything. He's not suffering in the sense that you think he is. There's a distinct possibility that Uncle Wiggily may be reacting to your intense observation. He could be picking up your anxiety about him. Give him room. Stop hovering over him for a while. Is he getting enough exercise? How are his bowel movements?"

Tom was waiting for me when I got home. I hadn't been to work in over a week. I hadn't been eating. And Tom was visibly shaken. He walked up and down, avoiding my eyes.

"I don't want to lose you," he said. "Please tell me what's going on. I know I haven't been supportive lately, but I kept hoping that if I ignored the situation you'd eventually snap out of this, whatever it is. If Uncle Wiggily's making you crazy, then maybe we should find another home for him. I love him, but I love you more."

I knew it was hard for Tom to express his feelings so openly. I also knew this meant that he was desperate. I decided to confide in Tom, to tell him everything, even about the Nirvana experiment. I hadn't mentioned Nirvana to Dr. Bruce because I was afraid that he would consider my actions to be cruel and selfish. Then, he might have had the SPCC remove Uncle Wiggily from our custody.

Tom, to his credit, listened thoughtfully to my explanation of the events that led me to believe that Wig was having flashes from his past life, and that he was as conscious as we were. Tom let me finish before he spoke.

"There's a good possibility that you created the images in the Nirvana state. No, listen to me, Kate. For just one moment. I know I don't know much about Nirvana, but I do know that you have never attempted a mindlink with anyone but your teacher. Most of the time you were left to practice on your own. It's been a long time since you passed the three levels of attainment. Isn't it possible that you distorted the images? It was hardly a scientific experiment if you were unable to control your end."

Tom had a point. And although I argued that I had never seen the woman in the photo taken from Nirvana, I began to have doubts. Tom looked at her and said, "She could be someone you met a long time ago and have forgotten. This whole experience could be wish fulfilment. Don't forget, you want Uncle Wiggily to remember his wife."

After this conversation with Tom, I decided to give Wig, no, Uncle Wiggily, some space. Dr. Bruce could have been right as well. I would no longer follow Uncle Wiggily around recording everything he did. I would give him his meds. I renewed my prescription as well.

Over the next few days, I spent time playing with him, running up and down in a bizarre form of tag that we had devised together. I bought Uncle Wiggily some body lotion from CryoCosmetics and a specially designed cryo outfit: T-shirt, jeans, and sneakers. At my suggestion, Tom took him for long walks around our living complex. Uncle Wiggily enjoyed the indoor parks. I put Uncle Wiggily's paints away. I decided that all of us, including Tom, needed a rest.

All went well for a while. Then, Uncle Wiggily began to crawl around on the kitchen floor in the exact location where I used to put his paper and paints. He would swing his right arm around, dipping his imaginary brush into imaginary paints. He would stop and look up at me as though waiting for a response. At first, he went through this routine for a few minutes at a time. Always stopping. Always looking up. Within a few days, he became obsessed, continuing the motions for an hour at a time. He ignored me when I asked him to stop. If I picked him up and carried him into another room, he would return to the kitchen and begin his ritual again. When I left the room, he would stop only to start upon my return. This went on for about a week. Eventually, I gave in. I returned his paints and paper.

He wasted no time going to work. He worked practicing strokes, reminding me of a Chinese calligrapher at one with the elements of brush, paint, and page. But when I tried to get his attention so I could bathe him and put him to bed, he pushed me away in anger. I was getting frightened. Tom had already fallen asleep, and I was reluctant to wake him. Reluctant to be accused of more nonsense. I sat up with Uncle Wiggily and watched his frenzied pace. At the end of a series of panels, he stopped. He sat on the floor and looked up at me. I bent down and looked at the sheet of paper. He had written: *Kill Wig.*

"Do you understand what this means? 'Kill Wig?'" I asked and pointed to the words.

Nothing.

"Write it again," I said.

Nothing.

Wig crawled into my arms.

I held him all through the night. When I heard Tom's alarm go off, I hid Wig's picture. I carried Wig to the bath and set the water and air pressure. I told Tom that I was sick and that I would log in absent at work. I promised to see a doctor and get a medical certificate for my team captain.

There was something final about that morning. Wig and I went for a walk that stretched into the noon hour. When we returned home, I took his painting out and placed it on the floor. I showed him the words again. This time he turned the paper over to the blank side. I was frozen. He began grunting and jumping like a chimpanzee about to perform a violent display.

For the first time, I was so frightened of him that I couldn't hide my fear.

"Stop Wig! Please. I can't take any more."

To my surprise, he did stop. He took my hand and kissed it. A real kiss. A human kiss. He had never done this before. Then, he went to the blank sheet of paper and wrote in his unsteady hand. There was nothing to distract or distort the words. None of the graffiti-like calligraphy that covered the other page. Again, he had clearly written: *Kill Wig*.

When Tom came home, he found me stretched out on the bed holding Wig in my arms. At first he thought we were asleep. But he couldn't wake us. A half-finished cocktail mix of our medications sat on the nightstand.

For the next week or so, no-one, not even Tom, would tell me how Wig was, except to say that he had been revived. Even in my dreams, I knew no matter how many psychiatric evaluations I could pass Wig would never come home. Finally, Dr. Bruce admitted that Uncle Wiggily had become extremely aggressive and violent. He had to be heavily sedated and restrained at all times, or he ripped chunks out of his own skin and banged his head on the bars of his cage. Dr. Bruce said that this sometimes happens to cryos.

LINDA DYDYK was born and raised in Montreal. In her youth, she was a rock singer and songwriter with a number of Montreal bands. She received her BA and MA from McGill University. She teaches English Literature at Dawson College in Montreal, including two classes she created, one on cyberpunk and the other on humour. Her poetry has been published in *The Journal of the Science Fiction Poetry Association* and in McGill University's *Scrivener Magazine: Journal of Creative Writing*. Her first short story, "Little Luella," appeared in *The Dinosaur Review* (Spring, 1988). Her story "Kaboom!" can be found in the archives of the online zine *The Journal of Apocalypse Fiction* (#7, October 2002).

Linda tells us: "My creative influences include Captain Beefheart, Patti Smith, Franz Kafka, Flannery O'Connor, Philip K. Dick, Kurt Vonnegut, William Gibson, Wu Tang, and Looney Tunes. I write about my observations concerning human behaviour and the Earth's survival. I'm a student of Zen Buddhism. Like the Dalai Lama (the Tibetan Spiritual Leader) and Kurt Vonnegut (the devout atheist), I believe that we need to 'Be kind.'"

Carrion Luggage

The ticket said he was on a connecting flight out of Haiti to New York. There was a lineup of passengers for flight 207 to LaGuardia, and they all needed to be on board in the next ten minutes. The security personnel had to keep the pace brisk if they were going to stay on schedule. Still, they had to stop and look. He only had one bag with him and that would be easy enough to pass. There was just enough time to spare him a good lingering stare.

Florida's Panhandle International saw more than its fair share of oddballs and weirdos. Half the time they were also boarding a flight for New York.

This one dressed like an undertaker, though not any undertaker of contemporary times. His clothes were black. Only the dress shirt under his vest and tie was a different colour: white. He had on an old top hat, dignified, but scuffed and worn by time.

His skin was almost as dark as his clothes, deeply coloured to the point where it nearly obscured the lines of his face in the poor lighting of the terminal. When his lips parted, the brilliance of his teeth drew the eye away from any less prominent feature. He smiled broadly. Too broadly. The smile didn't literally reach from ear to ear, but it came close, stretching right back to the hinge of his jaw as if his skin were too loose and his muscles too tight.

Margaret stood at her post next to the metal detector and waited for the man to approach. He looked down at her with yellow eyes magnified many times by the little circular glasses perched on the tip of his nose. The lenses were almost as thick as they were wide with dozens of tiny air bubbles trapped inside the glass.

"Just the one bag?" Margaret asked.

"Only the one. Yes," he said, barely moving his lips and never breaking his unsettling smile.

Margaret broke his gaze and placed the bag on the conveyor belt. She watched it disappear through the flaps of the X-ray machine and then pointed the man towards the metal detector.

"This way please," she said, gesturing at the open doorway when he failed to proceed. He was still carefully watching the machine his bag had just disappeared into.

Attracting his attention with a broad wave of her arm, Margaret ushered the man through the empty frame of the metal detector. He had to duck to clear the top bar. He repeated the motion after tripping the alarm with a plain steel cigarette case the first time. It was the only metal item on his person, and he was cleared on the second pass.

Sally, the youngest member of the security crew, watched the X-ray monitor. She gasped loudly as the man came through to her side. It wasn't a reaction to him, although he might well have elicited a similar response had she been looking his way. She was staring at the monochrome outline of the contents of his bag.

"What the heck are those things?" said Sally, although she'd already taken an accurate guess.

Rob, her supervisor, looked up from the handbag of toiletries he was picking through. He was as surprised as Sally, but didn't let on.

"Looks like bones," he said matter-of-factly.

Everyone at security exchanged glances. Sally was still staring blankly at the screen, which was now exposing the more conventional contents of someone else's luggage. Rob caught the tall man's bag as it came through the second set of flaps and dragged it onto the counter. Everyone did their best to look over his shoulder from where they were already standing as he pulled it open. No-one saw much, until Rob took out a darkened femur from the bowels of the bag for everyone to have a look at. The tall man watched the search carefully, but said nothing.

"That's a human bone, isn't it?" said Margaret.

"It can't be," Sally insisted.

Rob replaced it in the bag. When he withdrew his hand a second time, he had a human skull held carefully but firmly in his palm. Several gold fillings were clearly visible in the nearly complete row of teeth that hung down long and crooked. So was a wide fracture that spread across two of the skull plates in a jagged curve.

"My uncle," said the tall man in a tone that suggested he thought that would explain everything.

Everyone knew the flight was going to be delayed for sure now. The crew continued inspecting bags anyway as Rob telephoned the chief of security.

Eventually they had to let the flight go, forty-five minutes late, with one seat empty.

The tall man sat in the airport security offices. He'd calmed down only after he was assured he'd be put on another flight if everything was cleared in the next couple of hours. Since then, he'd been sitting perfectly still on a stiff wooden chair, with his hat in his lap. He'd offered no words or explanations since he'd handed over his passport. He just waited, politely.

Andrew Isaki returned to the desk where the tall man, identified as René Shanda on his passport, sat alone with only the video-surveyed door offering a way out. Andrew placed the passport on the desk and sat down on a couch across from Mr. Shanda. Shanda made no move to retrieve his documents. He sat expressionless, following Andrew with his eyes. There were answers to be had, and Andrew wasn't going to have an easy time of it.

It was Andrew's job to politely grill people detained from getting on a flight, usually until the appropriate officials arrived. He spent most of his time entertaining drug smugglers who were too stupid to know what kind of trouble they were in. Sometimes he was called on to testify in court, but not often enough to make the job interesting. Today's guest was an uncommon one. The police weren't on the way to take him off his hands. Not yet at least. Calls were still being made looking into the origin of what had turned out to be a complete adult male skeleton, cleaned of flesh, stuffed into one medium-sized travel bag.

"Mr. Shanda," Andrew smiled. Shanda didn't return his smile or greeting. Andrew tried again.

"I'm Andrew Isaki from airport security. I'd like to ask you a few questions about the contents of your bag."

Nothing.

"You said the bones in your bag were your uncle's."

"My uncle," confirmed Shanda.

"And what was his name?"

"Auguste Shanda."

"So," said Andrew, briefly considering how he could ask the next question casually. "What were you doing with his bones in your bag?"

"I was to take them to New York with me."

"Why's that?"

"Because that is where I am going."

"I see. Do you have any family there?"

Shanda hesitated a moment. "None living."

"You realize that it's generally considered ... inappropriate for passengers to be carrying somebody's mortal remains on a flight, don't you? Airlines are happy to transport a body provided it's in a proper coffin in the baggage compartment. They do that all the time."

Shanda tipped his head slightly forward and looked at Andrew over his glasses like he was a fool.

"The bones are to stay with me always."

"I can understand your reluctance to entrust them to baggage handlers, but still..."

Andrew trailed off. He could see Shanda's point. A body touching down in Hawaii on the same day it's to be put to rest in Iowa is an embarrassment to all involved and just adds to a family's grief. Extra care is usually taken to make sure coffins go where they're meant to, but mistakes still happen. The Hawaii/Iowa rerouting had stirred up a fuss only three weeks earlier.

Andrew switched tracks. "Were you very close to your uncle?"

"Where are the bones now?"

"We have them securely stored. Don't worry."

"Securely stored" meant "sitting under the desk of a secretary who was off sick." The airport staff lockers were big enough for most personal valuables, but couldn't quite fit Shanda's bag. Andrew didn't want to try to stuff it in. He didn't know how brittle the bones were.

"Are you planning to bury your uncle's remains in the United States?"

Shanda said nothing.

"Are you relocating his body? How long has he been deceased, if you don't mind me asking?"

"He has been dead these past eleven days."

"Eleven days?"

Shanda fell silent again.

"That's a pretty advanced stage of decomposition for eleven days."

Shanda furrowed his brow, questioningly.

Andrew explained, "Why is he ... why has he been reduced to bones already?"

"I boiled the flesh from them only yesterday."

He'd said it much as he might have explained that pants are put on one leg at a time.

"Why would you do that?"

"Easier to carry."

"Excuse me a moment, would you?" said Andrew as he got up. "Sure I can't get you anything?"

Shanda offered no suggestions, so Andrew left without another word.

"I don't know, Bill," Andrew was saying five minutes later, when he'd found Bill Mayer, his boss. "I don't know what local customs we could be dealing with here, but this sounds like some sort of weird serial killer racking up frequent flier miles."

"Just give me the name, Andrew."

"He said it was Auguste. Auguste Shanda. Same last name."

"All right. I'll check with the Haitian authorities. See what they say. You just watch him."

"Come on Bill, do I have to? He'd not exactly a sparkling conversationalist."

"Think of it as a cultural gap. Bridge it."

"I prefer the Haitian weed smugglers. They're chatty."

"Bring him a soda and give him a sugar rush. That might do the trick."

"It's creepy, Bill."

"It's probably nothing. Don't worry about it. Remember last time this sort of thing happened and freaked out everybody?"

"Yeah, but that was an anthropologist sneaking out of Argentina with twenty-thousand-year-old fossils. It's not the same. At least we were pretty sure he didn't axe murder his cargo in the dead of night."

"This one's probably not a murderer either."

"Tell that to the guy with the cleaved skull."

Andrew returned to his office to keep Shanda company until more calls could be made. He brought a diet soda for his guest and placed it on the desk, next to where Shanda was sitting. Shanda neither looked at the can nor acknowledged it being offered. Andrew took it in stride and sipped the foam off the top of his own opened can. He was getting used to the uncommunicative atmosphere in the room that day. When he sat down on the couch again, he drank quietly, neither looking at Shanda nor saying a word to him. When he finished his own drink, Andrew crumpled the can and accurately threw it across the room into the tin garbage can, where it clattered noisily. Only then did he look at Shanda once more. Shanda was staring back at him again, his attention drawn.

"How did your uncle die?" said Andrew casually once he'd regained eye contact.

Auguste Shanda had been the most feared houngan in all the villages that lined the shores of the Artibonite river in central Haiti. A high priest of a houmfor temple buried in the woods a mile back from the nearest road, he had been associated through rumour and hearsay with all the darkest dealings of voodoo lore. Presiding over traditional Saturday night ceremonies presented a legitimate front, but word spread through the towns and villages that on every other day of the week he was a boko, a sorcerer for hire, with no qualms about placing curses on friend or family for the right price.

The effectiveness of his doll curses was legendary, and it was well known he could cause anyone no end of misery with a wax and feather sculpture and as few as three of the intended victim's hairs — or a single toenail clipping. Folklore told of one occasion in Auguste's youth when he crossed paths with one of Duvalier's Tontons Macoutes, a policeman and thug who dared challenge the Shanda family's authority in their own village. The number of physical ailments the officer endured thereafter was limited only to the number of needles in Auguste's mother's sewing kit. Within a month, the policeman ended his own suffering with a spectacular self-immolation by gasoline and Zippo in the middle of the town square. The method of suicide, few denied, may well have been connected to the fact that Auguste chose to dispose of the man's figurine likeness in a smouldering barbecue pit.

Auguste was also implicated in several high- and low-profile disappearances. His penchant for poisons was apparent, considering the number of his enemies who died in their sleep for no good reason. But the missing persons, insisted the townspeople in whispered tones, had likely been recruited as zombies. Auguste was an obvious suspect, considering the formula for the fabled zombie drug relied almost entirely

on a poison thought to be understood by only a handful of boko —
most of them now deceased, most of them by Auguste's hand.

The recipe for the poison included an elaborate mix of natural toxins
and irritants that promoted swelling and severe itching. Intended victims
would speed their own demise by scratching madly at an infected area
until the skin broke. The poison, initially applied by sprinkling it on an
arm or a leg while the targets slept, would then infiltrate the bloodstream.
A catatonic and highly suggestible state of mind would result within a
few days, and the victims would become zombies ripe for the picking,
submitting themselves to slavery at the hands of the first person who
tried to command them.

Regular doses of the poison, administered by cut or pinprick, could
keep a healthy adult in such a state for years. A boko of Auguste Shanda's
skill was said to be able to extend a zombie slave's existence past any
form of natural life, creating a living death of tireless, endless manual
labour. The extra precaution of a doll curse might ensure the additional
fear and loyalty needed to maintain control over a slave forever.

Such cruelty was not thought to be beyond Auguste Shanda. Put
quite simply, nothing was considered beyond him. This belief in the
scope and malice of his reach kept a dozen villages in a grip of fear so
intense, it started to work against him. After so many miserable years
under his thumb, people began to believe Auguste's reign of terror had
to end some way. Any way.

René Shanda told Andrew none of this.

"Andrew."

The call came from the door. Bill was looking in, waving him over.
Andrew got up from his seat and walked over to Bill, who leaned in to
whisper.

"Is he giving you any trouble?"

"He's not too cooperative," said Andrew, "but he's behaving himself."

"Think you can handle him on your own?"

"Sure, why?"

"I just got off the horn with Port-au-Prince police. Your friend Shanda there is wanted for murder. Guess who he killed."

"Oh boy."

"Yeah. A car's on the way from downtown, but the highway's packed with rush-hour traffic. We've got him for another good half-hour."

"Okay."

"Packing?"

"Always."

"Good. I'll check in when the blue boys show up."

Bill dipped back out of the office, closing the door behind him. Andrew turned and saw Shanda staring intently. Andrew gave him a few moments of silence after he sat down again, then he spoke bluntly.

"Tell me why you killed your uncle."

Shanda answered immediately, calmly, like the question wasn't unexpected.

"You would not understand."

Andrew had convinced past guests to explain to him why they had tried to carry a gym bag full of hashish onto an international flight. Some had confided their reasoning for pulling a gun and shooting at state police who had them surrounded. He once even had a nineteen-year-old woman describe how she was coerced into carrying six latex condoms full of heroin in her stomach shortly before she died of an overdose when one of the condoms ruptured. The smuggling stories wore thin after awhile. He never had anyone explain why they'd caved somebody's head in with a bladed weapon, though. He was hoping Shanda would level with him. Shanda didn't say much, but what he had said so far sounded true. If the tall man indulged him, Andrew was sure he would have a good story to repeat at this year's office party.

"Try me," said Andrew.

Auguste Shanda's time on this Earth ended when he was quite old, but still strong of body and spirit. Despite the threat of an uprising from his fearful and superstitious flock, his end came suddenly and unexpectedly when an anonymous road worker took a break from laying fresh gravel long enough to march into the foliage and cleave Auguste's skull wide open with his shovel. The worker thought he'd seen the high priest giving him the evil eye from the path that led down to his secluded temple; he had panicked, daring a direct assault upon the voodoo sorcerer rather than risk the suffering of a prolonged curse. The irony was that Auguste had only come out of the woods to investigate the source of the noise caused by the idling city works truck parked next to the series of potholes that needed filling. He hadn't given the worker any sort of eye, for good or ill — had never even seen him, in fact, right up to the moment of his murder.

The worker had returned to his home without saying a word to anyone. He didn't dare tempt fate by talking about his crime, even though he would have been hailed as a hero for it. It was up to René Shanda to discover the body of his uncle days later, when he first started to emerge from his poison-induced haze.

René, like so many members of the Shanda family, had served as a guinea pig for Auguste's potions as he evaluated dosages and adjusted his ingredients accordingly. They were considered expendable. Whether they died outright or became mindless zombie minions didn't really matter to Auguste as long as they helped him find the correct dose for paying clients.

René had proven to be a particularly successful zombie. Strong and agile, he'd been a real workhorse for the temple, clearing the jungle undergrowth as it encroached on the compound with each new rainfall. But he had also been an unusually willful zombie. A wax figurine of him had to be pricked and tortured routinely to keep him from wandering off or disobeying. Combined with the poison, it had kept René in check for years.

However, once there was no-one to manipulate the doll or replenish the poison in his system, René began to wake up. He literally stumbled over Auguste's body as he walked through the woods, shaking off the last of his stupor. Another day went by before his head cleared enough for him to know what needed to be done.

René had been the only member of his family Auguste had bothered to keep at home. The rest — the ones who hadn't died outright from the poison — had been sold into bondage. There was a profitable demand for zombie labour among the Haitian red sects of Harlem. There were at least three restaurants operating in the north end of Manhattan that didn't need to pay their kitchen staff any wages. René had found out that a few of his closest relations numbered among the zombie dishwashers and floor-moppers. But before he could do anything about it, Auguste had made him his next victim.

Not that René had a plan back then.

He didn't know how the solution came to him. Perhaps in the years his conscious mind had been hidden away deep down inside, it still held enough of a spark to work on the puzzle. Ultimately, the answer was simple. René would make an antidote to bring to his enslaved family.

René knew just enough about Auguste and his perversion of voodoo rites to understand some of the principles behind his alchemy. He was sure, after dealing with poisons for so many years, Auguste must have built up a high tolerance to his own toxins. This immunity was in his blood, in his body, in his bones. The flesh was useless now — dead and rotting. But the bones could be recovered, the marrow dried and ground into a powder.

And the powder could be fed to his family.

That was the reasoning behind René's rapid departure from Haiti. He still had a passport, old and expired, but it could get him into America with enough tampering. A plane ticket was hastily purchased by selling off all of Auguste's possessions. By the time René was done pillaging his uncle's home, the only thing left of any value was an old cigarette case. René brought that along as his only personal luggage, ready to pawn it for cab fare once he arrived in New York.

The only thing left to pack was Auguste's boiled bones. Only now did René realize he should have waited until they were dried and ground to dust before trying to transport them abroad. It was the one miscalculation he had made in his haste — that, and leaving the rubbery stripped flesh of his uncle behind where police might find and identify it.

"No," replied Shanda to Andrew's simple request.

"Why not?"

"I have said. You would not understand. You are not from the islands."

And that was the last thing Shanda had to say. Andrew tried to get something, anything, out of him for a few more minutes, but his guest had fallen into a meditative silence he couldn't cut through. He eventually gave up and resigned himself to the silent watch until the police came. He passed the time reading an airline magazine that was seven months out of date.

It only took twenty minutes for the police to arrive in the end. When they came, there were just two of them, neither detectives. They were there to transport Shanda to the feds in the city — glorified couriers, nothing more. Bill showed them in and the two uniformed cops cautiously set themselves at either side of Shanda. One of them had cuffs at the ready. The other had his hand on his holstered gun.

"Mr. René Shanda?"

Shanda didn't so much as look up.

"We're here to escort you downtown. We're placing you under arrest for the murder of Auguste Shanda, pending extradition to Haitian authorities."

Shanda didn't break the vacant stare he'd held since long before the police arrived. The only indication that he'd heard the officers at all was his holding his arms out in front of him, wrists together. The first officer snapped the handcuffs in place as the second recited Shanda's rights under American law. When the legal speech was done, Shanda stood, holding his hat in his cuffed hands, and let the officers lead him out, one on each arm.

No-one could say how he spotted the bag on the floor when he was staring straight ahead the whole time. But suddenly, as they passed between the rows of office desks, heading for the exit to the terminal, Shanda pulled back sharply and broke the loose grip the cops had on his arms. The officers were slow to react, surprised by the sudden bolting of their formerly complacent suspect. Before they could turn, Shanda leapfrogged over the desk and landed on all fours next to his flight bag, which stuck out slightly from under the desk. The police had their guns drawn by the time he popped up from behind the desk again, his luggage in hand. They wasted a moment trying to tell him to freeze, but they probably wouldn't have been able to keep Shanda in place even if they'd fired at that moment or tried to jump him. He was moving fast, almost inhumanly so. He swung the bag wide, slapping both aimed guns out of his way with a sharp rattling of bones. In the same move, he stepped up on the table in front of him and was off, hopping from desk to desk as fast as a normal man might run across open land.

Shanda was out the door by the time the cops could get their guns pointed in his general direction. Neither of them fired. He was gone already, but they made chase.

Andrew and Bill followed the cops out. The police officers were waving people out of the way with their guns as they ran through the crowded terminal, leaving a clear path in their wake for the two airport security men. They knew there was no real danger, openly brandished guns or not. Shanda was unarmed, so there was no chance of a full scale shootout. But he was giving them the best chase the airport had seen since three teenaged smugglers bolted from officers in three different directions a decade earlier. None of them had gotten as far as Shanda already had, dexterously bounding through business travellers, baggage carts, and sluggish tourists. The number of obstacles he had to detour around slowed him enough for the police, parting the crowd more easily with the sight of their guns and uniforms, to make up the distance.

Shanda might still have evaded his pursuers long enough to get outside and lose himself in the parking lot, if only he hadn't glanced back to check how much of a lead he had. In the second it took him to look over his shoulder, a baggage trolley stacked high with luggage headed home after a two-week Florida vacation appeared in front of him. He ran right into it and pulled the whole works down as he stumbled over the top. Suitcases popped open, sending cheap souvenirs and sandy bathing suits flying. Shanda's bag opened up and spilled its contents, too. No-one had zipped it up since the search.

Half a dozen people were tripped up by the bones as they slid across the finely polished terminal floor. The skull landed right at the feet of a middle-aged woman fresh off the beach with a peeling sunburn and a Mickey Mouse hat to show for her travels. It took her a full second to realize what she was standing over, and another one to start screaming.

Screaming can disconcert a cop as easily as the next person, and, after hearing the shrill panicked cries of the woman, one of them fired before thinking. As Shanda sat up suddenly, appearing behind the scattered pile of checked luggage, the lone bullet hit him mid-chest, slightly off-centre, and sent him lying back down again just as sharply. Both cops were still covering him from a distance when Andrew and Bill boldly stepped over the refuse.

Shanda was sprawled out, looking quite relaxed. His eyes were shut, and his glasses were tipped up across his hairline. He looked like someone's grandfather who had fallen into a light sleep on the couch between sorting through the sports page and the world news.

Bill opened his vest, looking for a the gunshot wound. Not finding one, he immediately checked the inside breast pocket and pulled out what he suspected was there. The bullet had pushed through the first half of Shanda's sturdy cigarette case, but had flattened out on the second layer of steel. Loose tobacco from the destroyed stale cigarettes trickled out as Bill opened it to see the slug embedded inside.

"Lucky bastard. He'd be dead if—"

"He is dead," corrected Andrew who'd already taken Shanda's pulse twice, once at the wrist and once at the neck, and had come up with nothing both times.

"Can't be," said Bill.

"His heart's stopped."

"Call an ambulance!" ordered Bill. For the first time ever, he started using the CPR training he'd learned ten years earlier

He'd only pumped at Shanda's chest a few times before he stopped abruptly and felt the dead man's cheek.

"He's awfully cold for a guy who just sprinted halfway across the airport," said Bill.

"I know," agreed Andrew. "He feels like he's been dead an hour or so already. His fingers are already getting stiff."

The crowd who'd disappeared into the woodwork at the first suggestion of a shooting were gathering around again to see what sort of grisly results the gunplay had delivered. The ones who weren't busy discussing whether the bones were real people bones or not saw the next thing that was pulled out of Shanda's inside breast pocket. It was a doll, like a plaything, but uglier than anything anyone would ever give to a child. It was crude and barely recognizable as a human icon, made more grotesque by the ragged hole in its torso where the policeman's bullet had torn through on its way to striking the cigarette case.

"I don't think he bought that at the souvenir shop," said Bill.

Andrew wasn't listening. He studied the face of René Shanda, who had died only moments ago and now looked like a corpse exhumed after a month in the ground. He was wondering how best to word a report to the FAA that wouldn't get him fired.

Born and raised in a West Island suburb that has since been swallowed by the city megamerger, SHANE SIMMONS figures that makes him a native Montrealer. He has since moved closer to the centre of town to more closely fit the profile. Shane is best known for *The Long and Unlearned Life of Roland Gethers* and *The Failed Promise of Bradley Gethers*, a pair of epic comedies about the waning days of the British Empire originally published under the banner *Longshot Comics*. He tells us that "the first volume of the Gethers saga was recently translated and published as an award-winning book in Germany because Germans love to laugh."

Over the years, Shane has written for film, television, books, magazines, and comics, "but I won't be happy until I've also written for instruction manuals, road signs, and fortune cookies. I'm currently working on a number of projects I refuse to discuss for purely superstitious reasons, but I am at liberty to say that I've recently completed a vaguely facetious bio for an anthology called *Island Dreams*."

This past winter — 2002-03 — was a particularly cold one in Montreal. Shane has this to say on that subject: "I enjoy wind, cold, and snow; and I think Canadians who complain about the weather should have their citizenship revoked."

Mark Paterson

The Ketchup We Were Born With

Parker was born eleven years after the fourth epidemic of Mad Cow Disease, so he wasn't subject to the decade-long interim of confusion and recovery. He didn't take part in the endless Land and Casualty Surveys, argue in any Estates-General debates, nor was he a signatory to The Charter of Rations. Everything was already set up by the time Parker was born. He didn't have to worry. Stored in a warehouse near his home were his one hundred litres of ketchup; his allocation for life.

Two weeks before his eighth birthday, Parker was up in a tree playing Robins and Orioles with friends. Just when it became his turn to be the momma bird, Parker fell out of the tree and died. He hadn't even touched his ketchup.

Forty-seven people perished in the ensuing mini-war of succession. Parker's family and their allies claimed the ketchup for themselves, while the rest of the community said it rightfully belonged to society in general and, especially, to the unborn.

It was after Parker's family and their allies were defeated in war that Buddhism became the official religion of the post-Plague world. Supporters of ancestral ketchup inheritance were shown the error of their opinion when it was pointed out that Parker's reincarnated soul as a new baby would benefit from his ketchup being put back into the communal pot. The people were joyous, but not everybody was willing to chant and meditate. The leaders went easy on them.

The ketchup we were born with is the only certainty in this world. It's what we fall back upon in times of uncertainty or scarcity. It's what we use to trade for other goods that we've run out of like wooden boards or calendars or red pencils or cigarettes. Now, in a way, we are all born with Parker's ketchup and our world is wonderful.

MARK PATERSON was born in San Francisco and grew up in Montreal, where he lives, writes, and basks in the city's unique blend of pleasure, indulgence, and proper bagels. Mark's work has been published in various literary journals and anthologies. He also produces and co-hosts the Grimy Windows Variety Showcase, a monthly performance series featuring writers, poets, musicians, comedians, filmmakers, and wrestlers.

About "The Ketchup We Were Born With" he tells us: "I was having lunch at my parents' house when I got the initial idea for this short-short. I had just taken the ketchup out of the refrigerator when I noticed a *Peanuts* cartoon strip posted on the door. In one panel, Linus says to Charlie Brown, 'Ask your dog if he wants to come out and romp in the snow, and laugh, and act like we don't have the sense we were born with.'"

Brikolakas

The whole village had known. They'd called him a cuckold — keratomenos — behind his back, and they'd make the sign of the horn after he passed. Katina had been fucking a brute of a man — and that's what it was, fucking, because it wasn't sanctioned by the Church and went against the rules of God. Her lover was a beast and a brawler, a labourer who went from door to door begging for jobs that his betters refused. He was illiterate, a peasant with big meaty hands that hung like claws at his sides and leathery bronze skin from too many years toiling under the Mediterranean sun. He was an animal, and Constantine had dreamed of killing him. But he'd done just the opposite.

He'd never suspected his wife of having an affair. Katina was a good woman, a pious woman from a good family, and a churchgoer from childhood. At nineteen, she'd married Constantine — before he became a priest — and they'd been happy for thirty years. She had the perfect demeanour for a cleric's wife: pretty but demure, smart but soft-spoken, graceful and mannered. She was a perfect hostess, a delightful dinner companion, and an excellent dancer, able to go from a waltz to a tsamiko. But she was barren, at least in Constantine's mind, as they'd had no children and that couldn't have been *his fault*.

He sat in the parlour of his house; it was an austere room with an old chesterfield and carved wooden armchairs he'd inherited from an aunt. Black-and-white photographs lined the walls. Pictures of his family and of hers. The coffee tables were covered with doilies and knick-knacks, bibelots from weddings, ribbons from christenings, souvenirs from trips to Athens and Mykonos and Santorini. In the corner was an altar of sorts:

icons of Christ and the Virgin Mary drawn in Byzantine tones of bronze and brown and framed with cherrywood faced each other above a triangular shelf that straddled the corner and held a kantili and a censer. The kantili was a short red glass filled with olive oil and a burning wick that floated on cork. The censer was a tiny brass cup with a hinged-dome lid and cross-shaped vents that held incense and burning charcoal. The scent of incense and olive oil filled the room with a stifling ecclesiastic odour.

Constantine was dressed in his vestments. He was sitting uncomfortably on an armchair and sweating under the black robe. His beard was damp and beads of perspiration trickled down his forehead, stinging his eyes.

Bishop Sophos sat on the chesterfield. He was a tall thin man in his late sixties, with long white hair that was neatly slicked back and a beard that completely covered his neck. He was dressed Western style, in a grey woolen suit and a black shirt with a Roman collar. His chauffeur-driven Mercedes was parked in front of the house. He'd driven in from Athens and had worn the suit, rather than his robes, to show he was here on business. Children had run after the car and trailed it on their bicycles as it had wound its way up the mountain road to the village. Their parents had stopped too and had stood in the doorways of homes and shops to witness the vehicle's passage. It wasn't every day that a German limousine traversed the village, and soon a crowd had formed and followed it to the house.

Some of those who saw the bishop emerge from the car had run off to spread the news. The whispers were true, they'd said. Why else would the Bishop be here? There was no feast day to commemorate, and the tiny stone church of Hagios Nikolaos was in fine shape. And Father Constantine was a married priest, not a celibate archymandrite who was eligible for a higher office.

It must have been for *that* reason.

And in case there were some who were lackadaisical, Bishop Sophos had given his driver the morning off to spend at the local kafeneio, where he'd surely slip the tale to those villagers who were too lazy, too busy, or overcome by the summer heat.

Few had noticed the other passenger in the vehicle, an elderly monk dressed in a long black frock and wearing a tall black cap. The crone of a man was short and hunchbacked, with a pointy nose, large black eyes, and a shrivelled sunburnt oval face. He'd followed quietly behind the Bishop and now sat next to him on the chesterfield.

Katina came into the parlour carrying a tray that was laden with cups of thick sweet coffee and glasses of ice-cold water. Her long black hair was tied in a bun, and she wore a sober navy blue dress with a high neck and an ample cut that masked her feminine curves. She served the men one by one. She didn't look them in the eye. She didn't acknowledge the Bishop's thanks or her husband's weak smile. And she didn't take anything for herself; she simply served the others then sat in the armchair opposite her husband, demurely folded her hands on her lap, and stared blankly and intensely at a spot on the wall.

The Bishop took a sip and then wiped his mouth. He turned and looked at Constantine.

"By all rights, I can have you excommunicated," he said.

Father Constantine nodded.

"What you did to Mihali Tsatas was a crime of the highest order. You stripped him of his soul and of his eternal reward."

"I saved him from hell," said Constantine. "It was a charitable act to spare one so despicable."

"And you," the Bishop turned to Katina, "You should have known better. You're the wife of a priest."

Katina pursed her lips and spit on the floor. "That's what I think of your church," she said, "and of that impotent wraith of a husband."

"Do you know what you two have created?" the Bishop growled. "A brikolaka!"

"I don't believe in brikolakes," said Constantine, "They don't exist.

It's all superstitious nonsense and old wives' tales."

"People have been talking," said Bishop Sophos. "They've seen things. I've gotten a dozen phone calls in the last three days."

"Stupid old hags with nothing better to do than spread vicious rumours," said Katina.

"They were smart enough to catch you fucking that goat herder," said Constantine to his wife.

"You were too stupid to figure it out for yourself."

"I'm not here to play marriage counsellor," said the Bishop.

"So why are you here?" asked Father Constantine.

"I've brought Brother Theodore to undo the damage you did," said the Bishop. He turned to the wrinkled old monk.

"The brikolaka has been in this house." The elderly cleric's eyes widened. "I can sense it."

"This is the home of a man of God," said Constantine.

"A brikolaka can enter a church or the house of a man of the cloth," said the old monk, "If someone allows it to enter." He smiled and fixed his gaze on Katina, "Isn't that right, my young beauty?"

"I don't know what you're talking about."

"Yes, you do," said Brother Theodore. His voice was raspy and distant, dusty, like it came from a thousand years ago. "You knew that your lover was dying, but you weren't willing to let him go. So you let yourself become careless. You let your dalliance be revealed because you knew what your husband would do. You knew he'd deny Mihali the last rites. You know he would curse him and thus create a revenant, and, as a brikolaka, your lover would live on."

"You're as crazy as the gossipy old hags that stick their noses where they don't belong," said Katina. "You're a sexless old fool with an empty head."

"Am I?" grinned the monk. He turned to the bishop, "With your permission?" he said as he rose.

"By all means."

Brother Theodore dug into his pockets and pulled out a ruby-studded cross on a chain, which he slung around his neck. He kissed the cross then reached into his pocket and produced a pocket-sized folio bound in engraved gold leaf. He kissed it too and opened it to the first page. He began to read aloud, "Hagios o Theos..."

"What is he doing?" asked Katina. There was fear in her voice.

"I don't know," replied Constantine as he listened to the monk. "It's a liturgy that I don't know.

"Of course, you don't know it," said the Bishop. "The Church doesn't reveal *all* of its secrets to lowly parish priests like you."

The monk walked out of the parlour and into the bedroom; the others followed. He continued to chant, a long steady stream in the Koine Greek of the New Testament. He stood at the foot of the bed and drew a cross in the air as he read. "This is where the creature has last been," he said, interrupting his chant for a second and then resuming. He turned and walked through the kitchen and out the back door to the stone wall that separated the house from the neighbouring olive grove. "It came over this wall," he said to the others.

They walked around the yard to the front of the house. A mass of villagers was still huddled around the Bishop's Mercedes. They all turned to watch the procession of the monk, the bishop, the priest, and his wife. Teenage boys poked each other and whispered. The very young and the very old crossed themselves. A few came forward and bowed before the bishop, taking his hand in theirs and kissing it as he walked.

As Brother Theodore led the procession into the street, the crowd followed. He walked forward a few hundred feet and downhill to the crossroad. He finished chanting, put the golden folio back into his pocket, and turned to lead the crowd in the *Pater Imon*.

"What happens next?" asked Katina.

"We wait," the monk smiled crookedly.

"What is this?" asked Constantine.

"I've summoned the creature," said Brother Theodore.

"This is all a big theatrical production to you," said the Bishop to Constantine. "Isn't it?"

"I don't believe in this kind of thing."

"Of course you don't. You only believe in what is convenient and discard the rest. And you have lost your moral authority," said the Bishop. "I'm here to reclaim it for the sake of the Church."

As they stood, a figure emerged from the olive grove. It was a man in a suit, but his skin was a dull grey, so colourless as to seem almost invisible in the hot sun. The man walked forward and stopped before the monk. The gathered visitors watched. They gasped and whispered among themselves. A little boy remarked to his grandmother that a rotting corpse should stink. She immediately cuffed his ear.

Constantine stared at the creature before him. It had the face and the shape of Mihali Tsatas. It had the eyes and the nose and the ears and the hands, but its ashen complexion was not human. It was other. But it did not frighten him. It simply froze him, emptied him of anything that was feeling or thinking. He smelled it, and its smell was dust; dry nothingness and the residue of a thousand lifetimes. He felt it against his skin: a fine substance, a powder that slipped through his fingers. He tasted the dust. And it tasted of the desert, and of the sands that were washed away by the ebb and flow of the tide.

Katina let out a sob. "My love!" she yelled.

"He is not your love," said the monk. "He is a husk. Powdered bone sucked dry of marrow."

"No!" said Katina. She stepped to the side of the revenant. She stroked the brikolaka's arm. "Lover," she whispered, "keeper of my heart," but the creature stood silent, ignoring her. Its eyes were trained upon Constantine.

"What have you done to him?" she screamed at the monk. "Yesterday, he was in my bed. He brought me to life with his hands and his lips and his cock." She slid her hand between the creature's legs and cupped its balls. "My love," she said, "why won't you answer me?" Tears streamed down her face, and she buried it in the creature's arm. "Why?"

"It is a body without a soul. It answers to nobody," said the bishop.

"And he's a soul without a body," she pointed at her husband. "Please," she begged the creature. She took its hand and cupped it to her breast. "Please. Love me. Make love to me!"

"It wants nothing to do with you," said the monk. "It didn't come back out of love."

"It came back to destroy me," whispered Constantine.

"Now you're starting to understand," said the Bishop.

"No," yelled Katina. She turned the creature towards her and wrapped her arms around its wide shoulders. She hugged the thing and quietly begged. "Stay, Mihali. Please stay for me."

As she clung to the husk of her lover, Brother Theodore made the sign of the cross and whispered under his breath, "From dust ye came and to dust you return. As dust I consign thee to the four winds — North, South, East, and West — that meet at these crossroads. In the name of our Lord, I bid you depart."

There was a sudden gust, and the body that once belonged to Mihali Tsatas crumbled and was whisked away. Katina was left holding air, weeping. Constantine stood there, silent, expressionless like the thing he'd just seen dissipate. Husband and wife were covered in a fine layer of dust and had to wipe the grit from their eyes.

The Bishop turned to the crowd. The gathered villagers fell to their knees and crossed themselves. "Praise be to God," he said and smiled. It wasn't a friendly smile. It was a threatening smile, full of malice and contempt. "You have seen what happens to those that disobey the teachings of the Church. Go home!"

One by one the villagers concluded their prayers, rose, and walked back uphill.

Only the four remained, Katina weeping, Constantine drained, the old monk hunched over as if nothing had happened, and the Bishop grinning at his victory. They stood there in the swirling dust, and the bishop slapped Constantine's back.

"Why?" Constantine asked the Bishop.

"Because you're going to hell," said the Bishop. "And so is she. This is just a foretaste."

"What about love and forgiveness?" asked Constantine.

"Love and forgiveness?" snorted Katina. "You weren't man enough to love me. And you weren't man enough to forgive the man who did."

"Love and forgiveness?" chuckled the old monk.

"Did you see those fools on their knees?" asked the Bishop. "They witnessed the spectacle. They watched me humiliate you. And still they fell on their knees. It's never about love and forgiveness."

"Then what was it all about?" said Constantine.

"The same thing it's always about," said the Bishop. "Control."

Christos Tsirbas is a member of the SF writers' group, The Montreal Commune. "Brikolakas" was inspired by fellow member Glenn Grant, who quipped over supper that the Brucolac in China Miéville's *The Scar* was an example of how that author drew upon role-playing games to create his characters. Christos pointed out that a Brikolakas was actually a monster in Greek folklore. "I wrote this story to set things straight, but I've probably added to the confusion in the process."

Christos says: "I'm an avid cyclist. I love loud music, which makes me a lousy neighbour, especially in Montreal's Plateau Mont-Royal, which is known for apartments with paper-thin walls. My earliest memory is watching the skeleton scene from *Jason and the Argonauts* at the Rialto Cinema on Park Avenue. A native Montrealer, I spent part of my childhood in Greece, a period that can best be described as *Dandelion Wine* meets *My Big Fat Greek Wedding*. As a boy, I spent many afternoons at the Bloomfield branch of the Montreal Children's Library in Park Extension, where I discovered the writings of C.S. Lewis, Edgar Rice Burroughs, and Ray Bradbury. I've been known to drive like a maniac, and I hold the record for the fastest speed achieved on the southbound journey from Montreal to the Readercon SF convention in Massachusetts."

Endogamy Blues

Montreal was burning.

Joanie didn't need her eyespies to see the fires anymore. They'd roared through the suburbs and were consuming the downtown core like starving dogs at a fresh kill. It was almost as bright as day at the summit of Mount Royal, even though her wetset told her it was seven minutes past midnight.

She swept her ceps through her eyespy flock, and a seamless speedblur of horror flickered past her mind's eye. Floating gunbodies peppered the downtown streets with small arms fire, buildings burned, screaming people ran and trampled others and were trampled like tall grass. Mostly, there was fire and there was death.

And then, in the midst of all the horror and noise, there was a louder noise. Joanie's ceps were automatically shunted to the nearest eyespy, and she abruptly found herself in mid-air, looking straight down at the X-marks-the-spot shape of Place Ville Marie. "Oh no," Joanie whispered. "Please not..."

The eyespy timestamp reeled back fifteen seconds and was moving forward towards *now* again. Place Ville Marie swelled and burst like a pustulous tumour, spewing fire and broken glass in every direction. The shards of glass seemed to hang in mid-air for a moment, catching the light from the burning city like so many delicate pieces of fine crystal. Joanie caught her breath; this was almost beautiful, in a way, until the giant plus sign of the building's superstructure folded over on itself like a child's construction toy, ancient steel shrieking in anger all the way down to the ground.

Joanie pulled her ceps back into her own head, exhaled raggedly, and wiped her eyes with the back of her hand. She'd spent a lot of time in Place Ville Marie during her first self-directed semester at high school, when she still thought she might become an architect one day. It was one of only a handful of Modernist structures to have survived the greenpurges and the Downturn, and, as much as it was possible to love glass and steel and concrete, Joanie had loved that building.

Sniffling, she pinged a wetset utility.

<I'm sorry, Joanie, you haven't eaten in twenty-four hours and you're already above safe toxicity levels,> said the disconcertingly cheerful female voice inside her head. <Battlefield hormonal augments are not available.>

<But I need something! Just a little.>

<I'm sorry, Joanie,> repeated the headvoice. <Battlefield hormonal augments are not available.>

"Give me something!" Joanie shrieked, pounding the guardrail in front of her. "I'm going to die anyway. What does it matter anymore?"

The headvoice was silent.

"Bitch!"

Joanie screwed her eyes shut and tried to breathe. *You're a soldier,* she told herself. *This is war. Stop crying like a fucking baby!*

She opened her eyes and closed them again, but the afterglow of PVM's destruction was burned on her retinas as if she had witnessed it bare-eyed. She tried to visualize something else — anything else! — to chase away the afterburn. For some reason, she called up an image of the very spot where she was standing, of a giant steel cross that had graced the peak of Mount Royal. She'd only visited it up close once, on a rare family outing back when she was still little. "There's been a Christian cross here since Jacques Cartier claimed Montreal for France," her father explained, always the teacher.

"Christian? Like the Liberators?" Joanie asked mischievously.

Sandra looked down her nose in that *I'm humiliated just to be out in public with you* big-sister way. "The Liberators aren't Christians, dimmy," she snorted. "Don't you know anything? They're Christian*ists.*"

"Oh," said Joanie, as if there were any difference, and she shrugged. Back then, the war was a dark mystery happening in faraway places and Joanie was far more worried about the chocolate Chanukah gelt her grandmother was going to give her the next day. If grandma'd had a good season, maybe she'd even get a toy.

Her grandmother was gone, now. Sandra and Dad too. Even the giant cross was gone, destroyed in the first days of the invasion. No-one had had the time or the heart to put it back up again. Probably no-one ever would.

A contact icon flared in Joanie's left eye, and she blinked an acknowledgement through her tears.

<Outpost Four, report!> squawked a harsh male voice inside her head.

Somehow, it all seemed very stupid and very far away again. <Report?> she choked. <You want a *report*, Corporal Mitzger?>

There was stunned silence at the other end of the comm connection. <Outpost Four, this is Op One,> he finally repeated. <Report!>

<I'll give you a report. The city's burning, thousands of people are dying and we're *next*, Op One! That's my fucking report!>

<Any signs of thermonukes? Force weapons? Twisters?>

<Nothing, Op One! Just conventional weapons conventionally wiping out a conventional city. Everybody's conventionally *dead*! Out!>

She unpinged her wetset, and, for the first time in over a year, she was alone inside her own brain. It was a court-martial offense to unping on the battlefield, of course, but who'd be left to haul her off to the stockade? Whether the Liberators or Mitzger got her first was just a roll of the dice now.

With that thought, a shadow fell across her observation post. Joanie swallowed heavily, whispered "Hear O Israel, the Lord is God, the Lord is One," and looked up, expecting to see the last thing she would ever see. Instead, she made out the stubby silhouette of an airbody against the quarter moon, its Canadian Forces markings glowing brightly in a wavelength visible to Joanie's augmented ceps.

The airbody's underport opened with a soft hiss. A cable snaked down and a crewman braced by a waist tether fell partway out of the open port. "Come on!" he shouted. "We're bugging out!"

Relief and exaltation refused to come even as Joanie groped for the rescue cable. It was one thing to watch anonymous small prairie towns fall to the conquerors, it was something else to be there as your hometown died. There was no room left for any emotion at all.

"For Christ's sake, girl, get a move on!" The crewman gestured frantically at her.

Joanie shook her head and grabbed the red bobbin at the end of the cable. She locked it into the towjack on her chest pack and activated her bodyshield.

<Warning,> said her annoyingly cheerful headvoice. <You have only twenty shieldseconds of power remaining.>

"Great," muttered Joanie, giving the aircraftman a thumbs-up. Instantly, she shot into the air as if she'd been fired from a gun. She squeezed her eyes shut in terror.

Lifters screaming, the airbody rose into the sky and streaked north. Joanie swung in a wild arc beneath it as Liberator flechettes cracked and snapped against her bodyshield.

"Ohgodohgodohgod," Joanie moaned. "Let it end. Oh Jesus fucking God please let it end!"

The air exploded from her lungs as she slammed into the airbody's hull and rebounded. The aircraftman groped wildly for the loop on her chest pack as she arced past him.

"Careful!" Joanie shouted, slapping the big red shield cut-off button just as his hand closed around the loop. "Are you trying to burn your fucking arm off?"

"Sorry," he muttered as he hauled her into the airbody. He blinked twice and the underport slammed shut. The sudden silence assaulted Joanie like a blow.

"I'm so tired I don't know what I'm doing anymore," he said.

Joanie unhooked the bobbin from her towjack and held it above her head. "Cable free," she said.

"Cable free, aye," the aircraftman replied, and stepped back as it snapped into its sheath.

"Thanks," Joanie muttered, pulling off her helmet. She shook her head, but her curly red hair was so dirty and matted that it refused to spring back to its normal shape. Her rescuer was just as dishevelled, dark circles under dark eyes, jet black hair that needed a trim and a wash peeking out from under his flight helmet. Under other circumstances she might have thought him cute. Handsome, even. He looked sort of like that guy she'd dated a couple of times, the only one who'd ever kissed her. What was his name again? She'd been fourteen at the time, so that made it only three years ago, not the million-and-a-half it felt like.

"I really appreciate the haul-out," she said.

The aircraftman snapped to attention and saluted her. "My pleasure, ma'am."

To her own stunned amazement, Joanie burst out laughing.

"Sorry, ma'am," he stuttered. "I mean..."

"At ease," Joanie said, revelling in the forbidden lusciousness of officer-talk. "It's just that's the first salute I've ever gotten." She patted her dual-service shoulder flashes. "I'm just an enlisted girl. Private First Class Joanie Morgenstern, Canadian Forces and Ethnic Army of the Americas."

The aircraftman looked down at his feet in embarrassment. "Airbody Technician Second Grade Michael Cross," he said in a near-whisper.

Joanie painted a smile on her face and offered her hand. "Hi, Mike," she said. She took his hand and glanced at his shoulder insignias. He was also dual-service, but his second flash wasn't EAA, it was Iroquois Six Nations, with a Mohawk Warrior crest for good measure.

Their eyes met and Joanie smiled, for real this time. "From my tribe to yours, I thank you."

Mike laughed a sad laugh. "My tribe and yours are well and truly screwed," he said.

Joanie pulled off her chest pack and dropped it to the deck. "Again," she said, stripping out of her camolayer. It went grey and inert as it lost contact with the regulation uniform underneath. Mike looked away in embarrassment, and she absently hoped he wasn't too disappointed that she wasn't wearing lace panties and a frilly bra. Amazing how he had enough energy for the desire or the embarrassment. She just couldn't get her mind around it, or around much of anything, for that matter.

Joanie waited two seconds for her rank insignias and shoulder flashes to port to her uniform, and then she wadded the camolayer into a ball and shoved it deep into her chest pack. Strictly nonregulation way to handle it, but who cared anymore?

"So, not to sound ungrateful or anything," she said, just to fill the air. "But why did you bother to come get me?"

"Orders," he answered. "EAA Op One said you had comm failure and wouldn't know about the bug-out. Everyone else is evacuating over-land."

"Lucky me."

There was no way Mitzger thought she had comm failure; he knew she'd shut down deliberately. Maybe he wasn't so by-the-book after all.

"Do you have any idea where we're going?" Joanie asked.

Mike shrugged. "I don't know anything. I'm supposed to be bugging out overland with my unit, but I got grabbed at the last second by this Ermy officer—"

"EAA!" Joanie snapped. "Only the Liberators call us that."

"Sorry," Mike stammered.

"So this officer grabbed you. Did he tell you where we're going?"

"She," Mike corrected. "She said something about picking you up, and orders, and then she slammed the cockpit door shut. After that, you know as much as I do."

Joanie fell into one of the airbody's passenger seats. It was luxuriously padded and more comfortable than it had a right to be. Not standard Forces issue, that was for sure. "Orders to go where and do what?"

"I hear there are still some free pockets in the Québec interior." said Mike, settling into the seat opposite her. "Maybe they'll deploy us as guerrillas."

"No way," said Joanie softly. "Remember Guatemala and Arizona?"

Mike shuddered and nodded.

"They'll never risk it, not with the Liberators controlling the cities."

"What about..." he hesitated. "Could we make it to Europe?"

She sneered. "The Euros are afraid of their own shadows. They're still hoping if they make nice with the Liberator he'll leave them alone."

"Which leaves what, India and the China Sphere?"

Joanie made a rude, hopeless noise and sank deeper into her seat as Mike squeezed himself into the airbody's tiny galley.

Mike held up a big white mug emblazoned with a forgotten corporate logo, and Joanie could see his hand shaking. He asked, "Want a coffee?" She shook her head no, and with unpracticed movements Mike started to pour one for himself. He slipped, and the scalding blue stream slopped over the edge of his cup and over his hand. Mike cursed, dropped the mug, and caught the sugar dispenser on the backswing. It clattered to the deck, scattering sugar packets in every direction. Mike cursed again and fell to his knees right into the puddle of spilled coffee. Oblivious to the blue stains creeping up his uniform trousers from the knees, Mike desperately scrabbled for the sugar packs.

Joanie sighed and mentally kicked herself in the ass, very hard. Her battlepsych instructors would be proud of her, she was doing a bang-up job of keeping the noncombatants calm and focused.

It's the damn Warrior patch, she told herself. *That's what you get for believing in stereotypes.*

"Actually," she said, trying to smile. "I don't think either of us is really old enough for coffee."

Mike looked up at her and eyed the huge flechette gun holstered on her hip. He laughed again. One short, sharp laugh, more like a bark. He choked on the second laugh, and his eyes filled with tears. On his knees in the galley, his knees stained blue and his hands still full of sugar packets, the handsome young Mohawk Warrior started to cry.

"Oh God," he whispered, through his sobs. "Oh God, I'm so scared."

Joanie fell to her knees next to him and took him in her arms. The spilled coffee burned her knees and his tears burned her exposed skin as he buried his head in the crook between her neck and shoulders. She felt her own tears, and the raw, acid terror in her gut that she'd kept safely locked away for these long months.

"Me too, Michael," she said, holding tight and rocking him gently, like a baby. "Me too."

Joanie checked the time on her wetset again. Nothing had changed. She was still running late, and getting later by the second. She took several panting breaths and broke into a fast jog. The last thing she needed was to tick off the duty sergeant on her first day back on active duty.

It was just too easy to misjudge how long it took to get from one place to another at Post Val d'Or. It seemed impossible that a hole in the ground could be so big. Her body complained like an old woman's as she lengthened her stride into an all-out sprint. Back in the women's locker room, after her precious 3.2 minutes in the refresher stall, Joanie had looked in a mirror for the first time since she arrived at the Post — and what she'd seen was an exhausted, stooped stranger with stringy red hair, dark black circles under washed-out eyes, and a body so covered with ugly purple bruises that it was impossible to tell where one ended and the next one began.

"Private First Class Morgenstern?" growled the dual-service duty-sergeant standing outside Conference Room 6. He was a tall and broad man of South Asian Indian descent, with a shaved head and piercing eyes. Like all sergeants in all armies everywhere, he looked angry.

"Yes, Sergeant, reporting as ordered," she gasped, head down and hands on knees.

"You're late!" he snapped. "I don't care if you're an underager or not, this is the army, not high school! Not the prom! You *will* be on time for your duty assignments at Post Val d'Or!"

Joanie opened her mouth to apologize, but the sergeant cut her off and motioned at the closed conference-room door.

"Inside. They're all waiting on you."

Joanie's stomach spasmed in terror. Why would Captain Juarez hold up a whole briefing for a lowly private? She pushed the door open, and a half-dozen pairs of eyes turned in her direction. The feeble excuse she had been preparing died on her lips. Captain Juarez stood at the front of the room at the blankboard, watching her impassively. Three high-ranking women in Air Force blue stared unsympathetically in Joanie's direction, and, in the second-to-last seat, Mike Cross gave her a shy smile. Joanie's eyes widened in surprise at the sight of him; and, when her gaze fell on the tall man in the grey suit and ceremonial headdress sitting calmly at the head of the table, she gasped in awe.

"Yes, it's really me, Private," said Jerome Montour. "Let's fast-forward past the shock and the sputtering, please, and just get you in your seat."

Joanie saluted the Grand Chief of Canada sloppily, whispered "yessir," and slipped into the empty chair next to Mike. Everyone else in the room was a ranking officer and in their thirties at least. Bonita Juarez was somewhat older, a heavyset woman with sad brown eyes, dark brown skin, and a quirky Mona Lisa smile that appeared and disappeared without warning. Her uniform had a strange cut, black with white piping and a white peaked cap. On her shoulder, where the United States Navy crest had once been, she wore EAA Air and Sea Corps insignia. *No dual-service badges for her*, Joanie thought. *No divided loyalties. Nowhere else to go.*

"Now that we're all here," said Captain Juarez, absently tapping her stylus against the beige stackpack she wore on her left hip, "I would like to call this meeting to order. I remind everyone that the contents of this briefing are rated Most Secret, and it is a court-martial offense to discuss them with anyone of any rank not currently present in this room."

Captain Juarez waved her stylus at the blankboard, and a series of charts and graphs popped up under the Joint Command coat of arms. Joanie scanned the information quickly, and her heart sank.

"The numbers don't lie, ladies and gentlemen," said Captain Juarez. "We are not simply losing this war. In every way that counts, we have already lost it."

A collective sigh, almost a sob, rose from the table. No-one was surprised, but the words had never been spoken out loud before.

"Don't misunderstand me. The Chiefdom of Canada performed miracles building up a world-class military from virtually nothing, supplemented by whatever we..." she paused and searched for a word, "...*latecomers* could bring to the table, but we have been fighting the most powerful military force on Earth."

She waved the stylus at the blankboard again, and the black, white, and blue Liberator flag appeared above another collection of statistics. Joanie unconsciously ground her teeth at the sight of this sinister parody of the old Stars and Stripes, a clenched white fist on black where the blue field of stars was supposed to go.

"Our enemies have absorbed most of the military materiel of the former USA and the conquered republics of Latin America," continued Captain Juarez. "The Canadian Forces, the Six Nations Army, and the Ethnic Army of the Americas have fought fearlessly and well, but we have only managed to hang on as long as we have because the Liberators' attentions were divided between us and the Brazilians."

"Not to mention their sheer military stupidity," spat General Papageorgiou, one of the women in Air Force blue. "They've caused more casualties to their own side than we ever did."

"That's what purging your officer corps every six months will do to you," agreed Captain Juarez. "Paranoia has been a weakness of totalitarian states throughout history, and we took as much advantage of it as we could. It may seem strange to say this, but we should also be grateful that the Liberators were denied the high ground of outer space."

"To hell with that," snarled the Air Force woman next to General Papageorgiou. "The ThreeWorlders kicked Earth when it was down, and they've been holding us down ever since! I blame this whole war on them in the first place. They locked us in the asylum with the madmen and threw away the key!"

"Be that as it may, Colonel Wharton," said Captain Juarez. "The ThreeWorlds battlesats cost the Liberators a natural advantage in this war that we exploited to the best of our abilities, but we were still outmanned, outgunned, and outproduced. For every soldier we put on the field, the Libbies had twelve. For every airbody we built, the Libbies produced twenty. For every force rifle and shield harness we made, the Libbies made five hundred. Incompetence or no incompetence, they have crushed us with the sheer weight of numbers."

"How much time does the Joint Command give us?"

Captain Juarez flinched and looked to the Grand Chief. He sighed deeply.

"It is my sad duty to inform you that Ottawa has fallen," he said softly. "The Joint Command evacuated National Defense HQ four hours ago, and we've heard nothing from them since. We can only assume that they have been captured or killed. We've held off making an announcement to avoid panic and a complete collapse of morale."

The room fell silent. Once again, the nightmare images of Montreal's death-throes flickered past Joanie's eyes. She fiercely tried to push away the images of the downtown in flames, of PVM dying, of the storm of emotions that had exploded from her and Mike during their long airbody flight. Her chest laboured as if a huge weight was crushing her, and she struggled to draw in breath.

"The Great Longhouse in Akwesasne and the Old Parliament in

Ottawa are both in hands of our enemies," continued the Grand Chief. "The Prime Minister and her cabinet refused to evacuate Ottawa and are also presumed captured or lost. As of this moment, I am all the civilian government Canada has left."

Joanie pinged her wetset and kicked in her hormonal augments. She was abusing a battlefield-restricted augment, and there would be hell to pay in six hours when the effect wore off, but this time her headvoice did not object. She felt a giddy, surreal rush of happiness, and the weight on her chest lessened. She drew in a shuddering gasp and tried to focus on what the Grand Chief was saying.

"Traditionally, Canadian Grand Chiefs and the old Governors General before us exercised no real authority," he continued. "We were figureheads appointed to make long, boring Speeches from the Throne and cut ribbons at hospital dedications." The Chief paused and pointed at his ceremonial headdress. "At least that's the theory. The Constitution actually tells a different story. Under the law I am Canada's head of state and commander-in-chief of the Armed Forces, and for the first time in history I will be exercising that legitimate authority in the place of our elected leaders."

He looked at General Papageorgiou and then met the gaze of everyone at the table, including, to her shock, Joanie. "Before we continue I need to know that everyone in this room accepts my authority."

No-one said a word. Captain Juarez had obviously been forewarned, but the others at the table were frozen like statues. Despite her hormonal hit, Joanie still felt like she was sealed in an airtight box, like an escape artist whose trick had gone horribly wrong.

Suddenly, with a scraping sound, Mike pushed his chair back and rose to his feet.

He said something unintelligible and saluted the man in grey at the head of the table. <War chief,> translated Joanie's wetset. <Mohawk language, Kahnawake dialect.>

Shakily, Joanie rose from her chair. "Sir!" she said, snapping off the crispest, most military salute of her career.

The Grand Chief rose and nodded at Mike and Joanie. "Nia:wen," he said softly. <Thank you,> translated Joanie's wetset.

The three Air Force officers also rose to salute the Grand Chief, and Captain Juarez stepped around the table so he could see her. She saluted him in the old, pre-Liberator, American style.

"I am not Canadian," she said. "But I would follow you to hell, sir."

"Wrong direction," said the Grand Chief with a thin smile, pointing upward.

"What does that mean?" asked Colonel Wharton dully.

"Let's show you," said Captain Juarez.

During the long and bumpy ride through the maze-like tunnels of Post Val d'Or, Joanie and Mike stood in uncomfortable silence, jammed together on the passenger pad of a peoplemover built for one.

"Listen, about the other day. On the airbody, I mean..." As she said this, Joanie could feel Mike pulling as far away as he could go without falling off the peoplemover.

"I'm sorry," he whispered.

"Sorry? For what? For saving my life?"

"No!" said Mike hastily. "I mean, I didn't really save your life, you were already on the rescue cable. I mean, I'm sorry I ... you know ... lost it. That's not me. I mean, not the *real* me."

"You're kidding. You hung yourself upside down from a speeding airbody for me, and you're apologizing because you cried? I cried too, remember? Almost dying will do that to a person!"

Mike shrugged.

"You're an idiot," said Joanie softly, leaning in closer to Mike's broad back. "Just let the girl thank you for saving her life, okay?"

Mike said nothing, but he didn't he shrug or pull away, either. They stayed that way until the peoplemover slowed to a stop five minutes later. Joanie opened her eyes and saw Captain Juarez stepping down from her own peoplemover. She looked in their direction, raised an eyebrow, and briefly touched her EAA insignia, and Joanie hastily let go of Mike. Captain Juarez smiled an almost imperceptible smile and turned away. At the same moment, a section of bare grey tunnel wall in front of them silently turned sideways and sank into the floor.

"Ladies and gentlemen, this is the most tightly guarded and secret facility still under the control of the Joint—" she paused and put her hand over her mouth. "Of nonhostile forces," she corrected. "A fuzzyfield is active inside this service bay, making it virtually impenetrable to auditory, optical, and electromagnetic spying. Those of you with augmented perceptions should shut them down now," she looked at Joanie, who blushed furiously. "The field can cause some pretty nasty side-effects."

Why did she have to just blab it to everyone like that? Joanie thought angrily as she pinged her wetset and pulled her ceps down to baseline.

"Even those without augmentation may experience some momentary dizziness or disorientation, but it will pass. Please follow me."

They trudged through the narrow door in single file, like students on a field trip, and, with a stomach-dropping lurch, they crossed the fuzzyfield boundary. Immediately to Joanie's right, Colonel Wharton groaned and stumbled, and Joanie grabbed her arm to steady her.

"Thanks, Private," she said, pulling her arm away. "I'm okay now."

Joanie didn't hear. She was gaping at the impossible grey shape that loomed above them. She closed her eyes and counted to three, but it was still there when she opened them again.

A starship. It was a real, honest-to-God, Nspace-jumping, faster-than-the-speed-of-light *starship*. It was a creature out of myth, a legend from the history books, but Joanie knew it just as she would know a dragon or a blue whale if one suddenly appeared in front of her.

"Does it have a name, ma'am?" Joanie asked in an awed whisper.

"Not yet. EAA was pushing for *Rosa Parks*, but the Canadian Forces are dead set on calling her *Louis Riel*. The outer hull belongs to an old Canadian Navy submarine that was never completed, so the Forces will probably have their way."

"So that's what you've been up to in here all these months," whispered Colonel Wharton. "I can't believe it."

"Believe it, ma'am. As far as we know, this is the first working starship constructed on Earth in over a century. That's why I didn't want to even mention it outside the range of the fuzzyfield."

"Which raises an important question," said General Papageorgiou. "Why was it built? What's it good for?"

The Grand Chief cleared his throat uneasily. "We're going for help."

"Sir?" Joanie asked in astonishment, momentarily wondering if the fuzzyfield was interfering with her hearing. "Help? You mean, from the ThreeWorlds?"

"Actually, they're called the FourWorlds now," said Captain Juarez. "Carolus founded its own colony on a planet called Castille about thirty years ago."

"How could you possibly know that?" demanded Colonel Wharton. "The colonies haven't sent a starship to the Earth system since the Downturn, and Carolus is over five hundred light-years away. Their earliest signals won't reach us for another 150 years!"

The Grand Chief smiled. "Actually, Carolus sent an automated probe to check on the battlesats about twenty years ago. Apparently it malfunctioned and crashed in the High Arctic. We found it entirely by accident on a routine patrol."

"And a survey probe was just chock full of the latest ThreeWorlds news reports?"

The Grand Chief smirked. "Our cousins from the stars aren't the infallible *übermenschen* of Gesualdi's movies, Colonel Wharton. Whoever launched the probe tried to save a few bucks by growing the AI from off-the-shelf genecode, and it was, as you say, chock full of imprinted racial memory from earlier iterations. I'll bet it never even occurred to them that we might read it, or that it would matter if we did."

"But why would they help us, sir?" demanded Colonel Wharton again. "They call us the 'sick old motherworld!' They quarantined us like a bunch of lepers during the Downturn and left us here to rot!"

"It's been a long time — 127 years," replied Captain Juarez softly. "Circumstances change."

The Grand Chief sighed. "This may sound almost traitorous, but I don't completely blame them. The Downturn was like a plague. There was no law, no government, just factions fighting factions and refugees boiling offworld by the thousands, taking their feuds with them to the stars. The colonies did what they had to do to survive. I might have done the same thing in their shoes."

"And what do you think they'll make of the Liberators, sir?" asked General Papageorgiou. "With their marching and posturing and lunatic notions of racial superiority? The Liberators scare *me*, and I've been fighting them almost all my life. Isn't there a risk that we'd panic our enlightened star-cousins into sterilizing the whole planet just to protect themselves?"

The Grand Chief shook his head. "The FourWorlders aren't gods, and they aren't monsters, either. They follow the Eight Principles, just as we do. They tried to help during the Downturn, and they also tried to gain strategic advantage for themselves, and all of it just stirred up the chaos like a hornet's nest. The battlesats were an admission of *failure*, General. They cut and ran and slammed the door behind them. It must have been humiliating."

"If you say so, sir," replied the General dubiously.

"These are different times. We're fighting a conventional war against a nasty but conventional enemy. All the FourWorlders have to do is decide who they'd rather have in charge of their motherworld and pick a side. Far cleaner than genociding the whole planet, if nothing else. Probably cheaper, too, Eight Principles aside."

"And then what? Maybe they wipe out the Liberators and then decide not to go home again."

"Do you care? I mean, seriously, General. Could we be any worse off as a colony of the FourWorlds than in our current situation?"

General Papageorgiou chewed the inside of her cheek silently for a moment. "Even if I grant all that, sir, and I'm still reserving judgment, can we actually fly this starship? Can we get past the battlesats and navigate through Nspace? No-one on Earth has done any of these things in living memory."

"We'll do our best," replied Captain Juarez, "but it's a crapshoot. We simply didn't expect the war to go this bad this fast. Launch wasn't scheduled for a month, and now the entire flight crew is missing, along with everyone else at National Defense HQ. The ship's not prepped, and we have no-one to fly her. But that's where our young friends come in," she continued, nodding at Mike and Joanie.

Mike and Joanie stared at their superior in shock.

"You're not serious," said Colonel Wharton.

"If you'll excuse us, ladies and gentlemen," said Captain Juarez, "I think it's time for a private briefing."

"Obviously," said Colonel Wharton dryly.

Captain Juarez marched Joanie and Mike past the giant starship to an unpowered hinged door cut right into the wall of the service bay. It opened at her approach, and she led them into a small mess hall lined with stainless steel tables and chairs.

The fourth table from the door sported a full water pitcher and three glass tumblers. Captain Juarez poured herself a glass and sat down at the head of the table.

"Sit," she said, and Mike and Joanie sat. They stared at their superior wide-eyed as she drained her glass.

"Don't look at me like that," said Captain Juarez, putting the glass down on the tabletop. "I know what I'm doing."

"But, ma'am, I don't have any space experience," stammered Joanie. "I'm just a private soldier. An army grunt."

"Nobody has any space experience, child. I'm surface Navy myself, and I've never commanded so much as a rowboat, but I'm the closest thing to a starship captain the EAA's got. And you two are my only chance of getting her spaceborne."

"But we're not even noncoms!" sputtered Mike.

"I beg your pardon?" snapped Captain Juarez, suddenly all business. "Are you questioning my command decisions?"

"No, ma'am!"

"Good. Because I'd hate to lose you before we even begin, Aircraftman Second Class."

"Yes, ma'am!"

"Never underestimate yourself, Aircraftman. You bring some very specific skills to this table, skills we'll need to get that ship off the ground. You too, Private." She turned to look at Joanie.

"What skills, ma'am?" Joanie asked in a small voice.

"You're going to fly the ship, Private."

Joanie's chest was in a vise again. Her ears roared and the room started to swirl around her.

"Steady, Private!" said Captain Juarez, putting a hand on her shoulder. "Let's keep it together."

"But I'm just an eyespy controller, ma'am," Joanie stammered. "I've never—"

"Enough!" shouted Captain Juarez. "You're a Level Eight Augment, Private! We can upgrade your skillset in three hours."

Joanie flinched as if she'd been slapped.

"You're upset, Private," said the Captain.

Joanie just nodded.

"Say what's on your mind. Say it, and let's move on!"

"I'm not a toaster, ma'am. I'm a human being."

"You are the only person at this base who can use her wetset as anything more than a souped-up garage-door opener, Private Morgenstern. You're a good soldier, but there were lots of good soldiers who *didn't* get airlifted out of Montreal."

Joanie swallowed heavily and fought back the tears.

"You're here because there's no-one else who can do the job I need you to do. If I'm being harsh, it's because we have no time. Do I make myself clear? We have no time."

Joanie nodded silently.

"As for you, Aircraftman Cross—"

"Ma'am, all I've ever worked on are airbody secondary systems," interrupted Mike. "There must be hundreds of people with more training than me."

Captain Juarez slammed her glass to the tabletop. "I'm not going through this routine again! When I want an opinion out of either of you, I'll ask for it! Clear?"

"Yes, ma'am!" chorused Mike and Joanie.

"If all I needed was an airbody technician, Aircraftman, you'd still be trudging over the Laurentians on foot with a hundred-kilo pack on your back!"

"Yes, ma'am." Mike repeated.

"Do you remember the mechanical engineering project you did back at the Six Nations Military College?"

Mike looked puzzled for an instant. "You mean that model hydraulic lifter I fabbed for Professor Goodleaf? He *hated* it! I barely got a passing grade."

"I read your report card," said Captain Juarez. "He penalized you for a Third Principle violation."

"Sonofabitch," Mike whispered.

Joanie was astonished. "You violated the Third Principle for a *class project*?"

"I didn't violate any Principle!" shouted Mike. "My people had the Principles when your ancestors were still chewing the forests into toilet paper!"

Captain Juarez raised an eyebrow. "Let's leave that kind of ethnic superiority crap to our enemies, shall we?"

"Sorry, ma'am," Mike replied.

"Instead of shouting, explain it to Private Morgenstern, Aircraftman."

Mike shrugged. "It was just this dumb model of a hydraulic lifter I fabbed for mechanical engineering class. Before gravitics were invented, they used hydraulics for heavy lifting and construction."

"So where does the Third Principle come into it?" asked Joanie.

"I don't know. In the old days they used petroleum-based hydraulic fluid, but I used clean articulator lube instead. I mean, I'm not an idiot. All that matters is viscosity and compression, what the fluid's made of doesn't matter. Why would I get myself into stupid trouble like that for nothing?"

"Professor Goodleaf is an Eight Principles fanatic," said Captain Juarez. "He's one of those people who believes that all pre-Eight technologies are tainted. Evil by default."

"Jesus," exhaled Mike. "He almost cost me my certification."

"Forget Professor Goodleaf! Right now I've got a fifteen-thousand-ton starship lying on its side with no way to raise it into launch position."

"Gravitic lifters," said Mike.

"Right," said Captain Juarez. "Or we could just make a giant 'Please Come and Kill Us' sign. *Think*, man!"

Mike nodded sheepishly. "Of course. The rock over our heads—"

"—can't shield gravitons. If we were stupid enough to use gravitics now, the Liberators would vaporize us before the ship was two centimetres off the ground."

"But the primary drive, ma'am," protested Mike. "It's also got to be gravitic, right? Just like an airbody."

"Of course, but once we push the launch button, it won't matter. By the time they detected us, we'd be in orbit. The problem is getting the ship ready for launch without betraying our position before liftoff."

"So you want me to build some kind of hydraulic lifter to raise the ship."

"More like repair. We salvaged a mostly intact twenty-second-century lifter from an old mining site, plus assorted parts."

Mike was silent.

"Nothing to say, Aircraftman?"

"I was told to keep my opinions to myself, ma'am."

"That you were. Like it or not, you're Post Val d'Or's resident expert on hydraulics. The base cerafab is at your disposal. You have your orders, and you will carry them out to the best of your abilities."

"Yes, ma'am."

Captain Juarez smiled like Mona Lisa and stood. Joanie and Mike jumped to attention, but she waved Joanie back into her seat. "Sit. I'll have Corporal Dawson prep the Augment Suite, but that may take a few minutes. In the meantime, catch your breath and collect your thoughts. I'll send the cook in with something to eat. "Aircraftman," she nodded at Mike. "You're with me."

Mike cleared his throat uncomfortably. "Ma'am, do you mind if I stay here with Private Morgenstern for a couple of minutes?"

She looked at them both through hooded eyes. "Am I going to have a disciplinary problem with the two of you?"

"No, ma'am!" they barked in unison.

"Do I need to remind you of the distinction between 'on-duty' and 'off-duty' as defined in the Joint Command Code of Military Conduct?"

"No, ma'am!" they chorused again.

"Good. In that case, you can stay for five minutes, Aircraftman. Meet me by the aft starboard support strut."

"Thank you, ma'am," said Mike.

"Five minutes," she reiterated, stalking to the exit. "Not a second more."

The door slammed. Joanie and Mike stared at one another across the expanse of the steel table. A chef in Navy white drifted in silently with a tray of sandwiches and sweet-potato chips. She smiled at them and left without saying a word.

"This is too weird," said Mike.

"I think I'm going to be sick," whispered Joanie.

Mike smiled. "Fat chance. If the Air Force couldn't make you ralph, nothing will."

"Just thinking about the Air Force makes me want to ralph."

"Ouch!" said Mike, licking his finger and drawing a figure 1 in the air. "One point to the Army."

Joanie picked a bag of sweet-potato chips from the serving tray and tossed it from hand to hand.

"I *hate* the fucking Army!" she said. "Yes, ma'am. No, ma'am. Right away, ma'am." Joanie slammed the bag of chips against the tabletop. "Shall I open a goddamned *artery* for you, ma'am?"

"At least we'll get to see space," said Mike. "That's something."

Joanie crushed the chips viciously under the heel of her hand. "I don't *want* to go to space, and I don't want any more fucking witch doctors playing around inside my head! I just want to go home and sleep for twenty years."

Mike reached across the table and took the bag of chips from Joanie. "Shame to waste good food," he said, pulling the bag open and pouring the crumbs into his mouth.

"Are you an Augment, Mike?"

"Me?" he laughed. "No, I'm one of the garage-door people. Level 0.7. My wetset and I aren't on speaking terms, I've gotta do everything through the blink interface. You have to be, what, a Level Five to be considered a true Augment?"

"Four."

"Wow. And you're an Eight? I bow to your superiorness."

Joanie banged the table. "It's not funny! It's not bad enough that the Liberators want to grind my bones because I'm a Jew, but I have to be a freak among the freaks too?"

"I'm a freak?" asked Mike, quietly.

"I didn't mean it like that."

"That's what I heard." Mike's voice was tight with anger. "We let the fucking *Liberators* decide who's normal and who's not? I'm proud of who I am. You should be proud of who you are, augments and all."

"You don't understand..."

"We are what we are!" Mike insisted, crushing the empty chip bag. "The Liberators want to grind our bones because *they're* intolerant freaks who can't live with difference. We're in this base and having this conversation only because they exist. Whine about it all you like, there's no going home until we beat them."

Joanie looked away from him. "I'm scared," she whispered. "I don't want anyone mucking with my head again."

"You did it once..."

"I was fifteen and all alone and too stupid to know any better! They had me augmented and out on the battlefield before any of it had a chance to sink in."

"And now you're older and wiser," said Mike, taking her hand across the table. "And you've got friends to help you through."

Joanie's breath caught in her throat as Mike's skin touched hers. She looked up and saw his nostrils flare and his cheeks darken.

"The code of conduct," she whispered.

"We won't be on duty all the way to Carolus," he replied.

"Relax and try again," growled Corporal Dawson, Post Val d'Or's one-and-only Augment technician. "You're fighting the process."

The pressor field that held Joanie immobile in the augment-chair was badly calibrated, and lumpy bubbles of force kept rippling uncomfortably against her abdomen and up and down her legs. Worse, she was practically naked, stripped down to her combat bra and unitard, so the chair's ancient pickups could make better contact with the dermapoints on her skin. Or at least, that's what Corporal Dawson had claimed.

Perv, thought Joanie. *He'd have me out of my unitard too, if he thought he could get away with it.*

She desperately wished she could move, even a little. The derma-points on her shoulderblades and behind her knees itched crazily, and the wetport stuck to the back of her neck felt like it weighed tons.

"It's not working, Corporal," she said, fighting a crazy urge to blow her nose. "The pressure's worse. It's like the skillset doesn't fit. My head feels like it's going to explode."

"What did you expect? FruityFlies Chess? These skillsets are over a hundred years old! I had to run them through three separate converters just to make them minimally compatible with modern wetmemory. There's bound to be some feedback, it can't be helped. Just breathe deep and *do it*."

"I've been trying for three hours, Corporal. It *hurts*!"

Alien! Her mind was screaming. *Not me! Get out! Get out! Get out!*

Dawson grimaced and shook his head. "Listen, Private, all our necks are on the line because of you! I should be halfway to Nunavik with the second group of evacuees, but I stayed behind because I had a job to do. You're a soldier! Suck it up and do *your* job!"

She felt froth in her chest, and she struggled to inhale. "I can't breathe!" she shouted, struggling against the pressor field. "Let me out of the chair!"

"Relax, Private!" shouted Dawson. "Nothing's happening. It's all in your head."

"I'm suffocating," she wailed, struggling all the harder. "Let me out! Please let me out!"

"Get a hold of yourself, Private!" bellowed Dawson. "That's an order! You're not getting out of that chair until your skillsets are upgraded! Is that clear?"

Joanie panted and stared at Dawson. Her eyes were bloodshot, her pupils dilated as wide as they could go.

Dawson looked away. "I said, is that clear?"

"Yes, Corporal," Joanie whispered, closing her eyes and pinging her wetset.

"Are you crazy?" Dawson roared, slapping buttons on his control panel. "You can't trigger hormonal augments during an upgrade! You'll crash the whole process!"

With a jolt that felt like losing a finger, Joanie's wetset was suddenly gone. Even the ping utility itself went hard and cold like a dead thing inside her mind. Joanie wailed in terror and struggled against the pressor field.

"Let me out! Oh God, let me out of this fucking chair!"

"I'll have you up on charges!" Dawson yelled. "Insubordination! Dereliction of duty! They'll line you up against a wall and shoot you, Private!"

"Let me out! Let me out! God, please let me out!"

"Stupid Jewish cunt," Dawson muttered, still slapping buttons. "Liberators are crazy fuckers, but they're right about your kind."

Joanie heard a door slide open.

"Corporal," she heard Mike's voice from somewhere behind her. "Captain Juarez wants a word with you in the launch bay."

"Not now!"

"Right. Now." Mike repeated.

"You don't give me orders, you little sixer dipshit."

Joanie heard the velcro crackle of a flechette gun coming out of its holster, and Dawson gasped. "I'm not giving you orders; your superior officer is giving you orders. If you don't obey them, I'll shoot you for dereliction."

Dawson made a strangled noise, and then Joanie heard his heavy footsteps.

"You're lucky!" shouted Mike as the footsteps retreated down the hallway. "I put the last guy who called me a sixer in the medical bay!"

Joanie heard Mike's flechette gun slide back into its holster, and then he was in front of her at the control panel, pressing buttons.

"Where the hell is...?" he muttered, continuing to press buttons.

He turned to Joanie. "I'm sorry, I can't find the pressor..." The look of concern on his face suddenly transformed itself in a way Joanie didn't like. "Jesus," he whispered.

Joanie instinctively tried to cover herself, but her arms were still pinioned in place by the pressor field. "Stop looking at me like that!" she barked. "I'm not some fucking wankgirl!"

Mike flinched and hastily turned his attention to the control panel. "I'm sorry. God, I didn't mean..."

"Just get me out of this fucking chair."

"Augment techs are all crazy," Mike muttered, stabbing buttons at random. "We all hated them back at the academy. Only a total psycho wants to play around in other people's heads."

Joanie's world flashed, strobed, and burned. She screamed, and everything went black.

When Joanie awoke, the pressor field was turned off and her uniform shirt was draped loosely over her upper body.

"What happened?"

"The asshole neural-blocked your wetset," said Mike, studiously staring at a spot on the wall above Joanie's head. "I dropped the block, but I guess you're not supposed to do that cold."

"You *guess*?"

"I don't know augment tech very well. I'm sorry I hurt you. I was trying to help."

"It's okay," Joanie said in a tired voice. "It doesn't matter."

Mike looked down at the floor. "It matters to me."

"Stop staring at your fucking boots," said Joanie. "Look at me when you talk to me."

Mike shook his head and continued to stare at the floor.

"*Now* you're being a baby."

"I need you to know that I'd never think of you as a ... a ... wankgirl or anything like that. I—"

"Will you please *stop*? I was out of my head. I was talking bullshit. Let it go."

Mike raised his head slightly, but he still refused to meet Joanie's gaze.

"It's very important that you know how I feel and how I don't feel."

"Okay, let's change the subject," said Joanie, fighting back nausea. "Tell me something."

"What?" asked Mike.

"Anything. Take my mind off deep and painful things."

"Want to hear about hydraulics?"

"Anything but that."

Mike snickered. "Did you ever hear the one about the softbody and the pilot's—"

Joanie groaned. "No softbody jokes either. Ever since Victoria I just can't hear them anymore."

"Oh, come on! Captain Juarez's husband told me this one himself."

"I don't care who told it to you, it's just not funny." Joanie paused. "Captain Juarez is married?"

Mike blinked at her in surprise. "You don't know?"

"How could I know? I only met the woman three days ago. So what's he like? Tall, dark, and handsome, I bet."

"Carlos?" Mike laughed. "No, I don't think you could say that."

"Carlos? You're on a first name basis with an officer's husband?"

"No," replied Mike. "Not a first name basis."

Joanie grimaced and fought down a wave of nausea. "I've already got like a billion KPs of pressure inside my head. Unless you want my brain to explode all over your uniform, please don't play guessing games."

"Ever notice the beige stackpack Lt. Juarez wears on her belt?"

"Yeah. It's a commemorative stack. I've got one just like it my footlocker. For my family, you know."

"It's not a comm-stack. It's her husband."

"Oh, don't…" Joanie moaned as another wave of nausea surged through her body. She swallowed heavily and forced the bile back down her throat. "You are *so* gross, Michael Cross."

"His full name is SB Wellness Flowerspan Carlos. Very nice guy, funny as hell. He told me he wanted to be a comedian in the old days."

"Shut up!" shouted Joanie. "You are *not* making me believe that my commanding officer is married to a glob of genecode she wears on her belt!"

"So it's bad to make jokes about softbodies, but we still shouldn't marry them; is that what you're saying?"

"Oh God," moaned Joanie in a panic, hand over her mouth. "I'm gonna—"

Joanie retched and desperately tried not to vomit. Her blouse slid to the floor as she sat up abruptly, hands clamped over her mouth. Without looking up, without meeting her gaze, Mike grabbed a recycle bin and held it for her.

"It's okay," he whispered. "I'm here. Just let go."

Joanie threw up with such violence that she was afraid she'd black out again. Her whole body heaved, again and again as if it were trying to turn itself inside out.

"Sorry," she whispered when it was finally over. "Oh God, I'm so sorry."

Mike gingerly set the recycle bin down on the floor and pulled a handkerchief from a sleeve pocket.

"Oh don't," whispered Joanie as he wiped her mouth. "Please don't waste your—"

"Ssh." he said. "Don't worry. It's self-cleaning. Just take it easy."

Joanie breathed raggedly as Mike wiped her mouth and face with the cool cloth.

"Better?" he asked. She nodded. Mike wadded up the handkerchief, shoved it back into his sleeve pocket and withdrew a stick of mints.

"Want one?"

Joanie nodded.

"What flavour?"

"Whatever."

"Orange, chocolate, pesto," Mike whispered to the stick. He popped out the top mint and held it out to Joanie. She stared at it cross-eyed.

"You're crazy," she said.

"So pick your own," he said, dropping the mint to the floor and holding the stick up to Joanie's mouth.

"Chocolate, peppermint," Joanie said.

"Excellent choice," said Mike, popping out the mint and sliding it into Joanie's mouth. "Enjoy that slowly. God knows when we're going to get fed again."

Joanie closed her eyes and felt the candy start to dissolve on her tongue.

"You okay?" Mike asked.

"Now that I taste something other than puke, yeah."

"Sorry about that," he said. "I didn't mean to make you sick."

Joanie opened her eyes. "So you were serious?"

"Totally serious."

"A human married to a softbody? Is that even legal?"

"You and I aren't legal in most places."

"But you and I are *human*."

"So are softbodies. Carlos calls himself a man, and I take him at his word."

"But, I mean, he's *not* a man. I mean, not really. How do they...?"

Mike blushed. "I dunno. Maybe they don't."

Joanie shook her head. "This is too weird. I'm not even supposed to marry a gentile, let alone somebody coded in a gene-shunt. Can you imagine the look on my mom's face if I'd brought my boyfriend home in a shopping bag?"

Mike laughed. "I know what you mean. Even before the war started, the Six Nations were cracking down on people who married out. They were worried we were getting too assimilated."

"How did you feel about that?" Joanie asked.

"Didn't have much time to think about it. Don't really know. You?"

"Same," said Joanie. "I kind of understand it, but I kind of resent it at the same time. You know?"

Mike nodded.

"Do you think we have a chance of getting out of here alive?" Joanie asked.

"We have a chance," said Mike.

"But I can't make this work!" Joanie whispered, fingering the wetport hanging from the back of her neck. "I just can't stand these implanted thoughts in my brain! They're a ... a violation. Like someone—"

"Shhh," said Mike as he glanced at the control panel again. "Remember what you told me in the airbody? When I was sobbing in your arms like a baby?"

Joanie shook her head.

"You told me to just let it go. You just let me *be*. For the first time in my life someone just let me *be*. You got me off the testosterone horse, Joanie; don't you dare try to take my place in the saddle now."

Tears rolled down Joanie's cheeks. Mike tentatively reached forward, but instead put his hand in his trouser pocket.

"Listen," Mike cleared his throat, "I needed to do a test run on the cerafab so I ... I made you something. It's a little cheesy, because I don't really know much about art or about your people or anything, but..." He extended his hand. Dangling from his forefinger was a slim gold chain with a pendant attached.

Joanie's eyes widened.

"Don't get excited, it's not real gold," said Mike. "Just brass-plated ceratic."

With shaky hands, Joanie took the chain from Mike's finger. Blinking away her tears, she looked closely at the pendant. It was an impossibly thin and delicate circle, filled with a pattern of crisscrossing lines.

Hanging below the circle were a series of stylized feathers. Joanie looked at the crosshatch pattern again, and she realized that it formed a perfect geometric shape made up of two interlocked triangles.

"Oh Mike," Joanie whispered. "It's so beautiful. Is it a dreamcatcher?"

Mike nodded. "With the Jewish star. It's right, isn't it? I was working from memory."

"It's perfect. *Magen David*. Shield of David."

Mike took the chain from Joanie's hand, opened the clasp and leaned over to fasten it around her neck. "Shield of Joan," he whispered as he fastened the clasp and let it fall with a click against the wetport. Their faces were only millimetres apart, their eyes locked. "There's something I have to ask you," he breathed.

Joanie's voice caught in her throat. "Yes?"

"What are the galactic coordinates for the Carolus system?"

"Thirty-one point ten degrees longitude, minus twenty-four point seven latitude."

"I think your skillset upgrade has initialized," he whispered, and kissed her. An instant later she broke away, laughing hysterically.

"Bastard," she gasped between peals of laughter. "You miserable, sodding bastard!"

Mike grinned. "Hey, at least I made you laugh."

Joanie grinned back at him and swiped her pinky down the centre of her breastbone. Her bra fell open. She shrugged her shoulders, and it slid languidly down her body to her waist. Gooseflesh rippled up and down her arms and legs as she felt her nipples go hard.

"Made you look," she whispered.

Joanie sat in the astrogator's seat and ran her hands over the controls.

"Aft port thrusters," she said, touching one control rocker after another. "Aft starboard thrusters. Aft keel thrusters. Primary Ndrive..."

"That's fine, Private," said Captain Juarez, snapping her unipad shut and slipping it into a belt pocket. "You're not going to be using the manual controls anyhow."

"Yes, ma'am."

"We need to talk."

"Yes, ma'am," said Joanie cautiously. "It's my experience that nothing good can ever come after someone says that."

Captain Juarez sighed. "I wanted to apologize to you for leaving you in Corporal Dawson's tender care. I didn't realize the depth of his problems, or I'd never have left you alone with him."

"I understand, ma'am."

"This would never have happened in the old days. We had psych-screening, we had rules—"

"Ma'am, it's okay. It all worked out in the end."

"It's not okay, Private. I committed a serious error in judgement, and I take full responsibility for it. Will you accept my apology?"

"Yes, ma'am," said Joanie. "Of course."

"Good. Now that that's out of the way, do you have anything you want to tell me?"

Joanie froze.

"Something to do with a subject we discussed before? The Joint Command Code of Conduct, perhaps? Section 40, subsection 13A?"

"Ma'am, I—"

"You made me look it up, Private. I *hate* reading the Code of Conduct. It puts me in a bad mood."

"I'm sorry, ma'am. I—"

"This may seem very abstract to a seventeen-year-old, but having sexual relations with another soldier while on duty is an extremely serious breach of military protocol."

"But we didn't. I mean—"

Captain Juarez held up her hand. "Don't play semantics with me, Private. I'm not your mom, I'm your commanding officer. I could court-martial you and Aircraftman Cross both."

Joanie closed her eyes.

"If you weren't both underagers and vital to this mission, I'd do it, too."

"I'm sorry, ma'am," Joanie whispered. "It won't happen again."

"You're damn right it won't."

A voice crackled inside Joanie's head. It was male, and calm, and infinitely patient. Joanie could practically hear the smile. <For chrissake, Bonita, lighten up. The poor girl's been through hell.>

"Shut up and butt out," snapped Captain Juarez, speaking aloud. "You're way over the line."

<Bonnie...>

"I won't repeat myself, Carlos."

Joanie stole a glance at the stackpack on Captain Juarez's hip.

"Don't talk to him, don't look at him, don't think about him. This is between you and me."

"Yes, ma'am."

"I want something understood very clearly. My main concern is getting this ship off the ground. If I have to sacrifice myself and you and Mike and a truckload of newborn babies to accomplish that, I will do so. Do you understand me?"

"Yes, ma'am."

"Good, because I want you to understand that there was nothing personal or vindictive in my decision."

Joanie felt her stomach drop. "Decision, ma'am?"

"I've cut you a lot of slack. I've ignored a shitload of histrionics that would have landed almost anybody else in the brig. I expect you to keep your head now."

Joanie painted on her best military face. "Yes, ma'am!" she barked.

"Aircraftman Cross will not be coming with us to Carolus." Stars exploded behind Joanie's eyes, but her face didn't betray a hint of emotion.

"He was pretty much supercargo anyhow, and if his presence is likely to cause a disciplinary problem onboard, it's better not to bring him at all."

"Yes, ma'am!" barked Joanie again.

"I don't expect you to like this, Private. Frankly, I expect you to hate me pretty thoroughly. But you will learn to obey my orders."

"Yes, ma'am!" Joanie agreed.

Joanie flinched as the shapeless lump of ceratic clanged off the side of the hydraulic lifter. She and Mike were standing together in the shadow of the boxy, dull grey antiquity he'd refurbished with fabbed spare parts. The lifter was almost as long as the starship itself, and half-again as high.

Mike grabbed a heavy metal j-former and violently bulldozed tools and half-finished parts from his workbench. They clattered and crashed to the floor, uncured pieces of ceratic shattering as they hit.

"Bitch!" he shouted. "Fucking heartless bitch!"

Joanie approached him and pried the j-former from his hand. "Stop. Please stop."

"I can't," Mike sobbed, pulling Joanie close. "I can't do this again. I need you. I need you so much."

Joanie felt infinitely tired and infinitely far away. "Me too, Michael."

"What if, what if I tell her I won't finish the lifter if—"

"Sssh," said Joanie, putting her fingers over his lips. "You never said that. You never even *thought* that."

Mike said nothing. He just sobbed against her neck.

Tears squeezed slowly from Joanie's eyes. "Anyhow, the Nspace objective drift will work in your favour. I'll be back before you know it. It'll seem like I never went away."

"Don't leave me, Joanie." Mike whispered. "Everybody leaves me. Please don't go."

"AttenTION!" Joanie barked, and Mike leaped spastically into a semblance of military stance.

"Report!" shouted Captain Juarez, eyeing the tears and snot on Mike's face, but saying nothing. Mike stared back at her in undisguised fury, his jaw clenched so tight he couldn't speak.

"I said *report*, Aircraftman."

"Nothing's changed," he replied in a strangled croak. "Everything checks out. It should be working. But it's not. Ma'am."

"Show me."

Mike blinked. The lifter growled, but nothing visible happened. The growl went up an octave to a shriek, and Mike shut it down with another blink.

"I'm sorry, ma'am," said Mike, spitting out the word like a curse. "I don't know what's—"

"No excuses," Captain Juarez said. "Make it work, or tell me it won't work so we can decide on another course of action. We're running out of time."

"I crunched the numbers five times, ma'am. If I'd done this right, we'd have more than enough lift. There's probably some serious design flaw that I just missed. Ma'am."

"'Ma'am' me in that tone of voice one more time, and I'll have you up on charges, Aircraftman."

Mike looked at her for a moment. "Understood. Captain."

"And also understand this. You're doing a good job. There's just a gremlin in the works somewhere. For two solid weeks we couldn't understand why our model starship wouldn't fly, and then we noticed that someone had inserted a couple of minor power cells backwards."

"Understood, ma'am," said Mike, doing a better job of hiding his hatred.

"Just think it through. I'm sure you'll figure it out. In the meantime I've got to make sure the groundcrew doesn't push the wrong buttons and blow us all up."

Captain Juarez raised her thumb and blinked, and a lifting cable snaked down from the starship's prow port. She locked the tow bobbin into her chest pack and nodded at Joanie.

"Private."

Joanie returned the nod and saluted. "Captain."

Captain Juarez lifted her thumb again and shot up to the prow port. With a clang, she disappeared inside the starship.

"'Just think,'" mimicked Mike in a disgusted tone of voice. "Fuck *you*. Back in the old days they had teams of a thousand people to launch spaceships. How the hell am I supposed to do this all by myself?"

"Relax and think!" Joanie whispered. "Let's assume the basic design is fine. What else could be causing the problem?"

Mike blinked and called up a holographic status readout that floated between them. "I don't know! Look, it's not the electronics. The hardware is aligned perfectly, the hydraulic fluid is the right viscosity—"

<Private Morgenstern,> said Captain Juarez's voice inside Joanie's head. <Could you do a fast eyeball of the service bay, please? I'm reading too many warm bodies in there.>

<Yes, ma'am,> replied Joanie. She kicked in her ceps and gritted her teeth in pain as they momentarily clashed with the fuzzyfield. When the feedback cleared, she scanned the service bay.

<I'm counting fourteen people in groundcrew uniforms and four in ship's crew gear.>

<The whole ship's complement is onboard except for yourself and the Grand Chief,> replied Captain Juarez. <And I've got four members of the groundcrew up here, too. These numbers don't add up.>

Joanie took one step forward, and the world exploded. She was blown from her feet by a wall of force and slammed into the lifter's control panel. She tucked into a roll as she rebounded to the floor, her brain storing the pain and disorientation for later enjoyment. From a million klicks away, she heard Mike cry out, and she forced herself to crawl in the direction of the sound. She felt an arm. She opened her eyes, but all she saw was a blinding white afterspot of the explosion.

"Mike, are you hurt?"

"Bleed..." he replied in a ragged whisper.

She patted Mike's torso and head, but couldn't feel the telltale stickiness of blood.

"Hang on! Let's get to some cover, and I'll take care of the bleeding." She clamped her hand around Mike's upper arm, and half-crawled, half-scuttled behind the lifter's bulk. Mike groaned in pain as she dragged him.

"Mud people!" screamed a familiar voice, high and loud with self-importance. "You won't take your filth to the stars! The Liberators are triumphant! The Liberators are the chosen of God!"

Joanie's eyes cleared, and she kicked into overdrive, boosting her ceps and muscular augments to maximum. She could only hold there for a few seconds, but that would be enough. In an invisible blur, she stuck her head around the edge of the lifter and withdrew it long before the answering force charges burned through empty space.

Stepping down her augments, Joanie downloaded the captured images from wetmemory and slowed them down enough for her meat brain to make sense of them.

"Colonel Wharton," she hissed.

<What's going on down there?> demanded Captain Juarez's voice inside Joanie's head. <Why have the service deck doors been sealed?>

<We're under attack!> responded Joanie. <I make Colonel Wharton and at least six others with force rifles. They're traitors, Captain! Libbie agents!>

<The remaining groundcrew?>

<I don't know! Mike's wounded, and I can't see or hear any of the groundcrew from my position. Too much interference from the fuzzyfield.>

"I know you're hiding back there, Jew girl!" Wharton screamed again. "You and your dirty Indian boyfriend. Come out now and make it easier on yourself."

"Go to hell, Libbie traitor!"

"There's no way we're letting you unpeople go to kiss ThreeWorlds ass, Morgenstern! We'll launch our own starships when we're good and ready, and the only conversations we'll have with the ThreeWorlders will be the thermonuclear kind!"

"Bleed..." Mike groaned again.

"Easy," whispered Joanie. "I'll help you in just a second, Mike."

Joanie closed her eyes and called up a strategic map of the service deck. She'd never gotten around to changing her old FruityFlies icon set, so she was projected as a flashing yellow banana-bug, Mike was a potato-shaped ladybug, and Wharton was a praying mantis with a chili-pepper body. *Good choice*, thought Joanie, and then she shook her head in frustration. Wharton's six followers were nowhere to be seen, and the mantis shape was a good twenty metres away from her current position. Even on full augment, she could never cover that distance without being picked off.

<Is the fuzzyfield still active?> she thought at her wetset.

<Yes, the fuzzyfield is operating normally,> replied the faux-cheery female voice.

<Fuzzyfields work on the same principle as damperfields, right?>

<Yes, but on different wavelengths and at considerably lower power.>

<But if we pushed it way past redline, would it act as a damperfield?>

<Yes. At 300 percent output, fuzzyfields will interfere with the discharge of force weapons, but not with the effectiveness of a true damperfield.>

<How long will I have?>

<Between 10 and 17.5 seconds after mark, safety breakers will trip and the emitter array will shut down. This is hardwired into the unit and can't be overriden.>

<Okay. Get ready to push it to 300 percent on my mark...>

<Warning, Joanie. All fuzzyfield effects will be boosted by 300 percent. You'll be effectively blind and deaf for between 10 and 17.5 seconds.>

<Great.> Joanie pondered. <But so will Wharton, right?>

<Yes.>

Joanie took a deep breath and risked another augmented glance around the edge of the lifter. She transferred a flashshot of the service deck from wetmemory to true memory and studied it intensely.

<Do it,> she instructed her wetset.

There was no sound at all, or, if there was, the souped-up effects of the fuzzyfield blocked it out. Joanie was running at augmented speed in dead silence, with her vision rapidly narrowing to a thin tunnel right in front of her and gradually turning a deepening brown. The last thing she saw before the world went black was Wharton's force rifle, aimed right at her.

When Joanie's vision returned, Wharton was on the floor at her feet. Whether she was dead or just unconscious, Joanie wasn't sure, and she didn't take the time to check. She scooped up the fallen force rifle and signalled Captain Juarez.

<I've taken out Wharton, Captain. That leaves us with six hostiles on the service deck. Can you get the doors open?>

<I can, but I won't,> replied Juarez. <Post Command tells me there are pitched battles going on all over the base.>

<They had that many spies inside?>

<It wouldn't take very many inside a closed system like the Post. There could be ten, there could be fifty, and we're down to a skeleton crew. I can't take the chance of letting any more of them near the ship. We're on our own.>

Joanie was glad she was in augmented mode. She was immune to panic while her wetset controlled her endocrine system, but she knew there would be a price to pay when she stepped back down to normal. *If I live long enough to step down to normal*, she thought.

<So what do we do, Captain?>

<We launch, Private. We launch for Carolus!>

<But the Grand Chief...> Joanie protested.

<Here,> said another voice inside Joanie's head. <Don't worry about

me, Ms. Morgenstern. I have plenty to do coordinating the defense of Post Val d'Or. You just get my starship off the ground and out of the hands of our enemies!>

<How? The lifter is screwed up! Mike's injured and bleeding...> Joanie paused.

<What?> said Captain Juarez.

<He didn't say 'bleeding.' He said 'bleed.'>

<Yes?> prompted the Grand Chief.

<Wait,> said Joanie. <He said that the hydraulic fluid had to be uncompressible, right?>

<Yes.>

<But what if there's something else in the hydraulic lines? Something that *can* be compressed? Like air? Wouldn't you waste all your energy compressing the air?>

<And you have to let the air out!> shouted the Grand Chief. <I remember! I once read a twentieth-century novel where the main character had to 'bleed his radiators,' but it didn't make sense to me at the time. I thought it was just a literary metaphor!>

There must be some way to let the air escape, thought Joanie.

<I have to get back to Mike. Can you cover me, ma'am?>

<Hold on,> replied the Captain. <I'm not sure the weapons array was charged.>

<Private?> It was the Grand Chief's voice.

<Yes, sir?>

<If — *When* you make it into deep space, you'll find a number of documents in the ship's library that will help prepare you for negotiations with the FourWorlders.>

<Me, sir?>

<You, Private. You and your friend Mr. Cross. Captain Juarez can speak for the EAA, but it's not a sovereign state. She's not Canadian and cannot speak on behalf of our government. You are Canadian citizens, and I can delegate you to act in my place.>

<The port and starboard forceguns are useless at this angle. I'd blow us all up if I fired them,> interrupted Captain Juarez. <The keel guns only have the default charge. That's good for ten shots, maybe less. And I can't really depress them far enough to do much damage.>

<It'll do, ma'am.>

<Did you hear me, Private Morgenstern?> asked the Grand Chief in a voice far less sure than Joanie liked.

<I heard you, sir. I will find those documents when we make it to deep space. I will speak to the FourWorlders on your behalf.>

<You are a remarkable young woman, Joanie,> he said. <In peacetime there is no telling what you might have accomplished.>

<We may yet find out, sir. Captain Juarez, when you're ready!>

<Opening fire in mark three, two, one...>

The service deck exploded in light and sound. Fist-thick force charges scorched the air overhead and spent their energy uselessly against the reinforced walls of the chamber.

Joanie snapped off several shots from her own force rifle and raced back towards the safety of the hydraulic lifter. Answering fire exploded all around her, but it was instantly silenced by the starship's guns. With an acrobatic tuck and roll, Joanie dived behind the lifter and dropped by Mike's side. His eyes were closed, but his lips were moving.

"Mike, are you with me Mike?"

"Bleed..." he replied. "Gotta bleed..."

"Yes, Mike. I have to bleed the hydraulic lines. How? How do I do it?"

Mike's eyes opened, and he stared fixedly at the ceiling. His hand rose shakily, and he pointed at a tangle of hydraulic lines at the base of the lifting pads that supported the starship. Joanie kicked in her ceps and zeroed in on a small glint of silver almost lost among the jet black hoses.

"I think I see it, Mike! It looks like an old-fashioned — what do you call it — the things on old sinks?"

"Valve. Bleeder valve."

"Stay here," Joanie commanded.

Leaving the force rifle where Mike could reach it, Joanie crawled to the lifter base and began to scale it.

<Captain, in about five seconds I'm going to be totally exposed. I'll need whatever cover you can give me.>

<It's not much, Private. I only have about three shots left per gun.>

<Fire on my mark, ma'am,> Joanie said, only millimetres from the top of the lifter base.

<Mark!> she shouted, as she lunged for the tangle of black hydraulic lines. The roar and glare of the force charges was overwhelming this close to the guns, and Joanie groped blindly for the tiny bleeder valve.

<Got it!> she shouted triumphantly as her hand closed on cool metal. She twisted the valve, and foul-smelling air hissed from the hydraulic lines.

<How long will this take, Private?> asked Captain Juarez. <Down to the last charge!>

<I don't...> Joanie sputtered to a stop as thick red hydraulic fluid began spewing from the open valve. She cursed and frantically twisted the valve shut with one hand as she tried to wipe the fluid from her eyes with the other. <I think we're done, ma'am, but I've blinded myself with this crap!>

<Hold on. Catch your breath. I'm scanning with infrared.>

Joanie wiped frantically at her eyes with her jumpsuit sleeves until her vision cleared. Her eyes hurt, but at least she could see.

<I'm only detecting one moving target in the service bay; it's heading for the doors. The others are stationary, either lying low or out of action. If the traitor gets those doors open...>

<It's time to go, ma'am. I'm going for Mike.>

There was no reply.

Joanie stood on the edge of the lifter platform and kicked in her leg augments. <We have no choice, Captain.> She jumped to the floor, ten metres down.

<Cable down,> announced Captain Juarez.

Joanie looked up. The lifting cable and shield harness were falling from the prow port. <Cable down, aye,> she responded.

Joanie grabbed the shield harness as it fell past her and quickly pulled it over her head and shoulders. She bent down, lifted Mike's dead weight from the floor, and held him close. She slapped the big red button and a bodyshield crackled into existence around them.

<Godspeed to you both,> said the Grand Chief's voice in Joanie's head. <And Captain...?>

<Yes, sir?> responded Bonita Juarez.

<Since the starship is technically mine, Grand Chief's Ship and all, I'm going to make an executive decision about her name.>

The cable went taut, and Joanie and Mike rose from the service deck floor. Force charges burned at them, and the bodyshield glowed white as it deflected their energy.

<You do that, sir.>

<I think we should call her the *GCS Morningstar*. What do you say, Ms. Morgenstern?>

Joanie was calm. She didn't cry. She didn't gasp desperately for breath, but she knew all that would come later. <I think it's a little melodramatic, sir. Sounds like a spaceship from a vid show to me.>

<Be that as it may, that's what she's called. That's my decision.>

<Yes, sir,> responded Joanie.

<Yes, sir,> responded Captain Juarez.

Joanie held out her right arm as the cable reached its apex. Slowly — so as not to bang his head against the port frame — Joanie hoisted Mike through, into Captain Juarez's waiting arms.

"Small change in plans, ma'am," said Joanie, unable to prevent a smile.

Captain Juarez nodded. "I can see that, Private."

Mike stirred a little as he was moved.

"Bleed," he whispered again.

"The bleeding's over," Joanie replied.

MARK SHAINBLUM (www.northguard.com/mbs/) is a lifelong resident of Montreal, where he has worked as a columnist and feature writer for such local publications as *Hour, Mirror, Graffiti Magazine, MTL*, and the *Montreal Gazette*. The former editor and publisher of Matrix Comics, Mark is best known in his hometown as the writer of *Angloman*, a popular political parody comic strip co-created with illustrator Gabriel Morrissette. Mark and Gabriel also co-created the earlier comic-book series Northguard, which co-starred the Québec super-heroine Fleur-de-Lys, who eventually ended up on a Canadian postage stamp. In 1998 Mark and coeditor John Dupuis shared an Aurora Award for the alternate-history anthology *Arrowdreams: An Anthology of Alternate Canadas*. A founding member of The Montreal Commune SF writing workshop, Mark currently serves as president of SF Canada, the national association of SF authors and other professionals.

About the Editor

CLAUDE LALUMIÈRE is best known in Montreal as the founder and manager of the eclectic and idiosyncratic 1990s bookshops danger! and Nebula.

In 1998, he left retail behind and has since been working as a writer and editor.

He's penned some two hundred articles and reviews for various publications, including *The National Post*, *Locus Online*, *Black Gate*, *Montreal Review of Books*, *January Magazine*, *Fantastic Metropolis*, *The New York Review of Science Fiction*, *Blue Coupe*, *Strange Horizons*, and others.

His review column "Fantastic Fiction" appears in the book section of the Saturday edition of the *Montreal Gazette* and is archived online at www.infinityplus.co.uk/fantasticfiction/.

His own fiction can be found in *Interzone*, *Fiction Inferno*, *Other Dimension*, *On Spec*, and other magazines, anthologies, and webzines. His story "The Ethical Treatment of Meat" (from *The Book of More Flesh*) — inspired by his complete misreading of a previous (unpublished) draft of Dora Knez's contribution to *Island Dreams*, "The Dead Park" — was a final nominee for the 2002 Origins Awards. He was the featured "Foreign Author of the Month" for June 2003 at www.twilighttales.com.

In addition to *Island Dreams: Montreal Writers of the Fantastic*, he has also edited the anthologies *Telling Stories: New English Fiction from Québec* (Véhicule Press, 2002), *Open Space: New Canadian Fantastic Fiction* (Red Deer Press, 2003), and, in collaboration with Marty Halpern, *Witpunk* (Four Walls Eight Windows, 2003).

His website, www.lostpages.net, keeps track of his various publishing endeavours. (And there's lots more to come!)

Véhicule Press

www.vehiculepress.com